THE MAVERICK

JENNIFER MILLIKIN

JNM, LLC

ISBN: 978-1-7371790-0-9
www.jennifermillikinwrites.com
Cover by Okay Creations
Editing by My Brother's Editor

ALSO BY JENNIFER MILLIKIN

Other titles in the Hayden Family series (Standalone)

The Patriot

The Outlaw

The Calamity

Standalone

Pre-order Here For The Cake - releases May 2nd, 2024

Better Than Most

The Least Amount Of Awful

Return To You

One Good Thing

Beyond The Pale

Good On Paper

The Day He Went Away

Full of Fire

The Time Series (Standalone)

Our Finest Hour

Magic Minutes

The Lifetime of A Second

1

WARNER

TWO YEARS AGO

Everything it took to get to this point... well, it feels like it should've happened to someone else.

Peyton and Charlie sit opposite me in the booth, munching on kid-sized cheeseburgers. I have no idea how I'm going to handle this, only that I will.

Being a single father isn't something I pictured for my life, but then again, neither is any of what I've gone through the past few years.

We're on our own now.

2

TENLEY

IF I COULD CHANGE ONE DETAIL ABOUT THE WHOLE STORY, IT would be that he should've chosen better.

An *extra?*

It's so… so… *common.*

Plump lips, slim hips, fake tits.

He could have damn near anyone, and he chose the human equivalent of vanilla ice cream.

Celebrity Dirt broke the news. I don't read that trash, but others do. Like my best friend Morgan's aunt. Living alone in a double-wide trailer in Utah, Aunt Patty enjoys crocheting, her air fryer, and following celebrities.

On that Monday morning, she settled in her worn blue armchair, opened her phone, and navigated to her favorite celeb gossip site. The story was less than a minute old. Aunt Patty was the first to comment, a fact she mentioned proudly when she called Morgan.

It was Morgan who called me.

"Rule of thumb is never to believe this garbage, I know. But…" She stopped, as if she were gathering enough strength to continue.

It was her pause that made me jump from the treadmill. "Go on," I instructed through labored breathing, sweat matting my baby hairs to my neck.

"There are photos." Morgan's tone was an apology, as if she was the person who should be apologizing.

That was four days ago. *Four days ago.*

Ninety-six hours to disassemble a life we spent two years building.

The headline read *Tate Mack Caught Canoodling With Extra.* If it hadn't been for the pictures, I'd have written it off.

Just like I'd always done.

* * *

He came for his blender.

I sat at the dining room table and watched him. His tail should've been between his legs, but his ego is too large to allow such a thing.

He stands in front of me now, the high-powered blender cradled in his arms. The machine can make ice cream, soup, and macerate fruit. I feel as though my heart has taken a turn through its blades.

He stares at me. His shirt hugs his muscled arms, his sweats fit just right. Damn him for looking so good. I've been crying, and it shows.

"Tenley," he starts, stepping closer.

My hand leaps into the air between us, stopping him. "We both know you could have bought another blender. You could have bought one hundred blenders."

His features arrange into genuine sadness. "I wanted to see you."

His scratchy voice makes me feel the tiniest shred better, but I bat it down. I need the anger to stay in place while he is here. He cannot sweet talk his way out of this one, or apologize, or even grovel. But deep down, buried beneath the anger, my broken heart is there.

To the world, he is Tate Mack, box office god and sexiest man alive. To me, he was just Tate. My boyfriend.

Ex-boyfriend.

I blink and look away. "I hope she was worth it, Tate. I hope she was worth losing our relationship."

He rushes forward. The blender tumbles to the ground, plastic cracking, and Tate drops to his knees. He grabs my hands, pulling them to his chest.

"Please," he moans. "It was a mistake. A moment of weakness."

His words are like lemon juice in my fresh wound. They are acid, and they burn. There is no apology on this earth that could make me consider forgiving him. Extracting my hands from his grasp, I push my chair back and rise to my feet. "You made your bed, Tate. Now you get to lie in it." It would be so much easier to accept his apology, to move on. Nothing would have to change. His blender could stay on my counter. He could stay in my life.

But no. I can't have that. I can't live with myself, knowing I condoned that behavior. And what about next time? With a person like Tate, there will always be a next time.

"But we're so good together, Ten. Come on." He stays on his knees, his face upturned, his eyes big and pleading. Maybe for other women this routine would work, but not me, because I recognize that exact look. I acted opposite that same expression, in the movie we made right after we met. In the film, my character dropped to her knees and kissed him. But this is real life, and I'll stay on my feet.

Calmly, I walk to the front door. By the time I've reached it, Tate is off the ground and walking toward me. He passes through the door I've just opened. He doesn't stop. He won't grovel twice. The fact that he groveled even once could be labeled another *moment of weakness*.

I watch, stony-faced, as he guns the engine of his canary yellow Ferrari. The car creeps forward. His eyes meet mine in the rearview mirror. He looks contrite. For the first time since he showed up, I let down my guard. The tears fall. His brake lights illuminate.

No.

I step back, swallowed up into my foyer, and slam the door. The last thing I see is his Ferrari rolling forward through my gate.

An hour later, Morgan shows up with champagne and tacos. She strides into the kitchen and dumps her bags and purse on the counter. Her dark hair is wound into a wild bun on the top of her head, a pen shoved through the coil to keep it secured. She plucks at the end of the pen, and her hair tumbles down around her upper arms. Pen in hand, she grabs an envelope off the top of a stack of mail. "Let's make a list of everything you didn't like about him."

"Tacos first," I grumble.

Morgan waves a hand at the brown paper bag, where grease stains soak through the bottom. "Well, duh."

I reach in, coming away with a parchment-wrapped taco. "Heaven," I announce, biting into the warm picadillo. Sauce dribbles down my chin and she throws me a napkin.

Morgan looks down at the envelope she turned over. I peek. She's already written three things, and titled the list *Cons*.

"Where is the pros column?"

She shakes her head. "Cons only."

I read them aloud. "Ranch on pizza. Looks at himself in reflective surfaces every time he passes one. Sits down to pee." I shake my head, my finger poised above the third con. "He only sat down right after sex. He said the first pee was unwieldy."

She shrugs. "Still. It weirded you out the first time he did it."

"True."

She writes another and I read it out loud. "Tendency to tell dumb lies."

Morgan's not wrong about that. Tate had a problem telling inconsequential lies. Stupid stuff, like saying he went shopping for something when he hadn't. But once he told the lie, he would make good on it. He'd do what he claimed to have already done. More of an aspirational liar.

"You know why he did that," I point out, starting on my next taco.

"Right," she agrees, grabbing some food of her own, knowing I might very well eat it all. "Everyone has childhood shit. We all act out as adults. People can still choose to dislike us for it."

Tate once told me that if he had to grade his parents, they'd get a C-. An only child, he was fed, clothed, and mostly ignored. He began making up stories in his head, ones where fantastical events occurred. Some as simple as buying every type of candy the grocery store sold. One day he told someone his story, but delivered it in past tense, casting himself as the main character. It made him feel important and special, and he kept going, careful to keep it small so that it was attainable. He didn't see it as a lie, because he always made sure it came to fruition. I didn't have the heart to tell him it wasn't normal behavior.

But honestly, what do I even know about normal behavior anymore? I'm the one who just found out my parents, the famed actors who've defied divorce statistics for decades, are in seriously hot water. The kind that roasts you as you drown.

I glance at Morgan. She's been my best friend since her mom was my nanny. In a pinch, Morgan accompanied her mom to my house when she didn't go to school. We clicked, and I begged Margaret to bring her daughter every time she was out of school. Margaret cleared it with my mom, and I had a playmate for life. Even when my little sister Jasper came along, Morgan remained my best friend. She's tagged along on family vacations, joined me on movie sets, and was my roommate until Tate began spending so much time here, she couldn't take it and found a place of her own.

I swallow the last bite of my second taco and reach for the champagne. "You have a valid point," I admit, bracing the pads of my thumb on the cork and grimacing as I push against it. It releases with a loud *pop*. I drink directly from the bottle. It's that kind of evening.

Morgan takes it from me and sips. "Have you talked to Christian recently?"

"Not since this morning." My publicist called to remind me to stay off the internet. *For God's sake*, he'd said in that perpetually exasperated voice of his, *if there was ever a time in our relationship that you listen to me, let it be now.*

I listened. I'm too chickenshit to go looking for what people are saying. You'd think everyone would be Team Tenley, but no. The public is a fickle beast, it feeds and feeds and only wants more. As much as it eats, it's never sated. My saving grace is that I will only be top story on the homepage until another disaster befalls someone they deem worthy of talking about. And down down down on the page my story will go, until it eventually becomes a link in another story that mentions me.

I say all this to Morgan. She appraises me with her

watchful eyes, the ones that see past my public persona and deep into the soul I keep closely guarded.

"Is thirty too young to be jaded?" She hands me back the bottle and digs into the bag for another taco. I do the same. Food never tasted so good, like spicy salsa and soothed feelings.

"Possibly," I sigh, tipping my head to the side and biting down.

"Maybe it's a good thing you're leaving in a few weeks. Change of scenery and all that."

"Right," I agree, saying nothing about the fact that I'd be going to a small town in Arizona even if I didn't need a change of scenery. Not only have I signed on to do the movie, but my parents are betting the proverbial farm on its success. They are bankrolling the entire thing. No pressure there. Nope. None.

I didn't want the role. I'd just wrapped the final movie in a three-picture deal and was ready for a break. I'd even been toying with making the break semi, if not completely, permanent. But then shit hit the fan.

Morgan plucks the champagne bottle from the counter and starts for the glass doors leading out to the deck. I follow.

I'm tired of LA life, but I'll never tire of this view. Spread before us are the twinkling lights of a living, breathing soul. Places to go, things to do, traffic to sit in. This city has a pulse.

"Champagne was a weird drink choice," I murmur, taking the bottle from Morgan and bringing it to my lips.

Morgan chuckles. "I know, but it seemed appropriate. We're not celebrating that Tate cheated on you, Tenley. We're celebrating that you found out he's a cheater before it was too late and you had serious baggage. Before you invested any more precious minutes of your life with him."

I frown. "Seems like an excuse to drink champagne."

She sneaks a smile in my direction. "Well, I mean, yeah."

I pull one knee into my chest and stretch my other leg out. "Do you ever think about marriage? Or kids?"

"Sometimes. It's just"—she motions in front of herself—"out there somewhere. In the future."

"We're already thirty."

Morgan side-eyes me. "Are you insinuating we're *old*?" She says the word like it's gum on the bottom of her new shoes. "Women are having babies later than you think."

"Maybe." I shrug and watch a bug fly past the light next to the door.

Morgan reaches for the champagne but I hold her off and take another sip before handing it over. "I'm afraid one day I'll wake up and it'll all have passed me by. I won't fall in love again and I won't get married. I won't get to do everything different."

"I won't let that happen. I'll wake your ass up before all your opportunities are gone. You're going to get a redo. Promise." She does a wink and nod thing. "Did I look like a cowboy just now?"

Her antics make me laugh, and I feel grateful for her. How can I be fearful of a grim future when Morgan is here, working hard to make my present so damn enjoyable? I reach for her hand. "Thank you for coming over."

"Nowhere else I'd rather be. I'm going to miss you when you're on location in the Wild West."

I laugh. "I think the Wild West is a thing of the past."

"If that's true, I'm going to be very disappointed. I was planning to come visit you and meet a cowboy for the weekend. Maybe a bull rider." She wiggles her eyebrows.

I laugh again, and it feels good. I've been doing the opposite of laughing since I found out about Tate. An idea pops into my head. "You should stay here while I'm gone."

"You want me to move back in?"

I nod. "As early as tomorrow. Right now. Yesterday." It suddenly feels like the most important thing that Morgan moves back in with me. I've been moping around the house. I need someone to remind me that even if my relationship with Tate is dead, I am still alive.

Morgan's head tips to the side like she's thinking. "I don't know..."

"I have houseplants that need watering." The lie comes out smoothly.

Morgan frowns and thumbs back toward my place. "You don't have a single houseplant in there."

I hold up a lone finger, signaling *one moment* and reach for my phone. It takes a grand total of three minutes. I look up at Morgan. "In two days, I will be the proud new owner of two snake plants, one Ficus tree, two peace lilies, and something called a ZZ because its real name is too hard to pronounce." I toss my phone beside my thigh on the chair. "If you don't water them, they will die."

Morgan shakes her head, but the corners of her lips turn up. "Wouldn't want plant blood on my hands."

"Never," I agree solemnly.

"I have a lease," she reminds me.

"I'll pay the breakage fee."

"I knew you'd say that."

I take a drink of the champagne and hand it back to her. "Roomie?"

"Yes," she says, drinking. "You're quite persuasive when you want to be, you know that? Forget being America's sweetheart, you should have been a lawyer."

"Jasper's the lawyer." My little sister's working at a firm in NYC, as far away from the glitz and glamour of Hollywood as she can possibly be. She never tells people who her family is.

"You could've been one also." Morgan eyes me. She knew before she said it that she would strike a nerve, but she said it anyhow. That's how Morgan operates. She never treats me with kid gloves, like so many other people in my life.

I shrug. "All's well that ends well."

The following day, Morgan moves back in. For the next few weeks, I run lines with her and prepare to live in Sierra Grande, Arizona for the next three or so months. As for what comes after that? Well, I don't know. My future is one great big question mark.

3

WARNER

"I saw her this morning, you know. The Hampton girl in that SUV she used to tote those kids around in." Barb folds her hands in her lap and looks out at the street.

Shirley's eyebrows raise. "Don't you mean the Hayden girl? She married the middle one."

Barb snorts indelicately. "You know she ran off and left him with those kids. Poor children. They're the real victims."

Shirley eyes her oldest, closest friend. "You don't even know what happened."

"I don't have to. A mother never leaves her children. Never."

"Well then, I guess you're wrong, because she did."

It's old now, but I remember when it was new.

Shiny black, picking up every speck of dust. The new car smell only lasted a week. After that it smelled like Cheerios, the sweetness of a child's head, and sweaty toddler shoes.

I bought the SUV for Anna just before our son, Charlie, was born. Peyton was nearly two and sat in the center of the back seat of Anna's sedan. Our family grew and so did our vehicle. She whooped and hollered when I drove up in it and handed her the keys.

Eight years later, Anna used the SUV as a getaway vehicle.

I pass her car on my way up to Anna's parents' front door, tapping the taillight with an open palm as I go.

Knocking on the front door is awkward, but I do it anyhow. There was a time when I didn't knock, when I was family and the Hampton's told me knocking was for unexpected visitors and package deliveries.

And, apparently, soon-to-be ex-husbands.

The door opens and there she is. My wife.

It's been two years since she climbed in that SUV and pointed it south toward Phoenix. She stayed gone for a solid six months, and after that we saw her every other weekend. I'd take the kids down to Phoenix where Anna was staying, and we'd visit. The kids knew we were separated, and nothing more. Eventually Anna began making the drive back to Sierra Grande when it was her weekend, and I'd drop the kids off at her parents' home. Anna needs the safety net her parents provide. Personally, I'm not sure she needs it. Not anymore.

She looks good today. Every time I see her, I swear she looks better and better. Her cheeks are flushed a delicate pink, the same shade as the rosebush growing alongside the porch. She's had a haircut recently. Blonde hair that previously fell to the middle of her back now barely skims her collarbone.

"Hi," she says, her voice strong and supple, a melody to my ears. There was a time when she sounded hollow, or worse, when she said nothing at all. Days and days on end when she wouldn't get out of bed, when I'd lie and tell everyone Anna suffered migraines.

I clear my throat, trying to shake the onslaught of memories, both good and bad. "Hi, Anna."

She steps back, inviting me in. She's wearing jeans, white Adidas sneakers, and a white V-neck tee. For a split second, she is the old Anna, the one I pulled behind the bleachers in high school for intense make out sessions while my hand drifted into her shirt.

Seeing her like this, looking healthier than she has in years, it's almost enough to make me forget all that happened. But not quite.

The kids are in the backyard. I walk through the living room and kitchen, following their joyful yelling. Anna walks behind me. There was a time when it would feel like second nature to grab her hand and pull her alongside me, walking together like partners.

But that was before she needed help. Before she served me with divorce papers.

"Dad," Peyton yells, waving when she spots me. Charlie pops out from behind a tree, and Anna's parents look over.

"Sugarbear," I say in greeting, waving at Peyton. She lets the term of endearment slide, because our audience is safe. If she were with her friends, I'd have kept the nickname to myself. I know the rules.

Charlie races to me. He's ten, but he seems younger. He's not yet too cool for me, like his thirteen-year-old sister. He has no qualms about leaping up and letting me catch him. That will soon change, though, a lesson taught to me by Peyton. I hug my son and indulge in a quick sniff of his head. He still smells like a baby, but it's a thought I keep to myself. For Charlie, being likened to a baby is a fate worse than death.

"Brock." I nod my head at Anna's dad. "Hello, Susan," I say to her mother. I used to be as comfortable in this home as my own, but it's hard to maintain that when I'm in the middle of whatever the hell it is I'm doing with their daughter. There really isn't a battle, yet lines have been drawn, invisible as they may be. By default, Brock and Susan must choose their daughter. I understand. I'll always be on Peyton's side.

"How's your dad, Warner?" Brock gets up from his patio chair to shake my hand. I knew he'd ask this question. He always does.

"Refusing to slow down," I answer, my tone lightly admonishing. Not of Brock, but of my dad. Brock was almost certainly expecting my response, because it's the same one I always give. We stick to our scripts.

"Dad, guess what?" Charlie breaks in. "Mom says she'll buy me the new PlayStation when it comes out."

I smile down at him, bristling on the inside. "That sounds like a very nice gift, Charlie."

I look up into Anna's gaze and feel pleased when I see her guilt. She should feel guilty about staying in Phoenix. About not coming home when her treatment was finished. About blindsiding me with divorce papers.

Brock sits back down beside Susan, and Charlie runs to Peyton. Anna stands next to me, hips pressed to the back porch railing, watching our kids play. She doesn't mention the papers. Not the fact she sent them, nor the fact that it's been two months and I haven't signed them.

Peyton growls like a monster, curled fingers tapping the air on either side of her cheeks like piano keys. She takes off after Charlie. He yells, probably from excitement and happiness his big sister is paying attention to him, and scrambles across the yard. He runs for the safety of the tree, glancing back at Peyton as he sprints.

I see what's about to happen, and so does Anna. She moves sideways, foot poised to step into the yard, her hand raised and her mouth open with a warning that doesn't make it in time.

Charlie's forehead meets the edge of the ceramic bird feeder hanging from the tree, and he drops to the ground, screaming and holding his head.

Bright red blossoms immediately, pouring from the wound. Anna and I run for him, in step with each other, partners again.

Anna kneels beside him and I peel off my T-shirt, pressing it to his forehead to stop the bleeding. Charlie sobs and Anna soothes him while I stay quiet, applying pressure. When I think it's safe, I pull away the ruined shirt and survey the cut.

Anna blinks up at me, eyes horrified. Charlie looks at me. Teardrops stick in his eyelashes. I wink at him, determined not to let on how deep the gash is. "You've got yourself a good one, buddy. We're gonna get you fixed up, but I have a job for you, okay?"

Charlie nods, his lower lip quivering.

"Do you think you can keep this shirt pressed to your head? I wouldn't ask if I didn't think you could handle it, but if you think it's too much, just say the word and I'll ask Peyton for help."

"No," Charlie says quickly. "I can do it."

He reaches for the shirt and presses it against himself. Placing one arm under his back and the other under his knees, I lift him into the air. Susan holds the side gate open for me, and I stride through.

"We'll keep Peyton with us," she tells me.

Brock opens the back seat of my truck and I pause, looking at Anna. "There's a blanket in the bed, can you grab it?"

She does as I've asked, spreading the navy blue blanket across the leather. The Hayden Cattle Company logo embroidered on the corner faces me. I get Charlie buckled in and climb into the driver's seat.

Without a pause, Anna hauls herself into the passenger seat. For a second I stare at her, dumbfounded. We could be seventeen again, the way she just jumped into my truck and looked across the center console at me.

I shift into drive, one hand giving a terse wave out my open window, and head for the emergency room.

"You good, bud?" I ask Charlie.

Anna looks back at him.

"Yeah," he responds. "It stings."

I hold up a thumbs-up sign and hope he sees it. "They'll have something to help with that. Just hang on a little longer."

My forearm rests on my center console as I take the familiar turns through Sierra Grande. At first, it's a soft touch on my elbow. A gentle grazing down my arm. Then Anna's fingers slide over the back of my hand, coming to rest on my own, squeezing me.

I meet her gaze in the enclosed space. I don't need to ask her what she's thinking. I can see it plain as day on her face. *Thank you,* she says, *I'm glad you were there.*

In the end, Charlie gets seven stitches.

And me? I'm hoping Anna comes home and stitches our family back together.

4

TENLEY

"Are you sure?" Jasper asks, her nose scrunched and her eyebrows raised. Through the screen we're talking on, I watch her grab a cup of yogurt and a spoon.

"Yes," I answer, setting my laptop on the counter in my parents' kitchen. I face the computer toward the Malibu beach on purpose, to make my sister jealous. The effort is probably wasted. She prefers the view of the Manhattan skyline from her Brooklyn apartment. "Besides, I don't have a choice. I signed a contract, remember?"

Jasper gathers her dark hair over one shoulder. Like our parents, she has an olive complexion and dark brown hair. With my fair skin and blonde hair, I am the odd woman out.

For the past five minutes, Jasper has been trying to talk me out of filming. "Arizona, though? I just think of dirt and tumbleweeds." Jasper shudders and I roll my eyes.

"If you have suggestions regarding where I should film a movie about a woman who inherits a cattle ranch, I'm open to hearing them." My stomach grumbles and I cover it with a hand. I don't usually wait so long to have breakfast, but my mom asked me to come eat with her and my dad before I leave town.

Jasper lifts her hands. "Fine, you've made your point. At least you'll have Calvin with you, so you won't get lonely."

"True." Calvin Lawrence has been my friend since we acted in a teenage variety show, and I was happy to hear he'd signed on to play my love interest. He's a great actor, and I already know we have good chemistry.

"Is Mom excited?" Jasper holds the spoon in her mouth as she asks the question.

I purse my lips and look out to the living room, where my mom had walked through just before my video call with Jasper. "For the most part," I answer. It's the truth… kind of. My parents are very excited to get the movie filmed and distributed. My mom has dollar signs in her eyes, and I don't blame her. If the movie flops, my parents will lose everything. The Malibu house I'm standing in, the place in Aspen, and who knows what else. But Jasper doesn't know any of that. If I hadn't overheard their conversation two months ago, I wouldn't know about their current situation either.

They hadn't known I was at their house, and they'd come home arguing. It wasn't just a little disagreement, either. It was a balls to the wall, all cards on the table screaming match. Never, in the entire time I lived with them, had I heard them behave that way. They'd spotted me, frozen in place in my seat at the dining room table, and scrambled for everything except the truth. But I'd heard what I'd heard and there was no way to sugarcoat it.

"Anything new with Tate?" Jasper asks, making her voice light on purpose.

"He's called a few times, I let it go to voicemail."

"So that's it? You'll just never talk to him again?"

"Not if I can help it." I'm putting on a brave face, but I miss him. I think, anyway. Maybe I just miss the idea of him. The more distance I get from what happened, the more I wonder how much I actually loved him. My pride may be more wounded than my heart.

Jasper tucks a lock of hair behind her ear. "Good luck managing that in LA. Big city, small town."

"I know." I almost ran into him last week on a local hiking trail. I'd noticed him ahead and promptly turned around, got back in my car, and drove to a different trail.

"He's saying you were on a break at that time. That he was upset and made a bad choice, but he didn't cheat on you."

I nod. This isn't new information. Christian called me before it hit the news. He'd heard about it in the break room while brewing his K-cup. Perks of having publicists who work at the same firm, I suppose.

"Is that true?" The hope in Jasper's tone irritates me. Forget women all over the world, Jasper is Tate's biggest fan.

I give her a derisive look. "What do you think?"

She opens her mouth to respond but our mom walks in, interrupting her. "Jas, is that you? I can hear your voice but I can't see you. Tenley has you facing the water."

"She's trying to lure me back home right before she leaves," Jasper quips.

Mom rounds the island, stopping when she's pressed up to my side, and bends down so she's in the camera's view. They exchange small talk, and I stay quiet. There's been a shift in our relationship, although it has been hard to put my finger on it. Since finding out about their financial trouble, I've felt oddly parental toward them. I want to scoop them up, keep them safe, the way they did to me so many years ago. And then there's another part of me that feels disappointed in them. In my dad, really.

"She's insisting on driving that old Bronco out there," my mom complains, and I glare at the screen.

"What else should I drive out there? My Porsche? I'm not trying to show up in Sierra Grande like a princess. Besides, the set director thought the truck would be great in the film, so Pearl might just become famous after this."

"Infamous," my mom mutters, and I gently nudge her in the ribs. She smiles at me, but the smile doesn't move much of her face. All that Botox and filler. Needles will start coming toward my face soon too, if I stay in this business any longer. It won't be long before I'm considered old, and the roles I'm offered will become that of the mother.

"Anyway," I say pointedly, signaling it's time to move off the subject. "Start talking, Jasper. Take the heat off me."

Jasper tells us about spring in New York City. It's nothing we don't already know, having been there ourselves, but we enjoy the description, nonetheless. Changing seasons makes me wistful.

We maintain a few more minutes of chatter and then it's time to go. I say goodbye to Jasper and blow her a kiss, and she tells me to try and not get murdered on my drive through the California desert to Sierra Grande. I stick out my tongue and close the laptop, the virtual equivalent of hanging up on her.

Mom pulls a previously frozen quiche from the oven and sets it on the stove. She's not adept in the kitchen, and her personal chef is no longer around. She tried to tell me she wanted to learn to cook and that's why she let the chef go. *Trial by fire*, she'd said in this forced flippant tone. Even then I didn't believe her, and that was before I'd found out about the financial woes.

My dad walks in just as we're sitting down to eat. He kisses the top of my head on the way to his seat, and I want to ask him where he's been. What he's been doing. If he's sinking them even further into this pit they're in.

Before I'd overheard their argument, underground gambling had just been a thing I knew existed somewhere out there in the ether, like the mafia and organ trafficking. Things people talk about, but they don't feel real.

Until it hits you squarely in the center of the forehead, and you learn it has swept away all your parents' financial resources and your father has an addiction. I feel badly for assuming the worst, for being suspicious with how he spends his time. I've read about it, and trust is one of the most difficult parts for the family members of addicts.

"I saw Pearl out front," he says, setting a slice of quiche on his plate. "So I checked her fluids and tire pressure. Made sure you have an emergency kit in the back and plenty of water."

My heart swells with love, and a wide streak of guilt runs alongside it. "Thanks, Dad."

He smiles, his teeth perfect and white. "It'll be good for you to drive out there alone. Clear your mind a bit. Things look different when you add distance."

Mom makes a disapproving sound around the fork in her mouth. Dad winks.

By the time I've climbed into the Bronco and buckled myself in, they've each hugged me five times and wished me luck.

I pull out of their driveway, leaving the wind and surf behind. By the time I hit Palm Springs, I find my dad was right. Away from the glitz and glamour, the world feels different. Tate and my bruised ego are but a memory.

At the next gas station, I put the top down, secure my hair to the top of my head, and drive.

* * *

THIS IS NOT what I was anticipating.

I set up the last of my bright orange road triangles and tent a hand over my eyes, peering out in both directions.

There is nothing for miles. Nothing, nothing, nothing. And the cacti don't count.

"Shit," I mutter, kicking my tire. If this were a comedy, I'd yelp and grab my foot as if I hurt myself. This, however, is real life, so my foot is perfectly fine.

I dive into the front seat, reaching across for my bag and fishing out my phone. My optimism crumbles when I look at it.

No Service.

This isn't a surprise. It's not like I had service the other ten times I looked at it. I sigh and sit in the driver's seat, one leg dangling out of the open door, and lean my head back against the seat.

I'm two hours from Sierra Grande. In between towns, from what I can recall from road signs. I stretch my memory, trying to remember the last sign listing the miles to the next town.

It's useless. I wasn't paying attention. Fleetwood Mac was blaring from my phone and I was tapping my fingers on the steering wheel when my car began to sputter and jerk. I'd barely made it off the road when Pearl took what I hope is not her final breath.

I groan and push the hair back from my eyes. The strands are ratty from the windy drive and sweat has soaked through the band of my bra. On the bright side, I still have a majority of the case of water bottles my dad wedged between suitcases in my back seat.

I fight to get one out, then open it and drink half. Within five minutes, my bladder tells me what a bad idea that was. I look around, but since this is the desert, there is literally nowhere to hide and pop a squat. My luck, a person would drive by at the exact moment I drop my shorts. Maybe *Tenley Roberts Naked On Roadside* would be the headline to finally knock my breakup with Tate from its top spot.

I'm seriously considering pouring the other half of the water on my head to cool down when I hear it. An engine. I leap from Pearl and rush to edge of the road, arm stuck out. Not a thumb like a hitchhiker, but more of a wave.

The truck slows. It's white, new, with four doors and a set of double rear tires. I think there's a name for that, but I can't remember what it is.

It pulls off the road slowly, dirt billowing around the tires. I can't see the driver from here, but I know it's a man. He wears a ball cap. I walk a little closer, and he cuts the engine and gets out.

"Car trouble?" he asks, coming closer. He stops five feet from me, probably to let me know he's not a psycho who's going to kill me and wear my skin. *Try not to get murdered.* Jasper's words float through my mind.

But if this guy is the one doing the murdering? What a way to go.

He's arguably the most gorgeous man I've ever seen, and I think my opinion is pretty solid considering I spend a vast majority of my life around pretty people. His eyes are the color of toffee, and they twinkle. He's tall, broad-shouldered, his body tapering down to his hips. His jeans are on the right side of tight, and his T-shirt has the letters HCC on the left side of his chest.

"I think so," I answer, suddenly very aware of my rat's nest hair.

He inclines his head toward Pearl. "Mind if I take a look under your hood?"

I press my lips together and shake my head. Gesturing to the Bronco, I say, "She's all yours."

He comes forward, hand outstretched. "Warner Hayden."

"I'm..." I can't say my name. He doesn't appear to recognize me, thank God, but he might recognize my name. "Morgan Waller." *Thanks, Morg.* I place my hand in his, and that's when it happens. His warmth, his manly smell, his nearness. It swirls around until it's a heady mist enveloping me. It's been twenty-six days since I learned about Tate, and I hadn't realized how badly I missed the touch of a man.

Warner releases my hand. "Nice to meet you, Morgan." He starts for Pearl, his gaze roving over her. "1976?" he asks.

"Yes," I answer, following him. "Are you a vintage car guy?"

The palm of his hand traces her body. "Not really." He peeks in the open driver door and whistles, the sound low and appreciative. "Fully restored," he murmurs. He looks back at the soft top piled on the back. "With a Bimini top. And stuffed with suitcases."

He looks back at me, curiosity raging in those strikingly warm eyes. Whatever questions he has, he keeps them to himself and resumes his walk to the front of the vehicle.

He pops the hood and I join him. Heat radiates from the engine. To me, it looks like a maze of tubes and metal. Warner leans in, gripping the edge of the truck for leverage, his T-shirt tightening around his bicep. He pokes around, while I busy myself doing everything I can not to give in to my primitive instincts. Somewhere along the way biology programmed me to smell this attractive male and want to mate.

"I can't see anything obviously wrong. Nothing worn out or cracked." Warner looks at me, and there is so little space between us now that I smell peppermint on his breath, as if he'd been sucking on mint candy when he saw me. I take a breath and nod. Being this close allows me to see his finer details, like the small scar on his right brow bone. My fingers twitch at my side, aching to trace it.

It's official. Warner and I were lovers in a past life. There's no other way to explain the raw attraction I feel.

Warner, on the other hand, is either being overly polite, or I screwed him over in our past life and all of his biological instincts are issuing cautions. He appears to be altogether unaffected by me.

He nods toward Pearl. "Can you pump the gas?"

His request confuses me. There isn't a gas station anywhere that I can see. If there was, I'd have walked there and called for help. My eyebrows knit together, and my confusion brings a heat to my neck that isn't from the air temperature. He watches me wrestle with his words, a slow smile curving his lips.

Some men look better frowning, or stone-faced. Not Warner. His smile is like a dawning sunrise. And really, this is only a grin. I'm not sure what a full smile would compare to. Midday sun over the ocean, maybe?

He runs the pad of his thumb across his upper lip and wipes it on the shoulder of his shirt. "Sit in the front seat and try to turn on the engine. I think your problem may be the fuel injector, but the only real way to know that is to listen to the engine try to turn over. You have a new engine in here, which means you have a fuel injector. If you had the old engine, it'd have a carburetor, and I'd be able to see gas going into it when you pumped the pedal."

I do as he asks, hopping into Pearl and leaning out the door. The hood is blocking me from seeing him, so I say, "Tell me when."

"When," he answers.

I turn the key in the ignition. Pearl makes an attempt, but it sounds like the hacking cough of a lifelong smoker.

"One more time," Warner yells, and I do it again.

Poor Pearl. She sounds awful.

I reach into the back seat for two water bottles and startle at the sound of the hood slamming closed. I hop out with the water and hand one to Warner. He takes it, thanking me with a tip of his head, and unscrews the cap. His throat is covered in day-old scruff and it undulates as he downs the entire bottle.

"You've diagnosed her, then?"

"Fuel pump. Nothing else appears to be the issue, and the way it sounded when it turned over is a dead giveaway." Warner meets my eyes, and it dawns on me that he'd been avoiding looking at me directly this entire time. "There's a repair shop in the next town. If I had time, I'd grab the part from the auto part store and do it myself, but I need to pick up my kids from school."

The heat inside my body turns to ice. Of course. I hadn't thought beyond my own attraction for two seconds to consider this man may actually, I don't know, have a *life*. Kids. *Wife*. I look at his ring finger.

It's bare. But then, that doesn't necessarily mean anything. Maybe he forgot to wear it today. That would explain his apathy toward me. I'm not God's gift to man, but I'm attractive. Hollywood would've spit me out if I wasn't, no matter who my parents are.

I turn back to my car and grab my phone again, scowling at the words No Service.

"It's a dead zone out here," Warner says. "I'll drive you to Caliverde. The tow truck should be able to come get your car and take it back to the repair shop."

Get in a car with a stranger? That's first day of childhood lesson number one, on par with learning how to walk properly with scissors. I mean, yeah, I'm stupidly attracted to the guy. And, yeah, he's gorgeous, but Ted Bundy was attractive too. Being good-looking and a murderer are not mutually exclusive.

He chuckles softly, the sound deep and throaty. "I get it. I wouldn't want my daughter climbing into someone's truck. Not now, at thirteen, and not when she's an adult." He snaps his fingers and points at me. "I have an idea."

Without waiting for me to respond he starts further off the road and into the barren desert. He gathers small rocks into a pile beside Pearl and arranges them.

"Is that your license plate number?" I ask, studying the mix of letters and numbers.

"Yep. Do you feel safer now?"

"Yes," I answer truthfully. "Let me lock her up and grab my purse."

I grab a receipt from the passenger side floorboard and jot down his name and license plate number, and leave it tucked in the cup holder. Next, I pull up the top and lock the doors.

Warner is waiting for me in his truck. Cold air blasts me in the face when I open the door. For a moment I stand there, enjoying the rising goose bumps because it means I'm finally not hot. When I settle in and buckle up, Warner pulls back out onto the road. In all the time that passed since he pulled over, not a single car went by.

"Sorry about the new car smell," Warner says, glancing over at me.

"Is that on purpose?" I look around for one of those little tree-shaped car deodorizers.

He shakes his head. "It's new. My brother drove me out to pick it up this morning. He turned around and went back to work while I finished the paperwork."

I nod, looking back at Pearl until she's out of sight.

"So, where were you headed?" Warner asks, glancing over at me. He only looks at me for a second before he looks back at the road, and it's so refreshing I could cry. Staring is one of the milder things people do when they realize who I am. Shrieking, stuttering, and thrusting their phone out for a picture are other typical reactions. I used to love it. But that was when I was younger, when the recognition felt like a promise. Now it feels like a tornado and I want to drive the opposite direction.

And even though he doesn't recognize me, even though I'd probably be safe telling him at least the name of the town I'm due in by this evening, I lie again. Morgan Waller tells Warner Hayden that she's headed to New Mexico.

"Moving there?" he asks, probably thinking of the suitcases jammed in the Bronco's back seat.

"Temporarily."

Warner switches on the radio. We spend the next ten minutes listening to country, and I'm reminded why I don't prefer it. So much of it is about love, that pure, sweet and intoxicating kind. Unless you're lucky enough to be at that point in your life, the crooning melody is depressing.

I put my elbow on the door and look out the window as he drives, my good mood deflating with every revolution of the truck's tires. Warner is the kind of man Tate should have been. I don't have to know him any better than this. I can just tell.

Warner drives me to Caliverde Auto, and though the tow truck is out on a job right now, it will be available to get Pearl within the hour.

"Thanks for all your help," I tell Warner, reaching into my purse for my wallet. He doesn't seem like the kind of person who would accept money for his help, but shouldn't I at least offer?

When he sees my wallet come out, he shakes his head. "I should be the one paying you for the chance to look under the hood of a vintage Bronco. They're not exactly common." The curiosity is there again in those burnt caramel eyes. "You referred to the Bronco as 'she' and 'her.' Does that also mean you've named your vehicle?"

"Pearl," I answer, a hint of pride creeping into my tone. I love that car. She makes me feel free and untamed.

"Pearl," Warner echoes, nodding his head slowly. "I like it."

"That's good, because if you didn't, I'd have to change it."

His eyes draw together. "Really?"

I snort. "No, not really. Pearl is my girl, and her name fits her." Slipping the wallet in my purse, I come away with something else. "Candy?"

Warner stares at my open palm, then he meets my eyes. "Where I come from, candy has a wrapper."

"I know, it's unconventional." Unscrewing the lid to the wide-mouth Mason jar, I thrust it closer. "They're to die for. Spicy Peach Rings, and they make them in-house at this place in LA."

Warner eyes me. "LA to New Mexico? That's a haul."

I ignore the two little puzzle pieces he has just connected. It's not like he cares one way or the other. He is maybe or maybe not married, and he definitely has kids. "Just take one. You won't regret it."

He fishes out a peach ring and pops it in his mouth. I widen my eyes and lean forward, jokingly watching him. He nods and says, "Okay, those are good. Spicy, but good."

I eat one too, and tell him, "I told you."

He reaches for another. "I need one more for the road." He takes three and looks at his watch. "If I don't leave now, I'll be late."

"Thank you again," I say. He waves at me and turns around, and I watch him walk across the cracked asphalt parking lot to his truck. I will probably never see him again.

He doesn't belong to me, and he very likely belongs to someone else.

Still, I can't shake the feeling I've just lost something.

5

TENLEY

Shirley has brick red lipstick on her teeth, but the makeup faux pas can wait. Barb has something much more pressing to tell her friend. "Did you hear?" she asks in a superior tone, thoroughly enjoying holding court for her party of one.

"Hear what?" Shirley asks, curious but also reticent. Barb can be a terrible gossip.

"A whole parade of trucks came through town this morning. Big trucks," Barb holds her fleshy hands away from her body, motioning to show the size. "Hauling trailers. They're coming."

The corners of Shirley's lips dip with disapproval, and she taps Barb's hand, a physical tsk. "Would you stop? You sound melodramatic."

Barb leans forward conspiratorially, and Shirley smells a secret. "How's this for melodramatic? I heard they asked Beau Hayden if they could film inside his house and he asked them if they'd also like to crawl up his backside and set up camp." Unbridled pride skims her cheekbones and eyes, rolling over her face like a wave. Not much tastes as good as juicy truth.

Shirley laughs. "Now that, I believe. Nobody delivers a cutting line like a Hayden."

* * *

THE STUDIO HAS PUT me up in a big house close to a river. There is more land and privacy, but I would've preferred to stay closer in town, where the crew is staying. For looks, I'm supposed to be staying in the nicer place. Lead actress, yada yada. But I know who's footing the bill for all this, and the smaller the cost, the better. Still, I couldn't very well insist on a room at the town's hotel. Maintaining appearances is paramount to my parents. Despite the zeroes in their bank account (not the kind that come after a big number and are separated by commas), they need me to put on a show.

It's the least I can do for them, after all they've done for me.

Pearl is running like a champ again. Warner was correct. It was the fuel pump.

The sun has almost disappeared by the time I reach Sierra Grande. The GPS sends me around the town, so I don't get to see the details. From here, I see a lot of lights. Not headlights or brake lights, like I'm used to seeing, but streetlights. Lights from stores and houses.

Already I feel my pulse slowing, my anxiety ebbing. Everything about this place screams slower pace. Air swirls around me as I drive, and even that feels different from LA. I take a deep breath, trapping the oxygen in my throat, before I breathe it out slowly and loudly. Whenever I take a deep breath in LA, I'm left with tension and ambition. Here, all I feel now is calm.

The house my GPS directs me to is two stories and sits a couple hundred feet back from a riverbank. It's painted white, with light blue shutters and a red front door. It's obviously old, but maintained. From the outside, anyway.

My stomach rumbles as I pull up and park. I feel

supremely grateful my assistant, Gretchen, asked the scout who found this house and rented it to stock the kitchen before he moved on to the next city.

Gretchen emailed me before I left my parents' house this morning and assured me there was food waiting for me, and she also promised cold beer for when I finish my "cowgirl" lessons.

When my parents got the brilliant idea to use this film to save them from economic death, and the inevitable collapse of their social lives, I reminded them that I've never stepped foot on a ranch. My experience around a horse was limited to a single riding lesson when I was ten, and when it became painfully clear I would never be a skilled equestrienne, I quit. Which was fine, because that same day I got a callback for a commercial, and nothing made my mom or dad happier than to see me follow in their footsteps.

The solution to my lack of ranch knowledge was a teacher. A real cowboy who would show me how to rope and ride, teach me about the inner workings of a ranch.

Cary the Cowboy will be here promptly at nine tomorrow morning to begin lessons. Which means I need to get inside this house, eat, shower, unpack, and find a bed.

There's a lockbox on the door, and I use the code Gretchen included in this morning's email to open it and retrieve the key. Normally Gretchen travels with me, but her dad is undergoing chemotherapy and we both agreed it was more important she be there with him for his treatment. Besides, with this being my last film for the foreseeable future, I'm more than ready to be on my own.

I unlock the red door and use my knee to push it open, then shove my biggest suitcase over the threshold, followed by my two medium-size suitcases. Shouldering two duffels and holding my purse, I step inside and use the same foot to close the door behind me.

Gretchen said this house has been available for rent for a year, but it doesn't show. It has been freshly cleaned, judging by the aseptic scent in the air. I make a note to get a scented candle and drop the duffels so I can move freely through the house.

The first place I go is the kitchen. In the fridge I find everything I need to make a sandwich. There's also my favorite brand of sparkling water, so I grab one and walk through the house, alternating between bites of my sandwich and sips of lime soda water. It's fully furnished, but based on the outdated decor, my guess is that it came this way. Fine by me.

I keep waiting to miss my house. My bed. The skyline I'm so used to.

So far, it hasn't happened. All I can really think about is how relieved I am to be away from it. Because for a while, my house was also Tate's house. My bed was Tate's bed. In Sierra Grande, Tate doesn't even exist.

I finish my sandwich, find the master bedroom, and haul my stuff into the room. I text my parents to let them know I made it, ignore my mother's response that I should've texted her hours ago because there's zero chance I'm telling her about my car trouble, and send the same message to Morgan.

A light layer of dirt coats my skin, no doubt the result of hours of driving through dusty desert air. I take a long, hot shower and crawl into the bed. A large window faces out toward the river, the water visible in the light from the full moon. I'm going to regret it in the morning when the sun's rising, but I leave the curtains open. The stars are plentiful, twinkling like someone blew fairy dust across the sky.

My last thought before I fall asleep is how a man like Warner, and a man like Tate, can exist under the same sky.

* * *

"BROKEN PELVIS."

I drop my spoon in my chia pudding. "I'm sorry, what did you say?"

Gretchen stretches out, reaching for something I can't see. She straightens up and looks back at her phone screen. "Cary's wife called and said he fell from a horse yesterday and won't be available to teach you all the things."

"But... but..." My spoon flips over, sending chia pudding into the air. It lands on the kitchen table in an unappetizing clump. I lift my hands to my face, smoothing out my eyebrows with the pads of my pointer fingers, then keep the fingers pressed to my temples. "Okay. What are our options?" What I really mean to say is, *This cannot delay filming*. Being late costs money. Each day has a monetary value attached to it.

"I've already put in a call to the mayor of Sierra Grande and asked him for help. The largest cattle ranch in Arizona is in that town, there must be cowboys crawling all over the place."

I feel relieved enough to make a joke. "I don't think cowboys crawl."

Gretchen gathers her black hair over one shoulder. "*Riding* all over, then."

"Is Cary in a hospital nearby? Maybe I could visit him?" I've never met the man, haven't even spoken to him on the phone, but I feel like a visit would be a nice gesture.

"His wife said they'd had to drive two hours to the hospital, so I don't know what that means. I'm not sure if he was at home when it happened, or if he was somewhere else, like on a trail ride or something."

My eyebrows lift. "A trail ride?"

She shrugs. "I don't know. I'm *trying*."

"Well, let's find out where he is and send him something. Flowers seem awkward. Maybe a cookie bouquet?"

Gretchen nods, writing on the notepad balanced on her knee. "Got it. What else? Is the house okay?"

I look around at the kitchen. In the light of day, I can see everything better. The wall below the upper cabinets is painted a buttery shade of yellow. While I'd never choose that color myself, it looks good in here. It complements the view from the kitchen window, which is of a tree line comprised of skinny-trunked trees. "All good," I tell Gretchen, giving the screen a thumbs up. "Just call me when you hear from the mayor. I'm going to keep unpacking." Last night I'd been so tired I only unpacked the necessities.

We hang up and I eat my breakfast and finish unpacking. I still haven't heard back from Gretchen, so I wander outside and down to the river. It's not huge, or fast moving, and the sound is just right. Peaceful. I sit down and close my eyes.

I don't know how long I'm sitting that way, but it's a while. My ears have become attuned to the sound of the water, so when there's a rustling noise behind me, my heart leaps from my chest and I whip around.

It's gray. Small. Skinny. Its rib bones push against its coat. The dog stares at me, wary but hopeful. That's kind of how I feel about life right now. Wary but hopeful.

"Hello," I say quietly, sinking to my knees, hoping the dog won't see me as threatening. I hold out an open hand. It stares at me, and I feel it deep down in my chest. It's deciding if I'm trustworthy.

It must think I'm okay, because it takes a cautious step closer. Then two more, until it's only a foot away from me.

"I won't hurt you," I tell it. I can't believe I'm talking to a dog. Does it even understand me? It looks like he might. Maybe it's my tone of voice, not my words, that he comprehends.

It takes another step and I notice something I somehow missed. The dog has a limp.

"Are you hurt?" I stand up and it freezes. I look away, and start for the house, careful not to make eye contact with it even though I'm dying to look back. When I return, it's in the exact same spot and I take a peek between its legs. *Girl.* I break off a piece of cheese and toss it beside her. She gobbles it and looks at me for more. This time I throw the food a few feet in front of us. She's too hungry to be scared of me, or maybe she sees the food as a promise, because she comes forward and eats it. We do this over and over, until we're standing beside Pearl's open passenger door.

When I reach for her, my arms moving closer at an excruciatingly slow pace, she allows it. She's too blissed out on cheese to mind. I scoop her up gently and place her in the passenger seat. I stand back and look at her, realizing I've made a mistake. What if she goes to the bathroom on my seat?

"Stay," I instruct, though I have no idea if she knows commands. I sprint into the house and grab a bathroom towel, my heart banging against my chest by the time I get back to the car. She hasn't moved. I slip the towel under her and get in the driver's seat. I'm searching the internet for vets in Sierra Grande when I hear the sound of water that I know cannot be water because we're not close enough to the river to hear it.

The dog is peeing.

Thank God for the towel.

6

WARNER

My truck slows to stop in front of the homestead. I'm just about to hop out when something small and round rolls across the passenger floorboard and gets stuck under a book. I reach for it, tossing the paperback on the passenger seat and examining the small metal tube in my hand.

Mango flavored lip balm?

Must be Peyton's, though I don't recall buying it for her. It probably fell from her backpack when she'd grabbed it out of the front seat just now. She'd been in a rush, the first bell ringing just as we pulled up in front of school.

Or maybe it's Morgan's. It could've fallen from her purse when I gave her a ride yesterday.

I'd put the woman out of my mind the second I climbed back into my truck and got on the highway to Sierra Grande. Or, I attempted to, anyway. It wasn't easy, not with my fingers still tasting of that spicy sweet candy and my truck smelling like her. It was a mix, something flowery and vanilla, and it was enough to overpower the new car smell for a little while. It wasn't *bad* though. Not at all.

Twisting off the small tin lid, I bring the lip balm to my

nose and sniff. Oh, yes. And this. This was definitely a part of Morgan's scent. I don't want to leave it in here, so I pocket it with plans to toss it in the trash at my cabin. My brothers have a habit of driving my truck around the ranch. I complained once, and my older brother Wes asked me if I wanted a tissue to wipe my crocodile tears.

He's usually an asshole, but he's calmed down since he married Dakota. Can't blame the guy for his behavior before Dakota. Twelve years in the Army fucked him up. A few months ago, he told me he's been going to PTSD group therapy, though according to him it's really just a bunch of old broke dicks sitting around shooting the shit. His words, not mine. I don't know what a broke dick is, but I don't think I want to be one. Whatever he wants to call it, therapy has been about as helpful as Dakota in taming him.

Sometimes I wonder if my younger brother, Wyatt, needs something like that, minus the PTSD diagnosis. I don't know what he'd have to be traumatized by. He lived nearly the same childhood as me, and when Wes left for the military, we grew closer. Then one day, he stopped coming home every night. Fewer family dinners at the homestead. It was like one piece of our family unit broke off and traveled parallel to us instead of with us. Anna and I were knee deep in raising two little kids by then and I didn't have time to figure out Wyatt's problem. I feel more guilt over that now that my kids are a little older and I have more time. Whatever bothered Wyatt seems to have had a lasting effect, because he still comes and goes at random, doing whatever the fuck it is he does. The real mystery is why the hell my parents haven't kicked his ass into gear yet. I'd blame it on him being the baby of the family, except he's only the youngest of us three boys.

Jessie completes the Hayden siblings, our only sister

who's far younger than us all. She's nearing the end of her freshman year at Arizona State University. When it comes to her, I like to stick my head in the sand and pretend she's an angel, though that couldn't be further from the truth. She's always had a wildness about her, and I thank God every day that Peyton seems to be her aunt Jessie's polar opposite. I'd be dead of a heart attack before forty if my little girl were like my wild sister. There's a reason we call her Calamity Jessie, and it's not because she's meek or mild. I think having three big brothers made her tough and bold.

My palm brushes the tin of mango lip balm tucked into my pocket as I walk into my parent's house, and I picture the woman on the roadside in the middle of nowhere. That fully restored '76 Bronco, painted deep green with a black Bimini top, is a vintage car enthusiast's wet dream. And driven by a beautiful woman? Probably just about every red-blooded straight man's fantasy.

I'll admit to having thought of Morgan a handful of times since waking up this morning. Not only was she beyond attractive, but she looked familiar.

Now it's time to put the mysterious, gorgeous stranger out of my mind. Wes hates when I show up distracted, and since he's pretty much running the ranch now, he's technically my boss and won't hesitate to kick my ass. Figuratively. In the literal sense, we're a good match for each other.

Entering the ring with him might be something that happens sooner than later. Once he finds out what I've been up to, he's going to lose his shit. He depends on me. I'm the steady, the constant, the brother who has been here at the Hayden Cattle Company his whole life. I didn't serve in the military like Wes, or fuck off like Wyatt. I was the de facto head of the next generation until Wes returned. I was happy to relinquish my role to the firstborn, and it still surprises me that nobody asked one simple question: *why?*

Nobody in their right mind would think a man could step away from the role I'd occupied for years, unless of course he didn't want it in the first place.

I love the ranch, don't get me wrong. I love her beauty, her curves, the way it takes a whole crew of men to handle her. She is brutal and unforgiving, but generous.

I love her, but there is more out there for me. And when Wes finds out, we may come to blows. It wouldn't be the first time. It probably won't be the last.

But that is for another day. Right now, all I need is a fresh cup of coffee and then I'll get on with the morning's chores.

My eyebrows shoot up in surprise when I find Wes in the kitchen. "Late start this morning?" I ask him, but I don't for one second think that's the case. The man couldn't sleep in if he tried.

He shakes his head. "Refueling," he says, lifting his mug into the air.

I flash him a wicked grin. "Up late last night?"

He gives me a hard look, not one muscle in his face twitching. He doesn't tolerate any mention of Dakota in a sexual capacity, be it joke or innuendo. I had a lot of fun with that before he admitted he liked her. Wes makes it too easy for me to push his buttons.

"I remember those early days of marriage." I sidestep him and reach for the carafe of hot coffee. "It's like being drugged. You can't keep your hands off each other. Even better than when you started dating, because somehow her being your *wife* makes her even sexier."

Wes grunts in either agreement or acknowledgment, which is as good as I'm going to get, and I'm fine with that.

He sips his coffee and stares at me. "You seem chipper for someone who's been a dickhead since I got married."

"Don't sugarcoat it, asshole," I mutter, a twinge of resentment curling in my stomach. Anna served me divorce papers right before Wes and Dakota's wedding. I was less-than-pleasant to be around that weekend, and not-so-great since.

I lean back against the kitchen counter and glance out the kitchen window. The morning sun bathes everything in a soft, creamy gold. As it climbs higher, it will grow in intensity. I used to arrive on the ranch earlier than this, but that was back before Anna left. We had a house in town, and I drove out here for work every day. Now the kids are with me most of the time and we live in the big cabin a half mile from here. My workday begins after I take them to school and drive back out here.

"Things felt different the last time I saw Anna," I tell Wes, turning my gaze away from my family's land. "When we took Charlie to the hospital for those stitches, it was..." I search for the right word, but it evades me, so I shrug. "Different. It felt like we were on the same side again." I'll see her tomorrow morning when I take the kids to her parents for her weekend, and I'm praying it'll be the good experience we had last time. Minus the stitches.

Wes's lips purse, and I know he's exercising extreme control right now. He was furious when she left me and the kids. His opinion of Anna is very low, and I can see why. But if he knew the truth about why she left, he wouldn't be so upset. I can't be mad at him for judging her harshly. She knew it was going to happen, and so did I, but she made me promise to keep her secret. And as much as I hated it, as much as I didn't agree with her, it wasn't my place. So I went along with her lie, and two years later, I'm still going along with it.

"Is that what you want, Warner? To have Anna back, after she left you and the kids to *find herself*?" The last two words are so soaked with disdain, they're dripping.

I drag a hand over the back of my neck, rubbing at the tense muscle. "You wouldn't understand, Wes. You've never loved a woman for nearly two decades and made a family with her." Turning away from all that seems plain wrong.

Wes's lips straighten into a harsh line. I shouldn't have said that. Wes didn't do those things because he was off serving our country, and then when he got out, he was battling the leftover wounds.

Wes sighs. He opens his mouth to speak but our dad walks in. He's a big man, tall and broad-shouldered, physical characteristics he passed down to his three sons. He is soft around the middle now, and his face is deeply lined. He had a heart attack almost a year ago, and I spent the twenty-four hours that followed remembering every important thing the man taught me.

Dad holds up his cell phone, nods his head at it, and hits a button. "You're on speaker, Mayor."

"Thanks, Beau." Mayor Cruz's deep voice fills the kitchen. "Wes, you there?"

Wes glances with uncertainty at our dad, then says, "I'm here, Mayor. What can I do for you?"

"Cary Lindstrom fell off his horse and broke his pelvis. He had signed up to teach that actress about ranching before the movie starts shooting, and I need to replace him."

"Why you?" Wes asks. "Don't they have people for that?" He gestures flippantly in the air with his hands at the word 'people.'

"I'm sure they do," the Mayor says, his tone clipped. "But

I know people with experience and knowledge. A local from Sierra Grande makes for better publicity."

"Maybe they can forget shooting the movie here altogether and go torture another town," I mutter. I was late getting Charlie and Peyton to school this morning because of the increased traffic. They're everywhere, they don't know where to go, and they don't pay attention while they're doing it.

"That you, Warner?" Mayor Cruz asks.

"It's me, Mayor."

"We need the movie almost as much as the movie needs our scenery. I'm sure I don't have to remind any of the Hayden men about the bad press our town has had in the past year." He lets it hang out in the air, the reminder of the meth lab that exploded just off our property last summer.

"That wasn't on our land, Mayor." Wes's tone is even, but he sends a middle finger to the phone. One side of my dad's mouth lifts in a smile.

"All the same, it made the state paper, and a small town like Sierra Grande doesn't need a bad reputation. Wes, your wife has done a good job of bringing tourists to this town with The Orchard, and I'd like to see that continue. It's nothing but good for the local economy, even if it creates a little traffic." His jab is directed at me, no doubt. And then, Mayor Cruz takes it one step further. "Warner, I have a great idea. Let's have you become the actress's teacher. You can let her follow you around, teach her to ride, whatever else she needs."

I make a face and shake my head, even though he can't see me.

Wes lifts a stiff upright palm in the air, telling me he's got this. "Mayor, with all due respect, Warner is my right-hand man on the ranch. I need him."

"He can still work, Wes. He'll just have a shadow."

"I'll think it over and call you back," Wes says. He doesn't like being told what to do any more than the rest of us. It's a Hayden trait, and it's indiscriminate of gender. My mother, Jessie, and even Peyton will tell you where you can stick your commands.

"Don't wait too long," the mayor warns. "She's here and she was supposed to start this morning." The line goes quiet, and my dad tucks his phone back into his pocket, checking first to make sure the line isn't still active.

"He's right, Wes," my dad walks closer. His white undershirt peeks out from the top button of his denim button-up. He stops a foot from Wes. "You've got to start thinking about what's best for this ranch, and unfortunately that sometimes means doing things you don't want to do. You didn't want to sell that land to Dakota, and look how that turned out for you."

Wes scowls. A low sound that's close to a laugh rumbles in the back of my throat. "It's true, brother." I pat his shoulder. "You had no desire to sell that land, but it turned out well for every person in this town, and not just because you got a wife and the business out of the deal."

An old family rule made it so that Wes couldn't inherit the Hayden Cattle Company unless he was married. Dakota solved that problem for him, but had he refused the sale of the land, he'd still be single and pining for the family business.

Wes grins at me, and I know well enough to be alarmed by it. "What?" I ask sharply.

"Would you prefer your student call you Warner, or Mr. Hayden?"

My jaw tightens. "Wes—"

"Sorry, can't talk now." An exaggerated apologetic look

replaces his smile. “Gotta tell the mayor I’ve found Cary’s replacement.”

“Fuck you,” I snarl under my breath.

“Naw, I’m good, thanks. By the way, the new logos came. Make sure you grab one out of Dad’s office and put it on your truck.” He makes a kissing sound at me on his way out of the kitchen.

I start for him, but my dad stops me with a hand on my shoulder. I could easily push past him, but I don’t. Beau Hayden isn’t someone to be trifled with. He might look all of his seventy years, but that’s just a number. What it really means is that for seven decades he’s been kicking ass and burying secrets.

“Come on,” he says, lightly shoving me toward the back door. “Wyatt’s in the stable, helping the farrier shoe horses. Get your ass out there and help him.”

7

WARNER

"I'm excited to see Mom." Peyton glances at me from the passenger seat, assessing my reaction.

I hate that she does that. Correction: I hate that she feels the need to do that. She shouldn't be worried about how I feel.

"Does she know we're early?" Charlie asks, his feet bouncing against the seat.

My wink reassures him. "I sent her a text, buddy." She didn't answer, but I'm sure it's not a problem. The actress is coming to the ranch this morning to meet everyone, and I need to get back in time.

We pull up to Anna's parents' house. A car I don't recognize is parked out front. Something slick and fast. My truck dwarfs it.

Charlie and Peyton get out and run ahead. I sling their overnight bags over my shoulders and start for the house.

I'm halfway up the driveway when movement from the backyard catches my eye. It's probably Charlie, already back there running around. Sugar from the chocolate chip pancakes my mom made him for breakfast is coursing through his veins. It's a Saturday morning ritual, but it leaves me with a kid on a sugar high. He was bouncing in his seat the whole drive over. We don't need another close encounter with the bird feeder, so I walk to the gate, opening my mouth to remind Charlie to be careful.

But it's not Charlie.

It's my wife.

With another man's mouth on her neck.

"What the fuck?" I growl. From my limited view between the slats of wood, I see Anna's eyes widen and her head whip toward the gate.

"Warner," she croaks. My name sounds like sorrow, wrapped up in guilt and tied with a ribbon of apology.

I drop the kids' bags at the gate and stride toward my truck. I want to say goodbye to Peyton and Charlie, but I can't. I can't fake it right now. Behind me I hear the metallic clang of the gate latch.

"Warner, wait."

Her voice is a plea. My hand stalls on my door handle. This woman broke my heart two years ago when she left and didn't come back, but I understood. Right now, I don't understand.

Fucking *hope*. That's why I feel this way. I dared to hope.

"Warner." Now my name is a whisper.

I turn around.

Tears run down her cheeks, but other than that, she looks as good as she did a few weeks ago. Behind Anna the black BMW comes sharply into focus, and suddenly I understand just why she is doing so well. She has someone else now. That's why she sent me divorce papers. She hasn't mentioned them since she sent them, but that doesn't mean anything. What I hoped was a change of heart was actually just her treading lightly with me.

I stand there, waiting, my entire body trembling with anger, but Anna can't seem to get any words out. She meets my eyes and blinks rapidly. As angry as I am, as badly as my heart is hurting, it still pains me to see how much this is hurting Anna. And that, in turn, angers me even more.

"My lawyer will send the signed papers to you on Monday." I open the truck door and climb in.

"Warner." Her voice breaks.

My forearm rests on the open window frame. "Do our kids know him?"

Her head shakes in tiny, rapid movements. "I was going to introduce them today. I'm planning to tell them he's my friend."

My face twists in what I know is a nasty look as I recall his lips on Anna. I look toward the gate, but he's not there.

"He's driving back down to Phoenix this afternoon." Anna's adding this information to subdue me, but it doesn't help. I'm fucking floored.

I nod and bite the inside of my cheek, then start my truck and shift into drive. I don't say goodbye, because as far as I'm concerned, at this moment there's nothing more to be said.

We're through. Now I finally get it.

I WANT A BEER OR SEVEN. No matter that it's ten in the morning. It's a Saturday, it wouldn't be totally depressing to start this early. I think I deserve it, seeing as how I just received confirmation my wife did, in fact, mean it when she served me with divorce papers.

Before I can retreat to my cabin and lick my wounds all weekend until it's time to pick my kids up from Brock and

Susan's, I have to stop at the homestead and meet the actress. Wes just texted and said she's there. I'm only five minutes away. I can probably be back in my cabin watching ESPN with a beer in my hand in under an hour.

I still can't believe I was roped into showing this person the ways of ranch life. I'm positive she's going to be a pain. The whole plan reeks of certain headache. She'll hate the ranch. She'll spend the whole time complaining about the smells, the dirt, the hard work, her shoes getting muddy, the muscle fatigue, the calluses, and on and on and on. I swear to God if she has on high heels, I'm going to tell Wes to shove this idea up his ass.

I take the turnoff, easing my truck beneath the big metal Hayden Cattle Company sign, and drive the half mile of dirt road to the homestead. I could veer off now and go home to my cabin, but I don't. My anger has cooled to the point of simmering instead of boiling. I just have to fake it for a little while and I can go hide out for the remainder of the weekend.

There's Wes's truck, parked beside Wyatt's. My mom and dad's cars are parked on the side of the house, and beside them is *what the actual fuck?*

A green '76 Bronco.

I slow to a stop, parking beside the vintage car. What is Morgan doing here? Is she the actress? Is that why I recognized her? No. I mean, she's gorgeous enough, but wouldn't she have said something? Maybe Morgan is the actress's assistant? Which means that line about New Mexico was a lie.

The whole time I'm wondering all this, it's not escaping my attention that for the first time in thirty minutes I'm not feeling excruciating pain. It's...nice.

I get out and walk up to the Bronco. A dog is curled up

in the passenger seat, asleep. Where in the world did Morgan get a dog? It looks up at me, apparently not so asleep, and lets out a low growl. I walk away, shaking my head at the bizarre events of a day that began just a few hours ago, and walk into my parents' house.

I smell her before I see her, like I'm a goddamn bloodhound. Vanilla and flowers, minus the mango lip balm. I could still give it back to her. It never made it into the trash.

They're in the living room. Her back is to me, so she doesn't see me walk in. She sits on the couch beside Wyatt, and Dakota is on her other side. Wes and my parents sit on the couch across from them, and Gramps is asleep in the chair. Too bad Jessie isn't here, she's the one who was going on and on about a movie being filmed in Sierra Grande.

Mom meets my eyes. "There you are," she says, smiling up at me. All eyes turn to me, including Morgan's.

Her shoulders drop. Her mouth forms a tiny 'o.'

And just like two days ago when I pulled off the highway and stepped out of my truck, there's a weird tugging sensation in my chest. I'd chalked it up to her resemblance to Anna, but they really only have the basics in common. Blonde hair, blue eyes.

This feeling right now is something else entirely.

8

TENLEY

OH NO. OH NO NO NO NO NO.

Not the gorgeous man who rescued me. I wouldn't have lied to him if I thought I'd ever see him again.

Juliette, who I met fifteen minutes ago along with the rest of the Hayden family, is the first to speak. "Warner, this is Tenley."

The blush on my cheeks is unwelcome and embarrassing. I should be better at not showing what I'm really feeling, but this situation isn't exactly one I've found myself in before. I turn so I can see him. He wears jeans, a T-shirt, and a baseball cap, the same as he did two days ago.

I know he hears the name his mom said, but it doesn't register until he's halfway through saying, "Hi, Morg—" His eyebrows pinch together. "Wait, what?" His gaze shifts to his mom, as if he'd misheard her. I look over at her too.

"Tenley Roberts, Warner." Juliette gives him a *come on* look. "The actress you're going to be working with."

My gaze swings back over to Warner. His jaw is flexed, his eyes narrowed at me. "Right." The *t* sound is so pronounced it's all I need to know he's angry I lied.

I stand up and round the couch, my leg brushing Dakota's knees as I go. I extend a hand like I'm introducing myself properly, but my eyes are imploring him to understand. He was so kind to me two days ago, going so far as to use rocks to write his license plate number, and I lied to him. I know I had the right reasons for giving him a fake name, but I still feel badly about it. It's obvious honesty means a lot to him.

"It's nice to see you again, Warner." I'm sure every single member of the Hayden family is confused by my wording. "Thank you for agreeing to step in for Cary. I appreciate it."

My hand dangles in the air, waiting for him to take it. He stares at me, his toffee eyes dark and cold, nothing like two days ago. He places his hand in mine, and I try not to feel it everywhere. A zinging through my body, like an injection into my bloodstream.

Juliette clears her throat, not like she feels a tickle but more like she's giving Warner a proverbial kick in the ass.

Warner sucks in a breath. "It's no problem, Ms. Roberts. Here at the Hayden Cattle Company, we aim to please." He drops my hand, gives both me and his entire family a dirty look, and disappears the way he came.

Slowly I turn around to face his family. I'm mortified. They all look surprised and curious.

I explain. "Warner and I met two days ago on the highway a couple hours outside of Sierra Grande. My car broke down and he pulled over. He was so helpful and nice." My teeth capture my lower lip and I bite down, my gaze returning to the space where Warner was just standing. "I didn't tell him my real name..." I trail off, unsure how to explain my reasons to the Hayden family.

"You don't owe us an explanation," Wes says, walking over to Dakota and pulling her up off the couch. They make a striking couple, with her strawberry blonde hair and his dark features. "Please excuse my brother today. Normally he's the most good-natured of all of us." Wes looks at his parents. "Warner dropped the kids off with Anna this morning. I'm guessing it didn't go well." Understanding dawns in everyone's eyes. This person, *Anna*, has meaning. Wife? Ex-wife?

Juliette stands up, but Beau stays seated, his knee crossed over his other knee in a figure four. He runs his fingers over his jaw, thinking about something. From the chair, a snore drifts softly from the elderly man introduced to me as Gramps, and I smile as I remember what he'd said to me when we shook hands. *I'm so old I don't have a name anymore.*

Juliette touches my shoulder. "Tenley, I'm sorry about the way Warner behaved. Personal problems or not, that's not how I expect guests to be treated in my home."

"Get the switch," Wyatt says, smirking. Dakota laughs and Wes rolls his eyes. Juliette gives Wyatt an affectionate side-eye. Gramps snores again, louder this time.

"Well, thank you all for the meeting. I'll see you back here on Monday, like we talked about. Maybe Warner will be feeling better by then." I take a step back but Dakota pulls away from Wes and walks to me.

"I'll walk you out," she offers, looping her arm through my elbow.

We're through the front door when she says, "The Haydens can be terrifying, I know. I've had my own fair share of drama with them. But I promise you, Warner really is the nicest of the bunch. He's never been anything but kind to me. He's just going through a hard time."

"With his wife?" I ask, hoping I don't sound too interested.

She pauses on the top step of the porch stairs. "Yes." She

nods, but she doesn't offer anything more. As much as I'd like to hear about it, I also like that Dakota's not divulging. In my experience, trustworthy people aren't easy to come by.

I walk down the steps and look toward my car. Libby's on her hind legs, her paws on the dash, watching us. After the visit to the vet yesterday, where he removed a thorn from her paw and I learned she wasn't microchipped, I decided it was safe to give her a name. The vet said he'd never seen her before.

"Thanks for walking me out," I say, my gaze swinging back to Dakota. She's leaning against one of the two beams that flank the stairs.

"No problem. Maybe one of these days when you're finished shadowing, we can grab lunch at my place."

For a second I think she's talking about her house, but then she adds, "Sorry, I mean The Orchard. I own it, that's why I called it my place. It's a restaurant. Sort of." She waves her hand around and laughs. "Anyway, I'll see you soon."

She retreats back into the house and I go to my car. When I climb in, Libby scurries into my lap. She's part beagle, according to the vet, and a few other breeds. He said if I really want to know, I could get a DNA test, but I don't want to. I already love her, knowing her heritage isn't necessary. I considered putting up lost dog signs, but I can't list my name or phone number. For now, it's just me and Libby.

And Warner.

Who is apparently having trouble with Anna, the woman he dropped his kids off with. I can see this whole situation like a storyline, and it sounds as intriguing as the soap opera my parents starred in.

***

I've never had so little to do before. Or so few people to do it with.

I'm sitting on the back porch, my feet propped on the railing, when I make the decision to go into town. I'm hungry, and cooking for one is making me sad. I've spent the last two years cooking for two, or getting takeout for two, or considering another person in general. With Tate gone, I only need to think about myself. I know it's a healthy thing to be able to be alone, I just don't like it very much.

Once inside the house, I lock the door leading to the back porch and place my empty glass of iced tea in the kitchen sink. I change my clothes and coax Libby into the crate I bought yesterday at the pet store, which she definitely does not want to do. I feel bad for crating her, but this isn't my house. To make up for it, I drop in two of the toys I picked up when I bought the crate.

"Stop with the puppy eyes," I instruct her, but she doesn't listen. If anything, she turns on the pitiful look even more. "I'll bring you back a treat," I tell her, sticking two fingers through the skinny bars and scratching behind her ears.

It's a nice night and an easy drive to town. The air is a little cool, though the day was warm. I learned yesterday that there can be up to a thirty-degree difference between daytime and nighttime temperatures in the desert, so I tied a long sleeve shirt around my waist before climbing into Pearl. I also pulled on a hat and wound my hair into a bun at the nape of my neck. I don't have security right now, largely because I refused them when my dad suggested it. The last thing I wanted to do was show up in a sleepy small town with two big, burly, scary-looking men going everywhere with me. Sticking out like a sore thumb was not my goal.

And, as I meander through the downtown area with its cute streetlights and stores, I think I made the right call.

When I see the reddish pink lit-up sign for a diner, I pull into a spot and kill the engine. Though I don't know that I really need it, I keep the hat on my head. Better safe than sorry.

The diner is dated and smells like French fries. It's perfect.

I choose a booth at the back of the small room and slide in. I could keep my back to the place but I don't think that will be necessary. There are only two other families in here right now, and they didn't even look up when I walked in.

An older lady approaches me, her bottle-dyed red hair pinned on either side of her head with copper-colored clips. "Hey, darlin'," she says, sliding a plastic menu across to me. "Cute hat."

I touch the brim. "Thanks."

"What's it mean?"

"Oh, um..." My fingers bump over the embroidery. "It's the Japanese symbol for salvation."

She winks at me. "Well, it's cute. My name's Cherilyn." A sparkly deep purple fake nail taps the plastic name tag clipped to her shirt. "What can I get you to drink?"

I pick up the menu and scan it. Dried ketchup blocks the bottom of the list of shake flavors. "Chocolate malt, please."

"Sure thing." Cherilyn walks away and I look back to the menu. I have no business eating a cheeseburger, or drinking the malt I just ordered, but my trainer isn't here and thanks to this being a town without paparazzi, he'll never know.

A group of teenage girls walk in the diner at the same time Cherilyn is carrying over my drink. I pull my hat lower and look down at the cracked seat. The only thing worse than being recognized by teenage girls is having a stalker. I know both from experience.

"Here you are," Cherilyn says cheerily, setting the treat in front of me. "Do you know what you want to eat?"

"Cheeseburger and fries," I say, trying not to draw any attention to myself.

Cherilyn looks back at the entrance where the girls are standing, glancing over a menu. She looks back at me and leans down. "Honey," she says in a low voice, "I knew who you were the second you walked in here. Your secret is safe with me."

Then she walks up to the girls and corrals them, leading them to a table that's as far from me as they can get without being seated on the street.

Cherilyn meets my eyes and I mouth *thank you.*

When my dinner arrives, I dig in with gusto. Until today, the peach candy has been the only treat I've had in months.

I'm halfway finished when the door opens and more people walk in. I keep my head down, but the excited whispers are impossible to ignore. The door opens, one, two, three, four times, until it becomes too much to keep track of.

The chattering sounds like a buzz swirling around me. I'd forgotten how terrifying it can be, that feeling of being watched. In LA, only tourists are excited to see actors and actresses. Aside from paparazzi on the street, for the most part we're left alone, or maybe asked for an autograph a couple times. I lift my head just slightly, trying to see the room through my eyelashes.

"Excuse me." I hear Cherilyn's voice, but it's not sweet like it was when she came to my table. She sounds like a stern schoolteacher. "Move it."

I pull a fifty out of my wallet and hand it to her. I meet her eyes, and get a full view of the diner. It's a madhouse. All the tables are full, the booths stuffed with people. And though some are pretending to look at menus, many are blatantly staring at me. Fear coils in my stomach. They don't look particularly threatening, but I've seen how quickly crowds can go from passive to aggressive.

"I promise I did not tell a soul you were here," Cherilyn says. "It was probably those teenage girls. They get on one of those social media sites and it's like posting a billboard."

And far more effective with far greater reach.

I smile tightly. "Do you have a back entrance?"

Cherilyn glances down a short hallway. "Past those bathrooms, but I honestly don't think you should go that way. It'll dump you out into a place that's pretty secluded, and you'll have to walk a ways to get to your car. Your best bet is to go through it." She nods at the rest of the diner with her head. I look out again to assess the scene, and that's when I hear it.

I can't tell who, but someone says, "I bet it's the old Stephens house by the river. Where else?"

I freeze. People know where I'm staying? *Shit.*

And then, by the grace of sweet Jesus, I see an angel in the crowd. He might as well have a halo. I raise a hand and shout, "Wyatt!"

Wyatt has just stepped into the diner and is looking around, bewildered, at the scene. He finds my waving hand in the crowd and I change the movement so that now I'm beckoning him. He comes forward, sidestepping tables. He looks a lot like Warner in his jeans and T-shirt with a ball cap, but he's different too. I noticed it immediately when I met him earlier today that he has a restless energy.

Wyatt strides up to the booth and stands beside Cherilyn. "Ma'am." He nods to her. "Tenley, what's wrong?"

I tip my head slightly toward the rest of the room, giving him a silent answer.

He gets it. "Thought it looked a little busy. How can I help?"

"Maybe just walk me out of here? Be my bodyguard?" I laugh on the last part, trying to bring levity to the moment.

"You got it," he says.

I get up from the booth and startle when Cherilyn pulls me into her generous, warm body for a hug. "Honey, I hug my friends, and as far as I'm concerned, we're thick as thieves now."

"I'll be back," I assure her. "Just maybe for takeout."

Wyatt slings an arm around my shoulders, super casual like he's a friend and we're walking down the street. His posture is relaxed, but I get the feeling he could shift at a moment's notice.

We're almost to the front door when someone yells out, "Tenley, can I get a picture with you?"

I turn around. It's a young girl, probably seventeen. She doesn't look hopeful or sweet; she looks haughty and challenging.

I square my shoulders and look out at the sea of mostly young faces. "I appreciate you all coming out here to see me tonight." I smile my famous smile, the one that makes people call me a *sweetheart*. And I am mostly, but I'm also human.

"Just one selfie isn't going to hurt," the girl says again with a snotty look on her face. I remember what it was like to be her age, but I was damn sure never making public scenes like this girl. I left high school at fifteen and began homeschooling because I was working so much.

"Ella McFarland!" Cherilyn bellows, coming through the crowd. She levels a glare at the girl. "I am playing Bunco with your grandma tomorrow night and I will be telling her about you getting too big for your britches. You've been taught how to treat a guest in our town, so you should know better than to act like this."

The girl shrinks. I turn away, hiding behind a curtain of hair, so she can't see me smile.

Wyatt grabs a toothpick from the container on the counter and slides it between his lips. He tosses me a star mint and opens the door, waiting for me to step out first.

"Oh my gosh," I exhale loudly and squeeze my eyes tight as soon as we're on the sidewalk. It's dark outside now and the streetlights have come on, casting a light and shadow pattern on the sidewalk every twenty feet. I look up at Wyatt. He's using two fingers to roll the end of the toothpick that's sticking out from his lips.

"Does that happen everywhere you go?" he asks.

I shake my head. "Not in LA. People are so used to seeing industry people that they don't bat an eye anymore. Depending on where I travel for filming, like a big city for instance, I take bodyguards. I've never had to show up before filming to learn about cattle ranching, and I didn't think bodyguards were necessary." I smile crookedly, and he chuckles.

"No? Weird." Wyatt pulls his phone from his pocket like he's checking it, then drops it back down.

I clap my hands once in front of my chest. "Okay, well, thank you for coming to my rescue. I'm just going to go home and—" I stop short, remembering the talk in the diner, them guessing where I'm staying.

Wyatt cocks his head, waiting for me to continue.

"It's just that some people in there were talking about where they think I'm staying, and they were actually right, so..." I make a bare-teeth face. "I don't feel safe, but I have to go back and get my dog. And then," I look around like a hotel will magically pop out and reveal itself to me. "I need to find a place to stay."

Wyatt pulls the toothpick from his mouth. "I've got an idea."

9

TENLEY

"You're sure?" I ask, whispering, though I don't know why I'm whispering. There's nobody to hear us except all the pine trees and whatever animals inhabit them.

"Come on," Wyatt answers, which isn't really an answer at all but a directive. He reaches into the bed of his truck and retrieves my small overnight bag that he'd tossed in there. Libby squirms in my arms. I let her down and she runs to a tree, squatting beside it.

Wyatt watches her. "I'm glad she knows to do *that* outside."

Libby finishes and runs back to me. "I've only had her for a few days, but she seems to be trained." Which means she probably had an owner at some point, or maybe still does. I don't want to think about that too much. I'm getting attached to her. "You can still change your mind, you know. You can take us back to town and I'll smuggle her into The Sierra. She can fit in my bag." I'd looked up the hotel when Wyatt passed by it on our way out of town, and the website made it clear they had a no-dog policy.

"Just stay put," Wyatt says, slinging my bag over his

shoulder and walking toward the cabin. It looks just like the main house where his parents live, all wood and stone, but smaller. Wyatt told me they call his parents' house the 'homestead,' which makes me want to name my own parents' house in Malibu. He also told me his parents built a cabin for each of their kids, and that Wes and Dakota are currently building an addition because they hope to expand their family sometime soon. I didn't ask about Warner, even though curiosity is burning through me.

"Home sweet home," Wyatt announces, pushing the front door and holding it open for me. I step inside and find myself in the living room.

"It's small," Wyatt says, "a living room, a kitchen, one bedroom."

"As long as you have a couch."

"You can take my bed."

I shake my head. "I'm not going to steal your bed. You've done enough." He got me out of the diner, drove me to the house to get some things and pick up Libby, and brought me out here. He thought leaving Pearl parked on the street was the best idea because everyone who was in the diner was still watching me on the sidewalk, and he didn't want them seeing what car I was getting into. I pointed out my California license plate, and he pointed out there are a 'shit ton' of California license plates in town right now. The way he said it made me think their presence annoys him.

"You take my bed," Wyatt argues, striding to a small linen closet and pulling out a set of sheets. "Because if you sleep on the couch then my bed will be empty and there's no point in that."

"Are you planning to sleep under the stars tonight?" I'm being sarcastic, but also on the winding drive out here, past the lights of Sierra Grande and into the darkness of Hayden land, the night became brilliant, the sky shot through with twinkling light.

Wyatt shakes his head. "I was in town tonight for a reason, and I'm going back there." And that's it. Nothing more. No further explanation.

"Alright," I say slowly, chalking it up to a woman he doesn't want to speak about. "I guess I will take your bed."

He hands the sheets to me. "My mother would kick my ass for this, so don't tell her, but would you mind changing the sheets yourself? I'm late."

I take the linens, hugging them to my chest. "Of course. Go. I didn't realize."

"I didn't tell you," he says, shrugging. "I'll be back in the morning to take you to your car." He retreats to the open front door, pausing beside it. "You're safe, okay? There's no safer place than the ranch." And then he leaves, closing the door softly behind him.

I walk over, sliding the lock into place. Wyatt's engine comes to life, a single disturbance in the quiet of the night.

I switch the sheets, throw Wyatt's sheets on top of the washing machine, and change into my pajamas.

Libby snuggles into bed beside me, and though I'm falling asleep in a strange place for the second time this week, her warmth brings me comfort.

"Coffee first, Libby," I say, directing the words to my feet. Libby sits beside me, her paw resting on the top of my foot. I don't want to move it, so I stretch to fill the coffee pot with water from the tap. I let the coffee brew just long enough to pause it, fill one of Wyatt's cups, and then let it resume.

"Come on," I say to Libby, and she bounds in front of me

toward the front door. We step outside into the crisp morning air. It smells resinous, earthy, and pretty much just as good as any candle emulating it ever could. Every morning since I arrived in Sierra Grande I've gone outside and let the peacefulness of the landscape settle into me, but this is different. Taller trees filled out with needles. The trees around my place are skinny. It's more desert than whatever this is. I noticed it when I drove out to meet the Hayden family, the higher elevation that brought on the change in landscape.

I take a seat on Wyatt's front porch and watch Libby scurry out to the same tree she used last night. I sip my coffee and close my eyes, appreciating the absolute silence of the moment.

"It's a dog!"

My eyes snap open, my neck craning around to find the source of the squeal. Two children careen around the corner of the cabin, slowing as they get close to Libby.

Libby's eyes widen in terror, and she sprints back to me. I meet her at the bottom of the three front porch steps, my coffee sloshing over the sides of my cup. She leaps into my arms and I stand.

The kids are frozen in place, staring at me.

"Hello." I wave. "She's just a little skittish. She's a rescue." I think, anyway. Selfishly, I'm hoping she is.

The older child, a girl with brown hair and a guarded expression, points behind me. "Is my Uncle Wyatt home?"

I blink twice, the puzzle pieces falling into place. *These are Warner's kids.* Which means Warner must be around here somewhere too.

"No, he's not home." I shake my head and Libby gets excited. I think she's decided she'd like to say hi to the kids after all. I bend, setting her on the ground, and she trots over. Both the girl and the younger boy clap their hands and smile, bending down. Libby licks their faces, and they laugh.

"Charlie? Peyton?" a deep voice yells from somewhere nearby.

I turn my head in the direction the children came from, and just as I do, Warner strides into view. He's staring at the kids, wearing a confused look and those same jeans I swear are going to be the death of me. He hasn't seen me yet, and I'm afforded the chance to watch him.

Reverence softens his features when he looks at his kids. There is no question of his love and devotion, even from this distance. It radiates from his pores.

A pang, a longing, a sliver of hurt slices across my chest. I have good parents now, but I didn't always.

Warner glances toward Wyatt's cabin, and his calm, bemused expression is replaced with shock. His jaw flexes, his body stiffens.

I suck in a sharp breath. I know what this looks like. Me in pajamas, standing in front of Wyatt's cabin. I open my mouth to speak, but the words stick in my throat. Warner's coming this way, his lips pressed together and his eyes stormy. He stops a mere foot from me, his chest rising and falling with a deep breath, as if corralling his emotions.

The air around me might be refreshing, but the air between us is so tense it should be viscous, something I can sink my hand into and gather in my palm.

"Hi, Warner," I say, my voice kind, and I smile. He was a bit of a jerk yesterday but he had a reason. I get it.

He doesn't say anything, but I can tell that he wants to. Different responses dance through his eyes, and I'm almost positive none of them are very nice. Behind him, his children dart back and forth, and Libby chases them. What's happening over there is so different than what's happening right here.

Warner stares at me for another second, then sidesteps me and heads for the cabin. I sigh.

I lift my chin and say to the sky, "He's not in there."

I turn around. Warner has stopped on the second stair. "Where is he?"

I shrug. "I don't know."

He side-eyes the cabin. "Sounds about right," he mutters. He stomps past me. "Charlie and Peyton, let's go. We need to leave early if we want to make it on time." He shoots me a look. "Increased traffic in town these days. I'm sure you know where it came from."

My nose wrinkles. I understand being mad at me for lying, but seriously? I had a reason. A good one, too.

Warner's walking back the way he came. He glances at me as he goes. "Are you going to be done playing house in time to shadow me or should we put it off until tomorrow?"

My mouth drops open in shock. I cannot reconcile this rude man with the same person who helped me on the side of the road.

He disappears from view, his kids following him. Libby runs over and goes with me into Wyatt's cabin. My limbs are rigid, little sparks of anger shooting off inside me.

I get changed, strip the sheets, and check my phone on my way to throw them into the washing machine.

Wyatt has texted me. ***Sorry, I'm not going to make it home this morning in time to take you to town. Warner lives in the cabin behind mine, you can catch a ride with him.***

I exhale and drop my chin to my chest, then hurry to stuff the sheets into the washer. I don't have time to replace Wyatt's sheets on his bed if I'm going to catch Warner.

"Ugh," I groan out loud, double-stepping to my

overnight bag and zipping it up. With Libby in my arms, I leave Wyatt's place, walking around front and following the path I saw Warner take a few minutes ago. About a quarter mile away sits another cabin, a second replica of the homestead, but bigger than Wyatt's.

I wonder if Warner lived there with his wife?

I shake my head at the thought. It doesn't matter if he did. My first impression of him was obviously wrong.

His truck is parked out front, shiny and new, but now it has a decal on the side, the letters HCC in large font. If I'd seen that when Pearl broke down, maybe I would have put two and two together, or not seen him so much as a random person. He would've belonged to something, and maybe I'd have felt comfortable telling him my real name.

Would of, could of, should of.

I put my head down and hurry the last one hundred feet to Warner's home. There's no use in looking back now, I certainly can't change the past.

Peyton and Charlie step from the front door, backpacks slung over their shoulders, followed by Warner. He looks friendly again, his features back to the way he looked before he spotted me in front of Wyatt's cabin. That's bound to change once I do what I'm about to do.

I raise my hand and walk closer. "Warner?"

He stops dead in his tracks, his gaze shifting to me. His kids climb into his truck, doors closing behind them.

Warner raises an eyebrow at me, but at least he isn't staring me down the way he did at Wyatt's. Baby steps. "Do you need to borrow a cup of sugar?" he asks, his voice even.

I laugh like it was funnier than it really was. "Nope. Wyatt was supposed to drive me back to town this morning but couldn't, so can you please give me a lift?"

The corner of Warner's mouth quirks up like he's about

to smile or chuckle, but I can't see what's funny. He shakes his head back and forth slowly, just twice, and runs his thumb over his lower lip. "Jump in."

He walks to his truck, but instead of going around to the driver's side he heads for the passenger side, reaching out to open the door. He pauses, his hand on the door handle, and suddenly turns back to me. I put on the brakes, nearly bumping into the back of him. I smell him again, that same scent I picked up when he was leaning over my engine, and it ribbons around my chest, twirling and cascading through me.

I really should take a step back, maybe even two. I just... can't. It's as simple as that.

Warner looks down at me, and I watch his eyes shift, a tiny flex in his cheek muscles, his jaw going slack. "You should know Wyatt's not a commitment guy." His hand tightens on the door handle. "Unless that's what you're after, I suppose. No strings."

I shake my head. I need to set the record straight about me and Wyatt. "Warner—"

He lifts a hand. "Not interested." He opens the door and leaves it. I spend two seconds watching Warner walk around the front of his truck, then climb in.

I'm annoyed. I wish he'd let me explain about it all, but if he refuses to listen then I can't be responsible for the way he feels. He's wrong, and if he'd let me tell him the truth, he wouldn't have to feel the way he feels. Stubborn ass.

If it weren't for Libby, the drive into town would've been unbearably awkward. She sat in the middle between Warner and me, her front paws propped on the back of the seat, and happily accepted head scratches from Warner's kids. I learned his son, Charlie, just turned ten and is in the fourth grade. He loves his teacher, fishing, and might have a crush on his classmate Sydney but vehemently denied it when Peyton asked him about it.

Peyton is thirteen, and not nearly as excited to chat with me. I'd describe her as suspicious. Twice I noticed her staring at me, but not with fascination the way people do when they realize who I am. More like she's trying to decide how I fit into everything, and I don't want to utter a word. She's Warner's child, and in the interest of not stepping on his toes, I'll let him explain to her who I am and why the hell I'm on the ranch at all.

"Where to?" Warner asks me as we approach the outskirts of town.

"The diner on High Street," I answer. He looks at me, waiting for an explanation as to why my Bronco is parked there. He was probably expecting me to send him to a bar, because he's still operating under the mistaken impression that I met his brother somewhere and went back to his cabin with him for a wild night of no-strings-attached sex.

"Long story," I mouth. Explaining it in front of his kids would do nothing but create more questions.

Warner turns on to High Street, and I feel disappointed he's not dropping off the kids at school first. Now I'll have to wait until we're alone at some point on the ranch today to tell him nothing happened between me and Wyatt.

Warner pulls up behind Pearl. I say goodbye to the kids, thank Warner, and scoop Libby into my arms.

Just before the truck door closes, I hear Charlie say, "Dad, can we get a dog?"

Smiling to myself, I unlock Pearl and climb inside. I need to shower and head back out to the Hayden ranch. I'm nervous to go alone to the house I've been staying in, but I don't know what else to do. There are other movie people here, but I don't know them personally. Mostly it's the set builders and designers out here now, building out a large previously empty warehouse on the southern edge of Sierra Grande for all the indoor scenes. Calvin won't be here for a couple more weeks. He filmed a western a few years ago and has some experience already, so he's not clueless like me.

If I'm that scared, I need to get security out here. In the meantime, I'll check into The Sierra and smuggle in Libby. She's a good dog, she's not going to ruin their carpets or eat their furniture. I think.

On my way out, I call Gretchen and ask her to arrange for security to come out.

By the time I get to the house I'm feeling better, and even mildly foolish. It was a well-meaning crowd, not a dangerous one. Libby walks around the house with me, glued to my side as I check closets and look under beds.

"All clear," I whisper into her soft fur. She sits on the bathroom floor while I take a shower. I get out, towel off, and walk back into the room, opening a dresser drawer.

My hand flies to my mouth, covering my gasp.

All my underwear is gone.

10

WARNER

"Did you hear that actress is getting lessons in cattle ranching out on the Hayden ranch? Wouldn't it be a hoot if one of those Hayden boys fell for her?" Barb can see it now, one of those handsome cowboys falling in love with an actress.

Shirley frowns. "The younger one?"

"No, no, he's a bit of a scoundrel from what I've heard." Barb adjusts the collection of bracelets on her wrist.

"There's no one else. The middle son is still married."

"Not for long. I saw him walking into that lawyers office this morning."

Shirley makes a face. "You don't know what he was doing there."

Barb smiles her response. She knows she's right. She'd bet every last one of the flowers in her garden on it.

* * *

"That's it then, huh?" I sit back in the uncomfortable chair and toss the pen on the desk. It lands on the papers I've just signed.

Our family lawyer, Chelsea Banks, gazes at me across the desk. She is not one for emotion, which is probably why my dad chose her years ago. "Almost. They aren't turned in yet. You could still change your mind."

Considering my wife has moved on and didn't bother to tell me about it, I'm unlikely to have a change of heart. "I won't," I say gruffly, shaking my head and pushing up from my seat.

I say goodbye and leave her office, stepping into the bright desert sun. A day like this should be dark and gloomy, the air heavy with impending rain. Instead, it's yellow, the sun's rays reflecting off store windows. I slip on my sunglasses.

Two streets over is the diner where I dropped off Tenley this morning. I know I was a jerk to her, but I felt entirely unable to stop. Fury pulsed through me when I saw her standing in front of Wyatt's cabin, wearing those matching striped pajamas shorts and top. It wasn't like it was even sexy, but it was what it all represented. My wife chose another man, even after the two years I spent supporting her needs. Tenley chose my brother, even after... well, nothing. I have no claim to her, even though I saw her first. We're not children. Still, I feel slighted.

I reach up and rub my eyes. What a fucking day, and it's barely even started. I need to get back out to the ranch before Tenley arrives. I need to figure out how I really feel about those papers I just dropped off.

And I really need a giant cup of coffee.

From a diner two streets over.

***

"Hello, Warner," Cherilyn says to me before the bell

above the door I've just come through finishes its tinkling sound.

I walk up to the counter she stands behind. "Hey there, Cherilyn. Just need your largest cup of coffee."

"Been one of those mornings, huh?"

"Sure has." In my mind I see Tenley's flushed cheeks, knowing I saw her at Wyatt's, then the picture is replaced by the image of my own hand, moving across the signature line on my divorce papers. Cementing the ending of my marriage to my high school sweetheart, the mother of my children. The crack in my family is deeper even than the fissure in my heart.

Oddly, I feel numb inside. Maybe two years of being separated, two years of learning to be a single father, and many more years of slowly letting go of the person Anna once was, has prepared me for today. That's not to say it's not excruciating, but more like I'm watching a machete hack away at the life I thought I had, instead of actually *feeling* it.

Cherilyn walks away to get my coffee. Her back is turned, and I ask, "Did you work last night?" I'm going for conversational, but Cherilyn smells subterfuge. She turns one shoulder my way and throws me a look.

"Yes, I did. What is it you really mean to ask me?"

Cherilyn's take-no-shit attitude makes me grin. "Did my brother come in here last night?"

She lifts an eyebrow and turns back around, fitting a lid on my to-go coffee. "Which one? You have two," she teases.

I laugh as she places the coffee on the counter. "Not the one who never leaves the ranch."

"Ah, so that would be Wyatt you're asking about then? Yes, he was in here last night." She takes the five-dollar bill I've handed her and doesn't offer me change. I've been coming here to grab coffee long enough that she knows I don't want change. I could go to Marigold's, the fancy coffee shop at the end of the street, but I like the strong, no nonsense cup Cherilyn brews.

She rests her forearm parallel to the edge of the countertop and leans in a couple inches. "And it's a good thing he was in here, too, because the place was overrun by teenagers trying to get a glimpse of that poor actress. She couldn't even finish her food. Wyatt showed up in the middle of it all and helped her get out."

My brother, a real knight in shining armor. Nobody knows what he does half the fucking time and yet he somehow manages to be the one who beds a person like Tenley.

"Thanks for the coffee, Cherilyn. Have a good day." I push back from the counter with the hot paper cup in my hand, backing out the entrance and walking to my truck.

When I pull up to the homestead, I find Pearl parked out front. Tenley stands beneath the shade of a tree, her back to the yard, deep in conversation with Wyatt. Neither hear me walk up, and Tenley jumps when I say, "Hey there, lovebirds."

I'm aiming for playful, the way I'd normally be. The way I was when Dakota started coming around, and Wes was refusing to admit he liked her. But even I can hear how short of the mark I am. I sound brusque and grumpy. Tenley turns, and I see her dog in her arms.

I still haven't figured out how she came upon a dog since that day on the side of the road.

Tenley and Wyatt both look at me. Wyatt's lips stretch like he's fighting a laugh, and a shadow of irritation passes over Tenley's features.

"I'll be ready in a minute, Warner," Tenley says, in a voice that makes no attempt to conceal how she feels.

My jaw clamps. She... dismissed me. The same way

Peyton did this morning, when she asked me not to get out and hug her goodbye when I dropped her off at school.

Thank God for Charlie. He waited next to my truck for me to get out and come around, while his big sister walked on ahead.

I step away from Wyatt and Tenley's hushed tones, then whip around and bark, "You can't have that dog with you during shadowing." I didn't mean to sound so harsh, but there's no taking it back now.

The screen door slams and Dakota steps out. Tenley's mouth is open, preparing to retort, but Dakota gets there first. "She won't, asshole. Libby is staying with me while Tenley shadows." Dakota glares at me pointedly as she comes down the porch steps and walks over, taking Libby from Tenley's arms. "You'd know that if you weren't late." Her tone is even, her message clear, her delivery so much like my own mother's.

I shake my head and smirk. "You're going to make a good mom, Dakota. Already laying down the law with your brother-in-law." Brushing a swift, affectionate kiss on her cheek, I keep going across the yard.

The screen door slams again, and I look back, expecting to see Gramps. It's Wes, his arms crossed in front of his chest. "Don't let me catch you putting your lips on my wife ever again."

I hold up my hands like I'm innocent. "No problem, I won't let you catch me next time." I flip him off and keep walking. Wyatt's laughing, and so is Tenley.

"Come to the barn when you're done, Tenley," I call out. "We're getting ready to turn out the bulls."

She starts after me, but there's a good fifteen feet between us and she shouts, "What does that mean?"

All three members of my family snicker. I turn around

and form a megaphone around my mouth with cupped hands. "It means the bulls are going to spend the next month acting like they're on spring break in Cancun without condoms, regrets, or cell phones with video capabilities."

Tenley halts, her eyes wide, while Wes, Wyatt and Dakota shake their heads and laugh.

11

WARNER

Tenley is a mess. Mud on her boots, a swipe of it dried across her backside.

It does nothing to change how attractive she is, and I'm far from the only man who realizes it.

"Eyes on your work, Troy," I growl for the seventh time. The rest of the cowboys took the hint the first time I gave it, but Troy is slow on the uptake.

Tenley rode out to the pasture with Josh and Ham, two of our other cowboys, and Troy can't seem to stop staring at her as she climbs from the vehicle. I was a little annoyed when she didn't get into my truck, but I can't blame her. She can learn just as much from the other cowboys, with the exception of that shit-for-brains Troy, as she can with me. The only difference between us is that my last name is Hayden.

"Give me a break," Troy says, shrugging as he opens the passenger door. "She's famous and hot. Don't act like you've never jacked off to the thought of her."

My arm shoots out, shoving his shoulder. He flies

against the open passenger door, scrambling to keep himself from falling out, and doing a half-ass job. No shock there.

"Go unlatch the trailer, Troy."

He grumbles as he goes. He's damn lucky my fist didn't meet his jaw for a comment like that.

Josh is unlatching his trailer, too, and Tenley stands back, watching. Her golden hair is tied on top of her head, and she has just as much dust caking her clothes as the rest of us.

I walk over to where Tenley's standing. "Ham, go make sure Troy doesn't manage to fuck something up."

"No man should be responsible for that," Ham mumbles, but he does as I've asked.

I watch as the bulls walk off the trailer, their noises filling the air. The first two go into the pasture, and Josh and Troy open the gates in the trailer for the next two.

In the distance, the herd of cows have their necks up, watching.

Tenley clears her throat. "Is it just me, or do those cows look displeased to see their new roommates?"

Josh laughs out loud, and despite the sour mood I've been in all day, I chuckle. "How else is the species supposed to continue?"

Tenley does her best to hide her feelings, but I can tell she's not loving the breeding process. When the last bull walks into the pasture, she shouts, "Go get 'em, Tiger."

"Stud," I correct.

She turns to me. "Huh?"

"They're called studs."

"Oh, well, then," she adopts a raspy voice. "Tell me 'bout it, stud."

I don't mind that raspy voice. Nope, not one bit. Her

words, however, confuse me. "Is that a line from a movie?" It's a solid guess, considering her work.

She looks at me like I've grown horns. "Um, yes. *Grease*."

"Never saw it."

Her head rears back as if she was just slapped. "You've never seen *Grease*?"

"Warner, I've seen *Grease* four times," Josh interrupts. I give him a look and he backs off.

Tenley points at me. "That's your homework."

"To watch *Grease*?"

"Yes."

I shake my head. "Never going to happen. But I'm sure Wyatt will watch it with you."

Tenley narrows her gaze. "You need to knock that shit off. Wyatt and I aren't sleeping together."

"You were in front of his cabin this morning in your pajamas."

She nods. "Right. But nothing happened. He didn't even sleep at his place last night."

"Where did he sleep?"

"He didn't say."

"Why were you at his place?" Even as I ask, the answer forms in my mind. "Because of the scene at the diner?"

Tenley squints. She doesn't ask how I know about the diner, which is good because I don't want to tell her I was asking about her.

"Yes, mostly." She nods once. "I overheard people talking about where I might be staying, and someone guessed correctly."

"So you were too scared to go back?"

"Right."

My thoughts shift away from Tenley with my brother

and move onto Tenley's safety. "Do you have somewhere safe to go? Why don't you have bodyguards?"

Tenley sighs. "I didn't think I needed them out here. Wishful thinking, I guess. My assistant is trying to hire someone, but it turns out it's a little hard to do that at the moment. The agency I use doesn't have anybody available right now."

"What are you going to do?"

Tenley holds her hands out on either side of her in a 'ta-da!' stance. "Meet your new neighbor."

"You're moving in with Wyatt?" I've got a bad look on my face, I can feel it.

"Not really. I'm moving into Wyatt's cabin. He's going to stay at the homestead."

"Who knew Wyatt was so gallant?" I murmur, not quite feeling magnanimous yet even though I know he and Tenley didn't sleep together.

"Why do you even care?" Tenley's head tips to the side, and she shakes it slightly, her eyes tightening in confusion. "Aren't you married?"

"Ye—" I stop. "No. I'm divorced, actually." My heart feels like it's being pinched as I say the words. "As of this morning."

Tenley blinks. "I have no idea what to say to that."

I huff a laugh. "I have no idea what a response to a sentence like that should even be."

The corner of Tenley's mouth curves up into a suppressed grin. "Want to hear something ridiculous?"

"I guess. This day can't get much weirder."

"Someone stole all my underwear."

I shake my head, certain I've heard her wrong. "What?"

"You heard it correctly."

"From...?"

"The house where I was staying. That's what I was talking to Wyatt about when you drove up. *Not* about our illicit affair."

"Did you tell the police?"

She makes a face. "No. What will that accomplish?"

Honestly, I'm not really sure.

She keeps talking. "It's not like they can catch whoever did it, and I promise you someone in the police department will call one of the gossip sites, and it will be on the internet in no time. No thank you. I just got my name out of the headlines."

I'm dying to ask why she was in the headlines, but that can wait. I can answer my own question with some patience and an internet search.

"Alright, let's head back." I whistle at the group of cowboys, and they break apart.

"Can I assume you're not mad at me anymore, then? Because you've been a jerk and I don't appreciate it." Her hand goes to her hip, and her eyes challenge me.

"I'm not mad at you, Tenley. I'm mad at *Morgan*."

Tenley frowns. "Look what happened to my underwear. I can't run around telling every strange man I meet my real name."

"How many strange men do you run around meeting?"

She lets out a little shriek of playful irritation. "I'm riding with Josh again."

"I get Ham," I say, joking, until I realize what this means. "Never mind. Troy, you're with me."

* * *

ANNA: ***I received notice you signed the papers.***

Me: ***Right.***

Anna: ***Don't you think we should talk?***

Me: ***About what?***

Anna: ***I don't know, Warner. Everything.***

Me: ***We should've talked at some point in the last two years.***

Anna: ***Warner, don't. You know I couldn't.***

Me: ***Clearly I didn't know anything, Anna.***

Anna: ***I'm sorry.***

Me: ***I know.***

Is this how it's supposed to go? Shouldn't there be epic screaming matches or stubborn showdowns? Apparently not for us. We're ending on a whisper. Maybe divorces are like snowflakes, each one unique.

The kids are asleep now. I'm sitting on my front porch in the dark, my phone balanced on my leg, nursing my second beer. Across the quarter mile separating us, I see lights on in Wyatt's place. Or in Tenley's place, I suppose. For a little while.

Instead of stewing over the fact that my marriage is over, I grab my phone and type Tenley's name into the internet search bar.

The first result, and the dozen following, tell me nearly all I need to know. Tenley was cheated on. I click the first link and read the story.

Ouch. It was recent.

At least my divorce isn't splashed all over the place for people to read about, and then also comment on. I read the first three comments, then stop. *What the fuck is wrong with people?*

All three comments are from people saying Tenley is stupid to break up with Tate, even if he did cheat on her. I don't know how she does it, living in the public eye the way she does. She has people opining on her choice to expect fidelity from her relationship, and then some other crazy person stealing her underwear.

No wonder she didn't want to tell me her real name.

I look over to Wyatt's cabin just as the back porch light flickers on and Tenley steps out. From this distance I can't see any details, only movement. She walks the length of the cabin, as if checking something. Picking up my phone, I type out a quick message. ***All good out here. I'm keeping watch.***

Tenley looks this way, but without a porch light on, I know she won't be able to see me. A message pops up.

Are you watching me?

I sip my beer and respond. ***Not on purpose, but yes. I'm sitting on my porch.***

Tenley settles into one of Wyatt's patio chairs and bubbles appear on my screen. ***How are you?***

I got divorced today.

I was cheated on recently.

I know. I just finished reading about it.

I'm rolling my eyes right now.

I chuckle quietly, picturing her making a face. ***So am I.***

Why? she asks.

Because this Tate fool was obviously out of his mind. I press send and wait, knowing I've stepped out of the zone we've been standing in since I pulled over on the side of the road.

Tenley doesn't call me out, thankfully. ***Was he, though? Did you see the person he cheated with? She's eight years younger and has two cup sizes on me.***

Please. Tenley is gorgeous, and her body is perfect. I type out my response and hit send. ***Now you're the one out of your mind.***

Tenley responds. ***Anna was obviously out of her mind.***

She was, two years ago. She wouldn't get out of bed and I

was afraid to leave my kids with her. But now? I tip the bottle to my lips, swallowing the last of it. I'm not sure how Tenley knows anything about Anna, including her name, but I don't feel like playing detective. ***Maybe. Maybe not.***

Tenley responds immediately. ***Yes. Most definitely.***

She's seeing someone else. I saw them together last Saturday morning. Right before I came to my parents' house and met you for the second time. Sorry for being an asshole that day.

You're forgiven. I'm sorry I gave you a fake name.

What a dick I was. It was Anna who deserved my fire, not Tenley. ***No apologies necessary. Friends, then?***

An olive branch? I like it. Friends it is.

Friends. I stare at the word in our text conversation, a heaviness settling in my limbs.

Good night.

I respond the same. ***Good night.***

Across the distance, I watch as she gets up, pauses at the back door, then walks inside. The light turns off.

12

TENLEY

"THANK YOU FOR BREAKFAST," I SAY TO JULIETTE. IT'S MY third morning in a row having breakfast with her and Beau and Gramps while I wait for Warner to get back from taking his kids to school. Wyatt was here yesterday, but not today. Juliette told me Wes and Dakota join them on Sunday mornings, and Warner and the kids on the weekends when he has them.

From what I can tell, Warner has them the majority of the time. I'd love to ask, but I'm afraid I'd overstep a boundary. I'll remain in the dark about Warner's ex-wife until someone decides to turn the light on for me. It's none of my business, but I'm curious.

Dakota went to the store for me two days ago and helped me fill Wyatt's fridge. I can make scrambled eggs and bacon myself, but I like the company. Beau doesn't talk much, but Gramps makes up for it. He has stories for days, and he's eager to share them. Juliette doesn't love small talk, but she's happy to tell me about the ranch. I'm learning as much from her as I am from Warner and the cowboys. She's promised me a lesson in making goat cheese, and while I'm positive that's not in the movie, I don't care because it sounds like it would be cool to learn.

Another thing I've picked up is to eat a huge breakfast. Ranch work goes for most of the day and lunch isn't a priority. Mostly the cowboys eat whatever they've packed themselves. Shadowing Warner the past few days has been good, even fun at times, but it's not easy to be around him. I'm so attracted to him that it's distracting, and I make mistakes or forget what he tells me. He's patient, and sometimes I feel helpful, but mostly I think I'm in the way.

Like yesterday, when we took the side-by-side out to mend some fences. First off, I had no idea what a side-by-side was, but I kept my mouth shut and waited to be shown instead of asking. Second, I can't mend a fence to save my life, and I made more work for Warner than if he'd done it on his own.

We checked on the bulls on our way back, and he drove me around the property. Not all of it, because it's too massive to ride around in an ATV, but what I saw was gorgeous. At one point we rode up onto a small bluff and he ran a flattened palm parallel to the horizon. "That's all Hayden land. Everything, for as far as you can see." I didn't miss the hint of pride in his voice, and it reminded me of the words on the family crest above the fireplace mantel in the homestead. *Legacy, Loyalty, Honor.*

Warner walks into his parents' place just as I finish drying the last breakfast dish. He finds me in the kitchen, a dish towel draped over my shoulder, on tiptoe with my arm outstretched as I try to slide the last clean plate onto the stack in the cabinet. He comes up behind me, reaching above my head to help, and even though his scent is intoxicating, it's the care he takes not to touch me that really draws my attention. Bumping against me without thinking is one thing, but the deliberate action he's taking to maintain distance says more. All the air in my lungs disappears, replaced with a longing I hardly know how to fight. Instead, I choose flight, sliding along the countertop until I'm out of his range completely.

"Thanks for the help," I manage to say, despite the sudden shortness of breath. "All done in here." I toss the dish towel on the counter beside the sink.

Warner crosses his arms in front of himself. "How do you feel about learning to ride today?" He tips his chin up a fraction and raises his eyebrows.

I wrinkle my nose. I've done some unenjoyable ranch tasks over the past few days, but learning to ride a horse has been high on the list of things I don't want to do. I don't have a fear of heights, per se, but horses are really far up off the ground.

My hands clasp in front of me, and I stretch them out. "Well... what else is there to do?" My tone is sunny and hopeful.

He gives me a knowing look. "You're going to have to learn to ride sometime."

"I will, just maybe not today? How about tomorrow?"

A rumbling chuckle fills the air. "You could charm the skin off a snake."

"Ew."

"What? You don't have snakes in Hollywood?"

"We sure do. It's a word we use to describe bad humans."

Warner smirks. "Well, since you're refusing to learn to ride today, how about I ease you in?"

"How so?"

"Ride with me." Warner grabs two apples from a basket on the counter.

"Ride with you... on a horse?"

"No, on a tractor." He gives me a look. "Yes, on a horse. We'll go slow, I promise."

My lips twist. I really don't want to get on a horse, but I know I have to. It's required for my role, unless I put my foot down and demand a double. I don't want to be that person though. High maintenance. Plus, there's the cost.

"Alright."

Warner grins. Riding the horse might just be worth being on the receiving end of that grin.

"Come on then," Warner says, motioning me out of the kitchen.

I point down at my feet. Sandals aren't going to cut it. "I need to change shoes."

Warner rubs his hands together excitedly. "Meet me at the barn."

* * *

"Her name's Priscilla," Warner says, running his hand along the horse's side.

Priscilla is tall, muscular, and beautiful. Her tail flicks as I look her over. Her muscles are taut and defined under her coat. Raw power emanates from her. Maybe it's not the height that frightens me after all. Maybe it's the fact that she is filled with *potential.* At any moment, she could rear back. Gallop. Do whatever it is that horses do. The point is, she *could* do it.

"Come stand next to me." Warner motions me over with his head. "Say hello."

I step up beside him. The earthy scent of hay mingles with Warner's scent.

"Do what I do," he murmurs. I mimic his flat palm, running in long strokes down Priscilla's side.

"She's so still." I also copy his volume.

"She's our gentlest mare. The kids both learned to ride on her."

"Should be perfect for me then."

Warner crooks a smile and looks down at me. "Just right." I watch our nearness register with him. His jaw flexes under the shadow of his stubble, and his gaze travels over my face. I know I'm not imagining the tenderness, the longing, or the fear I see in his toffee eyes.

If he kissed me now, I wouldn't stop him.

Priscilla whinnies, and it breaks the spell. Warner drops his gaze. He walks around to face the horse and feeds her one of the apples he brought from the homestead.

"Another day, Priscilla. Tenley is afraid of you." Warner's teasing voice sounds forced. We both know something just happened between us, and he's trying to put everything back in its place.

It's you who is afraid of me. I keep that thought to myself.

I hang back and watch Warner bring out his horse. It's bigger than Priscilla, and I try not to let my worry show.

Warner leads him past me toward the exit and I follow at a safe distance. "This is Titan." Affection warms his voice. "I've been riding him for a decade."

Given how much I already love Libby, I can only imagine how much love Warner feels for an animal he's had for ten years.

The relentless Arizona sun reveals every muscle hidden beneath Titan's shiny black coat. He is solid power, and he makes Priscilla's potential energy look like child's play.

"Do you know how to get on a horse?"

I nod. Between my one riding lesson when I was young and seeing it in the movies, I know enough to stick my foot in the stirrup and swing my leg over the saddle. I slip a booted foot in the stirrup, but Titan is large and I'm petite, making it difficult for me to haul myself up.

"Let me help," Warner says. Before I can utter a word of agreement, Warner's hands are on my hips. He lifts me, fingers digging into my jeans. It's enough that I can use momentum to get my leg over. I'm pointedly ignoring the thrill of being touched by Warner.

"All good up there?" His voice catches on his question.

I look down at him. He holds one hand up to block the sun, and he looks conflicted. Something about all this, about *me*, is causing a disturbance in him.

"All good," I echo. Warner's up on the horse in mere seconds, his mount so quick and smooth I nearly miss it.

What I don't miss is him behind me. The heat radiating off his chest has nothing to do with the sun. It seeps into my back.

"We'll go slow, okay?" Warner murmurs. His voice is gentle, his assurance trickling over my shoulder. We've never been this close before, but I'm feeling greedy. It's not nearly close enough. I know we agreed to be friends, but this attraction is a force that may be entirely out of my control.

Warner makes a noise, and Titan starts. Like Warner promised, we go slow. I'm rigid at first, and Warner instructs me to relax. "Don't fight it," he says, and I resist the urge to throw those words back at him. After a while, my muscles loosen. The height stops feeling frightening. Titan begins to feel like a friend with a soul, not a wild animal with an agenda.

Warner takes me through the pines, and down lower where they stop growing. "This is pasture twenty-six," he says. I nod and look around, trying to figure out how he knows this. I don't see a sign or any marking.

"Look." Warner's voice drops so low it's nearly a whisper. He points out across the field. My eyes follow where he's indicating, and I suck in a breath.

"It's beautiful," I whisper. The big eyes staring at us, the lovely grayish brown color. "What is it?"

"An antelope."

It springs away, so graceful and buoyant, and just when I think it's going to run into a bank of trees and disappear from sight, it stops. Looks back at us.

"Huh," Warner says, sounding confused.

The antelope does the bound, stop, and look routine two more times.

"That's weird," he murmurs.

"What?" My eyes stay locked on the doe-eyed gaze of the animal.

"It's like she's trying to get us to follow her. I wonder if she has a baby over in the grass where she was standing." Warner eases forward, nudging the horse, and he starts.

Warner guides Titan slowly through the tall grass. I keep my eyes on the mother. Her expression doesn't change, nothing to indicate her fear, but I can't imagine she's not feeling something. If she cares enough to protect her baby by leading us away from it, she must be terrified watching us approach.

"There," Warner says softly, and I look down into the grass.

"Oh." I breathe the word, touching my lips with my fingertips.

It's tiny, so tiny, with its limbs folded underneath it. It's ears twitch as it watches us. "It's adorable. How old do you think it is?"

Warner leans forward to look closer, pressing into me, and even as taken as I am by the baby antelope, I can't help but be distracted by the feel of the hard planes of his chest.

"Probably not more than a week," Warner answers, his deep voice drifting over my shoulder. "They don't usually—"

The muscles in his forearms tense against my middle. "Fuck," he growls.

"What?" I ask, immediately alarmed even if I don't yet know by what. I lean slightly in the saddle just to get a side-eyed glance at his face. He's no longer looking down at the baby, but staring hard at something in the distance. Following his gaze, I see what has him so upset.

"Are those coyotes?" I've never actually seen one in person, but it was well-known even in the hills around LA that if a little dog went missing, you weren't likely to get it back thanks to the coyotes hanging around.

"Yes. They prey on antelope calves. They've even been known to hang around a pregnant mother, waiting for her to give birth. I understand everything has its place in the food chain, but I really hate those motherfuckers."

The coyotes stare at us with just as much singular attention as we're giving them. I always pictured them as rangy and starving, but this pair looks well-fed. The thought saddens me.

"Are they waiting for us to leave?" I ask.

"Yes." Warner shifts, looking back at the mother antelope. "She hasn't moved."

"I feel bad for her."

"Me too." He sighs. "I usually try not to interrupt nature. I know this is the way of things, and those coyotes might have little mouths to feed too, but..." He pauses, his hands tightening on the reins, and when he doesn't continue, I ask, "But what?"

His lips brush my ear so that I feel and hear his next words. "Do you trust me?"

Trust? My trust in men was recently shattered. But then, Warner is not just any man, or an everyman. I don't yet know who or what he really is, but I know enough about him to know what he stands for, and that I've already trusted him once on the side of a deserted highway.

My head turns so that his lips hover near my cheek, his breath warm on my skin. "I trust you."

His left arm leaves the reins, slides around my stomach, and grips my hip. He hauls me back against him, holding me firmly in place. "Hold on," he instructs.

My entire body stiffens in anticipation.

Warner leans forward, makes a noise with his mouth, and Titan shifts into action. I suck in a breath, my hair lifting from my shoulders, and hold tightly to the bucking roll on the saddle.

Titan begins to trot. "I've got you," Warner rumbles into my ear.

He's more right about that than he knows. My poor, foolish heart.

The coyotes still haven't moved. They're either brave or hungry, or perhaps their hunger has made them brave. "Yell," Warner commands.

At first I'm confused, but then he shouts, a wild and raucous sound, a long string of vowels, and the coyotes shift their weight, their posture changing from predatory to guarded.

I realize what's happening and join in, yelling like Warner, more animal than human. It feels good. It feels like what I should have done the moment I saw the pictures of Tate cheating on me.

The coyotes turn tail and sprint away. Warner keeps up

the chase, stopping once he gets to the tree line. He swings one leg over the back of Titan and hops down, shouting once more, but this time it's more of a cheer.

"We did it!" He reaches up, his smile stretching wide. He grabs me around the waist, lifting me right off the saddle and setting me on my feet in front of him.

I'm dazed and my legs are sore, but all of that pales in comparison to the high we're both riding on. I grin back at him, palming his chest. "That was insane," I laugh the words, incredulous, tipping my head forward and shaking it disbelievingly. "Can I add that to the script? Because that would be the perfect plot thrust for the main characters' love arc..." The words die on my lips. I blink up at Warner. The thrill of our adventure fades immediately, as if it were on a dimmer switch. Suddenly the air feels heavy, my unfinished sentence suspended in the ether.

Warner brushes my hair back from my face, his touch leaving invisible but permanent impressions in my skin. "What would happen next in your script?" Deep and rough, his voice digs into me.

"They would kiss." It is the simplest and truest answer.

Warner leans closer, our chests now separated only by the palms I still have pressed against him. His lips touch the corner of my mouth, hovering there, as if he's deciding if he should really go for it.

My heart hurts for him, for what he must be feeling in this moment. It isn't lost on me, what this means to him. Kissing someone who isn't Anna.

He drags his lips slowly across mine. Decision made.

"Like this?" he murmurs against me.

"No," I respond, shaking my head almost imperceptibly, so my lips brush back and forth across his. "Like this." My hands leave his chest, gliding up and into his hair, my lips press against his. He groans, urging me open with his tongue, sweeping across the inside of my mouth. His hands are on my hips, fingers digging in, crushing me against him, then sliding up my back. One hand continues up, up, up, where he works his fingers into my hair and holds my head in place. His other hand locks around my waist, and he holds me still, devouring my mouth. No kiss has ever felt so good, so right, so earth shattering. Beyond a shadow of a doubt, I will never be the same after this.

So I cling to the moment. I run my hands through his hair, scrape my nails softly over the back of his neck, hold on to his shoulders for dear life. And right this very second, it does feel like I'm holding on to life. *Real* life.

The kiss finally ends, and we both draw back, dragging in air, the only sound that of our heavy breathing. My hands go to my hips and I look up to the blue sky, cotton candy clouds stretched across it, as I try to slow my heart rate.

My head lowers. Warner watches me, his eyes half-lidded. He looks the way I feel. Astonished disbelief.

"That's how I kiss all my friends," I joke weakly, mustering a smile even though it's hard to call one up right now.

"Friends," Warner echoes, the word turning over in his mouth as if it's new to him. "It didn't take us long to go back on that agreement."

"True," I concede.

He offers his hand. I stare down at it. "Is that for a handshake?"

"Yes."

"Why?"

"To make sure we're still friends." His voice goes up at the end, like he's asking a question.

"After that?" My eyebrows lift. "We're still just friends?"

He has the decency to look embarrassed. "That kiss was probably a mistake."

Something in my chest breaks, but I don't want to show it, so I cover it up with a smile. I am, after all, a damn good actress. Placing my hand in his, I say playfully, "I should've known you'd be trouble from the second you pulled over to help me with Pearl."

He holds fast to my hand and looks me straight in the eyes. "Make no mistake about it, Tenley. *You* are trouble. Not me."

But he's wrong. He is so, so wrong.

13

WARNER

"Where are you headed?"

I startle at the sound of Gramps's voice. He's sitting in his new front porch chair, the one Wes gave him for Christmas last year. A glass of iced tea rests on the table beside him, the ice half melted.

I step closer. Gramps's hand trembles where it rests on his knee. I remember throwing a football around with him when I was ten, and thinking he was old. I had no idea what that word really meant. "Tenley has some photo shoot thing today and I told her I'd pick her up and take her to the archery range after. She needs to learn how to shoot a bow for the movie."

Things have been awkward as hell between us after that kiss. Tenley tries not to let it show, but it's impossible to ignore. A kiss that exceptional demands acknowledgment, and here we are trying to pretend it didn't happen.

Truth be told, I can barely look her in the eye. At a moment's notice I can recall the feel of her soft skin under my heated touch, how kissing her felt like sensory overload.

Touch, sight, sound, smell. Like an avalanche of pleasure meant to bury me.

Being around her now is difficult, considering what I really want to do is drag her into my bed and get so lost in her that I never dig my way out. And it pains me to know I can't. The timing and circumstances couldn't be worse.

Gramps nods. "She's a good one, that Tenley. A real good egg."

I smile. "Yeah, she's nice, Gramps." *Nice*. Hah. How about funny, beautiful, interesting, and hardworking, to name a few? Also, a mind-blowing kisser. I swear to God I can still feel her fingernails dragging through my hair.

Gramps leans back. "Your mom told me you signed the divorce papers."

I stifle a sigh. Divorce talk is one way to be jettisoned back to reality. "Can we not talk about that?"

Gramps frowns. "Don't be like Wes. Keeping it all tucked inside is bad for you." He waves his hand around. "Makes you angry and shit."

"Is that right?" I can't tamp down the sarcasm.

"Don't sass me, boy. I know what I'm talking about."

I sit down on the edge of a chair near him. "What do you want me to say, Gramps?"

He turns his face to me. Wrinkles pucker his skin, and age spots dot his forehead. His white undershirt peeks out from a missed button on his plaid work shirt. Suddenly, his age looks more pronounced than ever. I've been so busy these last two years, taking care of Peyton and Charlie mostly by myself, and in the years leading up to Anna leaving, I had to handle her. Gramps was there for every day of it, but I don't know how much I've really looked at him. Sure, I've seen him, but my focus was inward. The aging process was continuing no matter what, but this is the first time I'm really seeing it. I feel awful, and it makes me wonder who and what else I've overlooked while I was busy managing the slow implosion of my marriage.

"I want you to be honest with yourself about how you feel," Gramps says.

"Well." I turn my gaze to the front yard. "I'm sad, I guess. My marriage is over and my kids are officially from a broken home."

"Those are both shitty. What else?"

"I'm angry."

"What else?"

"That's it, Gramps. Really fucking angry."

Gramps shakes his head. "I've been alive long enough to know that anger isn't a primary emotion. It's secondary. Something else has to come before it."

I shake my head. I'm not sure what he means.

He continues. "When Janice died, I was mad too. It took me a little while to understand it went deeper than anger. I was afraid, Warner. Scared to live without her. It had been so long since I lived a life that didn't include her that I didn't know how to. I was angry that I was forced to live a life I feared living."

My lips purse and I nod my head.

"Warner, you and I are the only two Haydens who know what it's like to have a marriage end."

"Yours had a noble ending, Gramps."

"And what was yours?" he challenges. "Ignoble?"

"No," I answer quickly, but think about it and change my answer. "Maybe."

"Did you fight, Warner? For your marriage? Did you fight?"

My hands steeple under my chin, my elbows propped on my knees, as I think about his questions. There were years of arguments, of me pleading uselessly while I watched Anna slip away into herself and go to a place where she couldn't be reached. At the time I hadn't known the battle was really just beginning. And I knew nothing of how it would end.

"I fought hard, Gramps. But in the end..." I look at him and shrug. He watches me, and even though his skin shows his age, his eyes are bright. "I haven't been honest about Anna. About where she went when she left."

"I know."

I stare at him. "How do you know?"

"I put in my time as the operator of this ranch. I know the attention and energy it takes. Now, I sit out here and watch you all live your lives." He taps the armrest with two fingers. "I knew Anna when she was seventeen and you were taking her to prom. She may not have been a Hayden by blood Warner, but she was family. I took notice when she grew quiet. And when you started claiming she had headaches and couldn't make the family dinners? I noticed that, too. I never bought your story about her needing to leave you and the kids so she could find herself."

"Why didn't you say something?" I've been passing off that story for over two years now.

"Figured you'd tell the truth when the time was right."

I huff out a dry and disbelieving laugh. "Christ, old man. You are beyond words."

"You lot are so busy running around that you often don't see what's in front of you." He winks. "Lucky for you all, you have me. I have plenty of pearls of wisdom saved up for Wyatt and Jessie, whenever they get around to asking for them."

I nod but don't say anything. I'm still absorbing the bombshell that Gramps knew I was passing off a story about Anna this whole time.

Gramps coughs into his fisted hand. "Since we're airing the secrets you tell your family and yourself, might as well mention Tenley."

I look at him sharply. "What about Tenley?"

He shrugs. "She seems to bring out strong emotions in you."

My gaze sweeps down, focusing on the scuffed toe of my boot. "She was the unfortunate recipient of my anger, if that's what you mean. I had just come from seeing Anna with someone else."

He shakes his head. "I'm not talking about that day, although in my opinion your mother should've whooped your ass for how you treated a guest in her home."

"You were pretending to be asleep?"

"I woke up at the end." He swipes the air, like he's pushing that aside. "I'm talking about all the other times I've seen you with her."

"You mean picking her up here for work after I take the kids to school?"

"That, yes, but also how you've made it clear to the cowboys that they are not to look in her direction."

"I want them to be respectful of her. They're representing the HCC." *What a crock of shit.*

Gramps knows it. He makes a disbelieving sound with his lips.

"Doesn't matter what kind of emotions she brings out in me, Gramps." My head shakes, and I push aside thoughts of that incredible kiss a few days ago. Four days, to be exact, but who's counting? "We're just friends. The ink is barely dry on my divorce papers."

Gramps makes the sound again, making it all too clear what he thinks of my protests. "Your marriage was over a long time ago, Warner, and you know it. The only difference is that now the state knows it too."

I give him a withering look. "Tell it like it is, old man."

Gramps picks up his iced tea. "I'm too old to beat around the bush. You just remember the only person holding you back is yourself, Warner. When you get to be my age, something like waiting long enough after divorce to start dating again is just shit simple. Don't give the concept of time so much power over your life." He sips his tea and wipes a hand across his mouth when he's finished. "Don't you have somewhere to be?"

I nod and stand. Gramps sets the empty glass on the table and places the palms of his hands on the armrests. He stands up without too much difficulty, and I see now that the chair sits taller than the other set we have out here. I'm almost certain Wes did that on purpose, so that Gramps wouldn't struggle to get up. I'm even more certain Wes didn't tell him why he bought the chair, because if he had, Gramps would've set fire to it.

"It's time for my nap," Gramps announces, passing me. He stops at the front door. "Tell Tenley I said hello, Warner. And remember what I said. Time is relative, and if it's people's opinions you're worried about, well..." He shrugs. "Fuck 'em."

"Thanks, Gramps," I say, laughing. "I'll keep that in mind."

He goes inside, and I hustle to my truck.

* * *

THE PHOTO SHOOT is being held at the abandoned Circle B ranch on the far west side of town. I wouldn't even call it Sierra Grande, except that it is just barely inside the town's limits. I know the ranch well, because it was a prime party location in high school. It probably still is.

I park my truck alongside a line of haphazardly parked vehicles. There's a trailer off to the side, and a row of tents set up nearby. People walk around with purpose. They carry equipment, clipboards, and various items. One person wears something that appears to be an apron around her waist. It seems like a lot of work just to take some pictures. I'm as obviously out of my depth in Tenley's line of work as she is in mine.

I get closer and a trailer door swings open. A man dressed in jeans, a button-up flannel, and a cowboy hat steps out, followed by Tenley.

A long skirt floats around her ankles and she wears a top that looks a bit like a bra but also like a sort of shirt. It shows most of her stomach. Her blonde hair is big and curled, and there's more makeup on her face than she usually wears.

"Warner!" Her eyes light up when she spots me, her hand raised in the air. She meets me halfway, the man she walked out of the trailer with in tow.

"This is Calvin. My costar," she adds, assuming correctly that I have no idea who he is.

"Nice to meet you." I offer a hand to Calvin. "I'm Warner Hayden."

Calvin shakes my hand. He smiles, and his perfect teeth sparkle. "Tate who?" he says teasingly, glancing at Tenley.

She narrows her eyes. "Stop. You know Warner is letting me shadow him on his family's ranch. Showing me all the things so I'm familiar with them for the movie." She smiles sweetly at me.

"Tenley, Calvin, are you two ready?" someone yells. "The lighting is best right now and I don't want to miss it."

It takes me a few seconds to find the person yelling, but Tenley and Calvin look immediately to the source. It's an older man with wavy salt and pepper hair, his arms crossed and staring over this direction. I don't appreciate the exasperated look on his face.

Tenley squeezes my forearm as she passes by on her way to the guy who yelled. I watch her and Calvin joke with one another as they walk.

"Hi," a guy says to me, leaning into my line of sight. "Are you a friend of Tenley's?"

"Uh, yes." As a matter of fact, that's exactly what I am. A friend who kissed her four days ago and hasn't since, but not for lack of wanting to.

"Would you like to sit?" He leads me to a seat under a tent.

"Yeah, thanks." I take the seat and the bottle of water he's offered me.

"My name is Max if you need anything else, okay? I'm an assistant, which basically makes me everybody's bitch." He says it in a joking way, but it still takes me off guard. I can't imagine a universe in which I would ever describe myself as somebody's bitch, joking or otherwise.

"Thanks," I say, looking away. Tenley is at the entrance to the beat-up wooden round pen, and the guy who yelled is gesturing and saying something I can't hear. She nods, and so does Calvin.

What's the deal with Calvin, anyway? They're very friendly. Suddenly I wished I watched movies. I only know old-school action movies, like Die Hard. If Bruce Willis had stepped from that trailer, I'd have known who he was instantly.

The wavy-haired guy steps back from Tenley and Calvin. Someone hands him a big camera. He peers into the lens and adjusts something. He points it at Tenley, takes a picture, then looks into the screen. He adjusts something else on the camera, then tells another person who's standing off to the side to do something. They run over, grabbing a giant white concave thing near Tenley and moving it a few inches. The photographer takes another picture, checks it, and they do it all again. He must decide they are ready to go, because he starts directing Tenley and Calvin. They start funny, making faces at one another, like they can't believe they've been forced together. The photographer says something else I can't hear, and Tenley turns into Calvin, pressing into him and looking up like he was the first man to walk on the moon, not Aldrin and Armstrong.

My fingers curl into my palms. I can't believe I'm jealous. It's been so long since I felt this way. Did I even feel this way when I saw Anna with that guy? I don't think so. I was mad because she was my wife, because I hoped we could rebuild our family and my kids could have their mom again. But jealous? That's an emotion I don't recall feeling.

The photographer twists one finger in the air, making a spinning motion, and Tenley turns her back toward him, but angles her shoulder his way, glancing directly into the camera with a demanding and sexy look.

It makes me want to stomp over there, push Calvin and the photographer the hell out of my way and continue our kiss.

"Clarissa!" The photographer bellows, his moody eyes searching the area where I'm standing. "Cover up this fucking scar of hers! It's going to ruin my shot. Do you think people want to see a movie poster with this thing on her back?"

What the fuck is this prick going on about?

The woman wearing the apron hurries past me, mumbling something about photo editing. She runs over to Tenley and bends down, pulling tools and a bottle from her apron. She shakes the contents of the bottle on a sponge and begins dabbing it on Tenley's lower back.

I look up and catch Tenley's gaze. Her lower lip trembles. I don't know what the fuck this talk of a scar is, but I'll be damned if anybody is going to make Tenley feel like shit.

I'm up from the chair in an instant, but Tenley shakes her head quickly back and forth, a small but insistent movement. She plasters a smile on her face and calls out, "Warner? Would you mind grabbing a salad for me from the diner?"

I stare at her, willing my heart rate to slow, deciding if I'm going to listen to her and back off or teach the photographer a lesson in manners.

I can't go against Tenley's pleading expression. "No problem," I growl. I nod tersely at the bitch assistant and get in my truck. I highly doubt the diner has the kind of salad Tenley would eat, so instead I head into town and get an oversized brownie from Marigold's. I'm halfway through it, along with a cup of weak coffee, when Tenley texts and says she's finished.

She's standing beside the trailer when I arrive, Calvin's arm slung over one shoulder. I stride over, and Tenley smiles tentatively when she sees me. A flush creeps up her neck, and I don't know why it's there.

Before I can say a word, the asshole photographer walks up with an open laptop in his arms. He steps in front of me to show it to Tenley and Calvin. "This one is it. Good work, you two."

Tenley glances at the screen, then back up to me. The photographer turns and follows her gaze.

"Who's your friend?" he asks Tenley.

"Warner Hayden," I answer, sticking out my open hand.

"Hayden," the guy repeats, like he's trying to remember why he knows the name. He shakes my hand with a limp dick handshake that makes me dislike him even more. "Do you have a ranch around here?"

"I do." The arrogance in my tone rivals that of Wes's.

He adopts an obnoxious look. "We wanted to do this photo shoot on your ranch, but we were denied."

I keep my expression fixed. "Is that so?"

"It would've been a good move for you, to bring publicity to your ranch. You could have had attribution." He reaches up to pat my shoulder, the same way you'd placate an upset child. "We all make mistakes."

This motherfucker... I shrug off his hand. "Being a cattle ranch, we step in a lot of shit. I'm sure you can understand why we'd be careful about who we allow on our property. We don't need more pieces of shit than we already have." My friendly tone confuses him, and he's still trying to work out what I've said.

Not Tenley. She's holding back a laugh. "Okay, well, this was fun," she says, swallowing her laughter. She ducks out from under Calvin's arm. "Thanks for everything. Calvin, I'll see you on the first day. Call me if you want to run through lines before we start." Tenley wiggles her fingers at everyone standing around and grabs my hand, walking to the truck.

Her pent-up laughter fills the space as soon as the doors are closed. "Oh my God, Warner, that was the best thing I've seen in years!" She laughs into the fingers she has pressed to her lips. "Do you know who that photographer is?"

"No, and I don't give a shit if he can produce gold bricks from thin air."

Tenley laughs again as she clicks her seat belt in place. She spies the half-eaten brownie in the console and grabs it. "Oh Lord, that is good," she says around a bite, brushing crumbs from her lips. I pull away from the old ranch and Tenley finishes the brownie.

"Thank you," she says, after pulling a water bottle from her purse and taking a drink.

"For what?"

"I know what you were doing." Her voice has softened, and her hands are pressed together between her knees.

"You don't know what I was doing," I say lightly, teasing. We don't need to make a big deal of it. I couldn't deck the guy, at Tenley's silent request, but then he threw an insult my way, and I am under no obligation to let him speak to me the way he is clearly used to speaking to people.

I make a turn onto a busier street. "You and Calvin seem like you're close."

She waves a hand. "Yeah, he's been my friend for a long time. We acted together when we were younger, and he lives near my parents."

Her tone is casual, flippant, and I can tell there's nothing more there. She and her costar really are just friends. It's a little weird to know she's going to have to kiss him though. Will she kiss him the way she did me?

We're at a red light and I use the opportunity to study her. The warm sunlight soaks through the window, shining on her body, her hair glowing like spun silk. She's still wearing all the makeup from the photo shoot, but I prefer whatever it was she wore on her face all the other times I've been around her. This doesn't feel like the real Tenley.

She watches me watch her, and my thoughts drift back

four days, when I kissed her and felt it in my soul. It confused the hell out of me, and scared me too, if I'm being honest.

Tenley's head tips to the side, and she waits for me to say something. Behind me, someone honks their horn. I let off the brake and ask, "Ready to shoot a bow and arrow?"

She grins at me. "I've been waiting for you to ask."

14

WARNER

"Are you sure you weren't an archer in a former life?" I ask Tenley, sliding my bow into the bed of my truck.

"It's possible," she says, mimicking the form I just taught her and shooting a pretend bow into the sky. "Just call me Katniss Everdeen."

"Finally, a movie reference I understand."

"I still want you to watch *Grease*."

"Never gonna happen."

My phone rings and I pull it out to answer. "What's up, Wes?"

"Dakota and I are going to grab a beer from the Chute if you want to join. I'm assuming you're with Tenley?"

"Yeah, we're together." I look over. She's bent at the waist, stretching and reaching for her toes. "Let me ask her."

She twists her head, looking at me questioningly from her upside-down position.

"Do you want to get a drink with Dakota and Wes?"

She pulls upright, her hair messy around her head, and looks at her watch. "Sure," she says slowly.

"We'll see you there soon." I hang up and turn to her.

"We don't have to go." She didn't seem certain, and I don't want her to say yes if she doesn't mean it.

She picks at the frayed hemline of her shorts. "It's not that. The time corresponds to how busy the place is likely to be, and whether I'll face the same situation from the diner. No bodyguards yet." She shrugs and sends me a sheepish smile. "Did you know Dakota went grocery shopping for me last week?"

"Nobody will bother you," I assure her, opening the passenger door. "Not with me or Wes sitting with you."

She sends me a grateful smile and climbs in. "Wes seems nice."

I grunt a laugh and get in the truck. "He used to be a real dick. Dakota made him nicer, but he's still an ass. It's just his nature."

She lifts three fingers into the air. "So, Wes is the serious brother." She folds down one finger, leaving a peace sign in midair. "Wyatt is the restless brother." Another finger folds down, leaving the one pointer finger. "What does that make you?"

My lips twist as I grapple with an answer. "I don't know. I used to know exactly who I was, but I don't anymore. The only role I kept was dad. And son, I guess. And brother." My thumb taps the steering wheel. "So, I guess I kept most of my roles except one."

"A role that eclipsed the rest. Except maybe dad." Tenley's hand drops from the air and brushes over her thigh. "I know how that feels. Roles, I mean."

"Well, yeah. You're an actress."

She laughs softly. "I don't mean in movies. I mean in life. My real-life role is that of a perfect daughter. My parents wanted me to be an actress, and I wanted to please them. I couldn't stand disappointing them. I still can't." Her body presses into the seat, like the admission is heavy, and I get the feeling there is more she isn't saying, more to the story of why she refuses to disappoint them. I wonder if it has something to do with her scar.

"So you decided to become an actress? Just like that?"

"My mom and dad were big in daytime television. I don't expect you to know them, but they played a couple on-screen in a soap opera. Cassidy and Jonah Malone. For almost two decades." Tenley smiles. "They died and came back to life many times."

"Lucky them."

Tenley snorts. "I suppose. But I think if I could come back to life, it would be as something else."

"Like a hummingbird?"

She stares at me across the console. "Why would you choose a hummingbird?"

I shrug. "Just seemed like something you could be. Kind. Unassuming. Sweet. Non-predatory."

She laughs, the sound bouncing around the truck, shooting through me. "Thank you, but I meant I'd come back to life as someone with a different backstory." She looks down, her lips twisting, and she says, "Obviously that's not possible, but a metamorphosis might be nice."

"You want to change into something else?"

Her answering shrug is one-shouldered. "Maybe."

I wipe my palm on my thigh and focus on driving. Because the thought that just slammed into my head wasn't one I was prepared for, but now it's there, ping-ponging around, and I can't escape it.

I want you to be who you are, no matter what it took to get you here.

This thought conveys more than it's seventeen words say. It is a book, a poem, a tome.

Its message reverberates through me, inciting just as much exhilaration as it does fear.

* * *

"Look, look, there they go." Barb grabs Shirley's arm hard enough to make the old woman wince.

"Goodness, Barb, keep your sweater on." Shirley squints in the direction Barb's pointing, but all she sees is an HCC truck passing by, and that's hardly enough to yammer about.

Barb ignores Shirley's whining. "I had a feeling that actress was going to get on with the middle one. Gut feeling." Barb pats her generous middle.

Shirley chooses not to say what she's really thinking, which is that Barb watches too much daytime television.

* * *

"Please, please, please tell me you dance," Dakota says, grabbing Tenley's hand across the table.

"Nope," Tenley answers, sipping her beer. "But I'm teachable."

"That's all I need to hear." Dakota grins, drinks half her beer in one gulp, and stands. She looks pointedly down at Wes. "If Wyatt were here, I'd have a dance partner."

Dakota pulls Tenley out to the corner of the mostly empty dance floor.

"What did she mean about Wyatt?" I ask Wes, taking a pull from my bottle.

"Apparently he can dance."

I make a face. "He's lying."

Wes shakes his head. "I've seen it firsthand."

"Where'd he learn?"

"Mom."

My frown deepens. "When?"

"When I was busy fighting in a war and you were busy playing house and procreating with Anna."

"We weren't playing house, asshole. We were making a life, kind of like what you're doing now with Dakota." I scowl at the label on my beer.

"Mom told me you and Anna are officially divorced. Is that why you've had your dick in the dirt lately?"

I rub my palm across my face. Another military term, to be certain. "What the hell does that even mean, Wes?"

"It means you've been feeling sorry for yourself." He rounds his shoulders, hunching, mimicking a moping posture.

"I hope to hell you're not this blunt when you talk to Dakota." On the empty dance floor Dakota is pointing down at her feet as they move and Tenley watches, nodding.

Wes straightens. "Sometimes I am. And it gets me in trouble."

I watch as Tenley laughs at something Dakota has said, her head tipping backward, sending her blonde hair sailing down her back. With my beer poised at my lips, I say, "Gramps told me my marriage was over a long time ago, and I'm just having trouble accepting it."

"Gramps is usually right." Wes finishes his beer. "Do you want to hear what I think?"

I side-eye him. The problem with listening to Wes is that he doesn't know the full story about Anna. Still, I motion for him to continue.

"I think you haven't been in love with her for a long time —" He stops me when I open my mouth to argue. It's automatic, this rebuttal. Wes presses on. "I think you were just used to being in love with her because you'd been together for so long. I was with you the night you asked Anna to be your girlfriend. And when you asked her to marry you. And I stood next to you at your wedding." Wes leans forward, tapping the bottom of his empty bottle on the table. "Warner, shit happens, okay? You think life is going to go a certain way, and then it falls on its fucking face and you learn the hard way that you're in control of none of this." He rolls the serrated ridge of the empty bottle around in a slow circle. "You can plan for all outcomes, and then something will happen that you never saw coming."

Wes glances up, looks me square in the eyes, and I see how certain he is of his words. It's knowledge gleaned from experience. Experience I don't have, because my whole life has been planned. I met Anna, I wanted her, I got her. I wanted to marry her, I asked, we said *I do*. We planned for kids, we had two. Then life started going sideways, and it hasn't straightened up yet. The train jumped the tracks, that's for damn sure. And me? I feel like a shirt drying on a line, pushed around in the breeze.

My thumbnail scrapes the corner of the bottle's label, lifting it. "What now, big brother? Where do I go from here?"

Wes leans back against his chair, lifting a leg and crossing it over the opposite knee in a figure four. His eyes are on Dakota and Tenley. Dakota calls out an eight-count and Tenley keeps up with her. "I'd say," he starts slowly, choosing his words carefully, "that you should do whatever feels natural to you. If you like Tenley, then let yourself like Tenley. If you need to spend some more time grieving the final ending of your marriage, then do that too. Just be honest with yourself."

Wes doesn't say anything more, and I let his advice soak in while we watch Dakota and Tenley. When they come back to the table, Dakota sits right down on Wes's lap. Tenley takes the seat beside me. Her cheeks are slightly flushed from exertion, and she's wearing the biggest smile I've ever seen on her face.

"Fun?" I ask, the corners of my own mouth curling up in response to hers.

Her hair slides into her face as she nods excitedly. She pushes it away and takes a drink of her beer. "I can see how much fun that would be with lots of people on the dance floor and live music."

"We'll come back another time when the band is playing," Dakota says. Her arms are wound around Wes's neck and she presses a kiss to his temple.

We finish the drinks and pay our tab. On the drive back to the ranch, I explain all I know about Dakota and Wes's relationship. Which is, admittedly, very little. Wes is close-lipped when it comes to Dakota.

"So they just happened to meet again after five years' time? That's so romantic. It could be a movie."

I grunt a laugh. "Good luck getting Wes to agree to that. He's very private."

"I gathered that. He seems protective. Was he always that way?"

"Always. When he was a freshman in high school and I was in seventh grade, Wes heard about this kid who was being an asshole to me. I told Wes not to interfere, because I didn't need his help and fighting has never really been my thing, but Wes wouldn't listen. He found out who it was, met the kid on his walk home from school, and taunted him until the kid hit him first. Our dad always said we weren't allowed to start a fight, but if we had to fight then we better damn well finish it. After that, it was game on. The kid didn't come near me again." My head shakes as I think about that day, the way Wes came home and didn't say a word, and I learned of it on my own the next day at school. "It's in his DNA, honestly. In a past life, he was a leader of a nomadic tribe or something like that, where the entire village would perish if not for his protection."

Tenley laughs. "I can see that."

I pull up to Wyatt's place and she opens her door, pausing with her hand on the frame. "Shoot. I forgot I ran out of coffee this morning. I'll have to pick some up tomorrow. Or ask Dakota to get some for me." She rubs her eyes, as if the idea exhausts her.

She is probably sick of having to hide out or feeling like she needs to. I'm going to put a stop to that real quick, but for right now all I can fix is the more immediate problem.

"I'll bring you coffee in the morning, before I take the kids to school. Sound good?"

She gets out, turning back for her purse and winding it around her. "That would be incredible. Thank you." She closes the door and walks up to Wyatt's cabin, using his spare key to let herself in. She sends me a last wave before the door closes.

I back out and drive the short distance to my place. I text Wyatt and tell him to make sure everyone in town knows that Tenley is not to be fucked with. As much as I'd like to be her knight in shining armor and relay the message myself, Wyatt is the better person for the job.

Wes told me to be honest with myself. And, *honestly*, I like Tenley, but I also can't fully grasp the concept that it's okay for me to like her.

It feels like a betrayal to a life that is no longer mine.

15

TENLEY

As promised, Warner is at my door (Wyatt's door?) with coffee. It's in a tall stainless steel carafe, and I can smell it even with the top securely fastened.

I step back from the open door, ushering him inside. He brings the chilly morning air in with him, swirling around my bare legs as he passes. I shudder and nudge the door closed with my foot.

Warner walks straight for the kitchen, setting the carafe on the table and removing two cups from a cabinet. It's clear he knows this kitchen, and his familiarity makes me think of my own kitchen in my own home. Where, presumably, my underwear still sits in my drawer, not stolen by some unknown person doing God knows what with it.

"Were you awake already?" Warner asks, his eyes on my hair.

"Yes," I lie, my hand smoothing the hair at the back of my head. It's lumpy and wild, I can tell just by running my palm over it.

Warner smirks, somehow knowing I've just fibbed. He pushes a cup across the table from where he sits. He's wearing a zip-up hoodie sweatshirt and jeans, and his hair has been combed.

I snag a throw blanket from the back of the couch, and drape it over my shoulders like a cape, then settle at the table. My fingers wrap around the mug, absorbing its warmth.

“Good morning,” I say, after I’ve taken my first sip.

Warner grins. “Good morning.”

He doesn’t say anything else, just sips his coffee, and I’m okay with that. I need this jolt of caffeine before I can converse. Each time I’m around him feels more intense than the last, teeming with growing emotions, feelings that ebb and bend.

He’s pouring my second cup when he says, “Ready to ride today?”

I suck in a breath, my brain automatically going to our ride almost a week ago, and the antelope, and the kiss. *The kiss*. The kind of kiss they ask for at the end of the movie, the one where the main characters have realized they love one another at all costs, the kind of kiss that needs multiple takes to get right.

Or just one, with Warner. When it’s genuine.

I clear my throat and lean back in my seat, propping my foot on the empty chair to my right. All movements meant to make me look like I’m chill. Nonchalant.

I look at Warner, but his gaze isn’t on me. I watch his eyes sweep over the entirety of my leg, from the hem of my sleep shorts to the tips of my toes, then looks away.

Friends, my ass.

I’m too old to play games, but for Warner this isn’t a game. These are the first timid steps, a shaky confidence on unstable feet. I won’t push him. If he wants me, he can come for me. The decision must be his. I can, however, stop putting up a fuss about learning to ride a horse.

"You just tell me where to be and when, and I'll be there," I nod my head and pretend to touch the brim of my nonexistent cowboy hat.

A smile plays at the corner of his mouth. His face is a touch darker than yesterday, the product of a missed shave. "Nine o'clock. Meet me at the stable." He drains his coffee and rises from his seat. He takes his carafe, removes the glass coffee pot from Wyatt's countertop coffee maker, and pours the remaining coffee into it. He flicks on the Warm button and replaces the pot on the burner.

"Wouldn't want you under-caffeinated," he says with a wink. "See you out there."

He walks to the front door, then pivots as if he has remembered something. "Wear jeans," he instructs, his gaze dusting my bare legs again, but much faster this time. Then he walks out, leaving me behind with the coffee and my feelings.

***

"Mom, hi." My voice is breathless as I hop up and down, trying to fit the tight jeans over my hips.

"What are you doing?" she asks.

"Freshly washed jeans," I explain, sucking in my stomach to button them.

"Squat," she tells me. "Deep squat. Works every time."

It's a trick I'm well aware of, but I don't tell her that. "Thanks," I say, bending my knees and pressing the speaker button. I slide the phone onto the dresser and continue to stretch out the jeans.

"How are you? I haven't talked to you since you got a new ranching instructor."

I look out the window at her mention of my new instructor, my gaze swinging toward his cabin. "I'm good. Getting ready to learn how to ride a horse."

"Kind of important." The way she says it makes me picture her with a wry smile.

"Just a smidge."

"So everything is okay, then? You're okay?" Worry trickles into her voice. And guilt too. Probably a sliver of embarrassment. She feels bad for how they've pulled me into this mess. She doesn't need to feel that way. I'd do anything for her and my dad. Anything.

"Mom, I'm good." I haven't told her about having to leave the house I was staying in. I don't want to worry her. She put up such a fuss about me driving out on my own, and she'd been right. I mean, yeah, I lucked out as much as a woman could when Warner stopped to help me, but what if I hadn't? She'd also fussed about me staying in that house on my own, in a town I didn't know. Turns out, she was probably right about that too.

"How are you, Mom?"

"Good, good. Just going through my closet. Getting rid of some things."

I pause, a mascara wand in my hand. My mother's closet is her treasure. She keeps everything, and I mean *everything*. My sister and I learned the hard way that Mom's closet was not for dress-up, no matter how much we wanted it to be. Once, while she was out of town, we snuck in and tried on her red carpet gowns, and even though we'd been meticulous about how we'd rehung each item, she knew. So her offhand comment about going through her closet is complete and utter bullshit.

"Oh, cool," I say, arranging my voice to be light and airy. She is a pot of water just before it boils, the bubbles swirling under a calm surface. She is acting also. "What are you doing with the items you're getting rid of?"

"Oh, you know, maybe give it to the local women's shelter. Might sell some of the designer pieces on consignment."

There it is. What I'd assumed all along. I don't say this though. I know better. "That's great, Mom, but don't you dare give away that white pantsuit. I've had my eye on it for years."

She laughs, and I recognize the throatiness, the way it curves around the edges. It's her Cassidy Malone laugh. The character she is most known for playing.

I understand how that can happen. You can move on from a character when filming wraps, but the character stays inside you, hooks set. I suppose I am Brooke from *Single and Loving It*, Janine from *Little Black Book*, and Jody from *Worst First Date*, among others. The characters have brought out parts of me hidden in shadow, facets unseen because of larger, brighter sides of my personality. And as much as I appreciate what each character has meant to me, I'm looking forward to my next chapter, whatever that may be.

Mom assures me she's saving the vintage pantsuit for me. I want to ask why she's preparing to sell her closet. Does she think this movie won't do well enough to pay off my dad's gambling debt? We end up making small talk, and then she says, "I won't keep you, hon, I was just checking in."

We promise to talk next week when filming begins and say goodbye. I slather sunscreen on my face and pull my hair back into a ponytail, then head out to meet Warner at the stable.

* * *

WARNER ISN'T HERE YET.

I contemplate hanging around out front, but decide to go inside the stable to wait. I step in, nose slightly wrinkled, expecting to be hit in the face with the smell of manure.

Oddly, it smells good. I mean, the manure scent is there, but it's buried under layers of rich leather, wood, and something I can't identify but I know I like. I walk past each stall, peeking in as I go. Most of the stalls are empty. It's midmorning, so that makes sense. The cowboys are working. Earlier this morning I saw a group of five riding out, perpendicular to Wyatt's cabin. I was sitting on the front porch after Warner left. I don't know if they saw me, but even if they did, they'd be too polite to gawk. Except maybe Troy. He's a handful, but I think he means well.

I go to Priscilla, knowing Warner will probably put me on her. The honey-colored horse nudges her head forward, as if prompting me to do something. I'm nervous because I don't know what she wants from me, but happy to know she likes me enough to make a request.

"She wants you to pet her. She remembers you."

I startle, my shoulder blades squeezing together. Warner stands in the open door. The sun shines in from behind him, turning his dark hair into a lighter, warmer brown. He moves toward me, his eyes on me at first, and then the horse. It was only an hour ago I saw him, but a thrill runs through me.

"Thanks for not giving me a wild stallion to learn on." I hear it after I say it, but it's too late. I can't take it back, so instead I laugh. Warner's shoulders move as he chuckles. "I don't often sidestep an opportunity to tease, but this time I will."

"Gee, thanks," I say dryly.

Warner nudges me aside, and I step away from the stall. He unlatches the gate and swings it open, striding in and pulling a saddle down off the wall.

"Peyton usually rides Priscilla, and this is her saddle." His gaze runs over my body. "It'll work for you."

I feel hot, as if his gaze holds actual heat. To alleviate the feeling, I say, "Are you telling me I have the body of a thirteen-year old?" It's a bad joke, but I'm uncomfortable. It makes my brain short-circuit.

His fingers, busy buckling the straps around the horse's middle, pause. He looks over at me, his eyes pouring into mine and his expression hardening. "No, Tenley, that's not what I'm getting at." He goes back to what he was doing. "You're petite, and these things aren't sized like jeans."

I don't say anything more. I don't understand why he sounded gruff just now. Warner leads Priscilla from her stall, and I fall in beside him as he walks from the stable. We pass what looks like a barn on our way to wherever it is Warner is taking me. The wood of the barn looks newer, not as weathered as the stable, and I ask Warner about that, simply for the sake of having something to talk about.

"A fire burned it down last summer. This new barn was finished about six months ago."

"How did the fire start?"

Warner glances at me, his eyes wary. "The official story is that we don't know what happened."

"And the unofficial story?"

Warner looks down at the rein in his hand. Priscilla's rhythmic steps are the only sound, until Warner says, "Arson."

I gasp. "Wyatt said this was the safest place to be in town. Apparently not."

"It is now."

It is now. His words turn over in my head. "Did something happen to the arsonist?" The tone is there in my voice, the apprehension, that conveys how I might not really want to know.

"Let's just say he won't be lighting anything else on fire."

I stop short. Warner senses I'm no longer beside him and pauses, turning to look back at me. Morgan's comment about the 'Wild West' floats through my mind. I'd told her that concept didn't exist anymore, but now I'm thinking maybe I was wrong.

"Warner, did you,"—I look around, and though nobody is in sight, I still whisper my next words—"kill him?"

"No." He shakes his head, and my whole body sags in relief. I want to ask more questions, but Warner's walking again and I get the feeling it's not a subject he wants to talk about.

We reach a circular pen, surrounded on all sides by wooden fencing, and Warner opens the gate. "This is called a round pen," he explains, stepping through with Priscilla. "You used one at the Circle B on the day of the photo shoot."

I nod, giving them some space and then follow. I remember very little from my single riding lesson when I was younger, except the strict instruction to never walk right behind a horse.

Warner slows to a step in the middle of the round pen. He faces me, one hand stroking the side of Priscilla that isn't covered by the saddle.

"Do you remember how I showed you to climb on Titan last week?"

I nod.

Warner steps away from the horse and gestures, silently asking me to show him.

I'm nervous, but I'll never let on. I lift my chin and walk to Priscilla's left side. Sliding my left boot into the stirrup, I pull myself up and swing my right leg over, grateful she is smaller than Titan.

"Good," Warner says, looking up at me. He takes off his hat and pushes back his hair, then replaces the cap on his head. "Remember to relax. Horses can sense if you're nervous." He steps up to Priscilla's head, reaching for the reins. "Now, I'm just going to walk her around the pen a couple times to get you used to the feel. I know you rode Titan with me, but that was different. I was in control."

That day floats through my mind. But not actually that day, more like those few minutes near the end of our time together. Right before Warner declared our kiss a mistake.

We're about halfway through the second lap when Warner looks back at me. "What do you think?"

"Honestly?"

"No, lie to me."

I give him a look and he grins. "This is really boring."

Now he laughs. "That's what Peyton says too."

I frown. "Why do you keep comparing me to your daughter?" I know I might upset him, just like my earlier comment, but I don't care. I don't particularly appreciate being likened to a tween.

He stops, and so does Priscilla. He looks me in the eye, and after an interminably long moment, says, "I'm trying to forget you're an attractive woman."

The blunt honesty takes me off guard. I blink twice. "Oh, uh. Okay."

Warner starts walking again, the horse underneath me moves. But something inside me is moving too, something hot and prickly.

"Actually, no." I call out, my voice raised. "Not okay,"

Warner stops and turns around. He looks at me, wary. "What's not okay?"

"It's not okay with me that you're trying to forget I'm an attractive woman."

A pained look creeps across his face.

"You kissed me, Warner, and it was the best damn kiss I've ever had. And not to make you uncomfortable, but I've kissed the kind of men women the world over would pay to kiss." Full disclosure, many of those men were terrible kissers. Not the point. "So fine, I get it, you need us to just be friends. And maybe I do, too. I'm not that far out of a relationship either. But please stop trying to look at me and see something else. You don't have to give in to your attraction to me, but at least stop denying its existence."

Warner blinks up at me. I realize how ridiculous this looks, me on a horse and Warner holding the reins. Warner opens his mouth to say something, but decides against it. He's all business after that. He teaches me how to hold the reins and give directions, how to position my body. I tell him about a scene in the movie where the horse spooks and gallops with me on the back, and when he makes a worried face, I assure him there will be a stunt double that day.

When we're finished, Warner has me lead Priscilla into the stable and put her back in her stall. I remove the saddle and replace it to the spot where I saw him grab it earlier. I finish by brushing Priscilla, just to show him I'm not completely inept.

I'm latching the gate on the stall when he says my name in a quiet voice. I pivot and he is there, all six-feet something of him, broad-shouldered and well-muscled and conflicted as hell. "I'll stop denying it."

There's nothing I can do but nod. I hear him loud and clear. He'll stop *denying*, but it doesn't mean he'll start giving in. It's the best he can do right now, and I like him enough that I'll take what I can get. Even as strictly friends, I enjoy spending time with him.

I take a look at my watch. "Do you want to come over for a sandwich and a beer? I have a lot of lunch meat to use up."

"I'd like that." He ducks his head in the quintessential cowboy way, even though he's wearing his standard ball cap. "Wes asked me to stop by the homestead, so I'm going to do that and then I'll be over."

We go our separate ways. I assemble lunch and realize I don't have beer. I shoot a text to Warner and he replies telling me he'll be over in ten and he'll bring the drinks.

* * *

I'M STANDING in the kitchen, looking through the back window out toward Warner's place, when my phone rings. I saw his truck pull up a minute ago, so I know he'll be along soon. Reaching out to my phone on the counter, I hit the speaker button.

"Hey, Gretchen," I answer, placing each sandwich on a plate.

"Tenley, hi. Bad news."

I frown at the phone. Bad news comes in so many forms. "What?"

"It's about the security guards. No luck. Still." Her tone is apologetic, not that she has anything she needs to apologize for. It's not her fault the security agency is fresh out of bodyguards.

Movement out the window draws my attention away from the phone. Warner, in a clean shirt and what I imagine is a fresh pair of jeans, strides across the distance between our cabins, two longneck bottles gathered in one hand.

Sunlight turns his dark brown hair the same burnished color as his eyes. God, that man is sexy as sin.

"That's okay, Gretchen. Thanks for letting me know."

The back door opens and Warner steps in. He opens his mouth to speak but Gretchen's voice fills the kitchen and his confused gaze swings to my phone.

"I can't believe your birthday is tomorrow. I'm bummed. I wanted to make your usual, but obviously we'll have to wait until you get back home."

I take the phone off speaker and hold it to my ear. "I'll be missing yours next month too. Let's plan a birthday night when I get back. You make my red velvet, I'll make your lemon coconut."

We chat for a minute more, then say goodbye. Slipping my phone into my back pocket, I turn around to face Warner. He's leaning against the counter, his feet crossed at the ankles. One half of his sandwich is already gone.

"You weren't going to tell me tomorrow is your birthday, were you?"

"Nope." I brace my hands behind myself on the counter and hoist myself up to sit.

Warner shakes his head and opens a drawer, removing a bottle opener. He flips the tops off, swinging the metal opener like a bat and making contact with each top. They hit the tiled backsplash and drop into the sink.

"Did you play baseball?" I take the beer he's offering.

Warner nods. He plucks the tops from the sink and drops them into the trash, then leans back against the counter. He's across the small kitchen, about as far away from me as he can get without tucking himself into the fridge, but he may as well be next to me. My body's awareness of him is embarrassing.

"I played Little League growing up and made the varsity team my freshman year of high school."

I sip my beer. "Did you ever think about continuing after high school?"

Warner looks down at the bottle, tipping it just slightly like he's reading the label. "I was offered a scholarship to a school back east."

"From your tone I get the feeling you didn't take it?"

Warner glances up, his dark eyelashes thick and partially concealing his gaze. "Anna didn't get in."

My breath sticks in my chest. It's the first time he has really mentioned her, the very first time he has said her name to me. I swallow and say, "That must have been a tough choice."

Warner's head moves back and forth slowly, as if he's stuck in the time period. "It wasn't, not really. I knew what I wanted more than anything, and it wasn't baseball."

I'm not sure what to say, or where to look, so I drink the beer and look up at the ceiling. When I right my head, I find Warner's gaze on mine.

"How did you meet Tate?" His voice is deep and even, and he looks genuinely curious.

"At an award ceremony. On the red carpet. I was in the middle of an interview, telling the reporter who made my dress, when Tate interrupted." The memory turns my lips into a wistful smile. "He asked me on a date right then, on camera. It was incredibly romantic. The stuff of movies, but in real life." My fingers play with the hem of my shorts. "LA is the land of hard work and broken dreams, but some dreams slip through the cracks and come true. And it's easy to get caught up in the fantasy that true love exists." I feel my wistful smile dripping, rearranging into a grimace. "That's what I sell in every movie I make. True love. It's a product, and it sells well. And for a period of time, even I bought what I was selling. Until, well, you know..." My eyes flicker up, catching on Warner's face.

He's listening intently, his eyes squinting as he focuses. "True love, huh? You thought you had it?"

I lift one shoulder, then drop it. "Looking back, I'm inclined to say no. Hindsight being twenty-twenty, and all that." My heels bump the kitchen drawers softly as I consider my next words. "Tate was probably right for who I was at the beginning of our relationship. But as time went on, I started to feel... stuck. Stifled. Like there was more for me somewhere, out from in front of the camera. Tate's not like that." As I say it, I see him in my mind, looking at himself in a store window as he passes. He's on his way to the gym, and then meeting the mobile tanning person. It's not that he's so in love with himself he'd fall in a pool of his own reflection and drown, but Tate understands the industry and doesn't mind living up to its standards. I mind. I care. I'm sick of it.

Warner chews his bottom lip. It's as if I can see the thoughts in his head, feel their weight. "What are you thinking about?"

He releases his bottom lip, head turning slowly back and forth. "I've been so focused on what Anna did to our family, and blaming her for giving up, but what you just said makes me think." He crosses his arms in front of his chest, still holding a half-full bottle in one hand. "We were right for each other for a long time. But we were young. So young. And when Anna started having trouble"—he glances at me, knowing he's said more than he meant to—"I haven't thought of it like you said. Like maybe we were right for the person we were at the time. But things are different now.

The experience changed her. Me too, in ways I'm not prepared to examine just yet."

I nod, my fingers gripping the edge of the countertop, and stay silent. I know so little about Anna, this mythical creature, Warner's ex-wife. A small part of me is irrationally jealous of her.

A loud, high-pitched sound screams into the air. Warner and I both jump, and he reaches into his pocket and grabs his phone.

"Alarm," he says apologetically, pressing a button and quelling the insistent noise. He tucks the phone into his pocket and grabs the other half of his sandwich, eating it in three bites. "That is exactly why I set it though. So I wouldn't forget to go get Charlie. Not that I would forget, but..." His voice trails off.

I can't help my smile. I slide down off the counter and walk slowly closer, craning my head overdramatically. "Warner, is that... a blush on your cheeks?"

His face scrunches, trying to tell me how wrong I am with just an expression.

"Ohhh yes it is," I tease. "The big, bad cowboy is blushing." I back off a little, so he doesn't get embarrassed, but honestly, it's nice to have something to lighten the conversation.

Warner dumps the leftover beer in the sink and places the bottle in the trash. Wyatt doesn't have a separate bin for recycling. He pauses at the back door. His blush has faded to a light pink. "I've noticed that sometimes you and I get to talking and time passes a little faster than I'm used to, and I didn't want Charlie to be waiting for me. That's all."

"You're a good dad, Warner." I smile and offer my hand for a high-five.

Warner stares at my offered palm as if he'd like to smack it away. "What's that?"

"A high-five. Ever heard of it?" I use my other hand to complete a demonstration for him.

"No, never," he responds sarcastically.

"It's what *friends* do, Warner."

He steps onto the thick, braided mat outside the door, turning back to respond, but I don't think he realized that I've followed him out the door. I'm not expecting the sudden stop and do my best to avoid falling into him, which means I'm going to have to fall into something else, and there is nothing but the floor.

His hands catch me, wrapping around me and steadying me. I grip his arms, my inhale sharp. We freeze, caught in the pause between seconds, uncertain and surprised.

Warner sucks in a deep, slow breath. He takes a step back, releasing me, and I swear to the man upstairs I can feel, taste, hear, and see his reluctance.

"Right." His voice is charred. "Friends." He takes another step, then two more, turning and walking back to his truck.

No high-five. He left me hanging.

16

WARNER

I've always been good with words. In high school I considered being on the debate team, but decided I'd rather use my talent to have good conversation, not win an argument.

What happened just now with Tenley was the opposite of being good with words. I think it was because I touched her. Caught her. Felt her softness in my hands and lost the connection between my brain and my mouth.

Yes, that's what it was. My brain couldn't focus on responding to her high-five in the appropriate and expected manner because it was too busy going haywire.

Against all good sense, I don't want to be her *friend.*

It seems impossible, but I want more. From someone who isn't Anna. That's what really has me hung up. Wanting someone who isn't Anna is inconceivable. This is the part of me where fidelity lives, deep inside in the inner sanctum of my heart.

Therein lies the problem. My brain and my heart are in disagreement. My brain knows it's okay to like Tenley. To see her face and feel happy, to see her smile and automatically produce one of my own. That kiss was a snap decision, a choice not made with my heart or brain, but with my desire. Sneaky devil.

I pull out onto the road that leads to town and grab my phone, dialing the number of the one person who can help me out of the clusterfuck inside me.

"Warner? Is everything okay?" Worry threads through her voice. I don't blame her. There's no reason for me to call her, except about the two things we share. *Our kids.*

"Everything is fine, Anna." I'm quick to assure her, because she's always been a worrier. Anxious. "I just... well..." I don't know how to say it, and now that I've called her, I sort of wish I hadn't. Too late now, though, so I go for it. "Who is he?"

She sucks in a breath. I can hear it through the phone, sharp and surprised. "His name is Jordan." She sounds reluctant. I don't blame her. I don't particularly *want* to be doing this either, but it doesn't take away from the fact that I *need* it.

I press on. "How did you meet him? Jordan." I say his name, trying it on. It feels like prickly pear cactus in my mouth.

"Warner, I—"

I can tell she is about to implore me to stop, and I can't let that happen. "Anna, I think you owe me this much."

She's quiet. She knows I'm right. Her sigh pushes through the phone, heavy, and she begins. "He struggled also. I met him at Harmony."

My breath sticks in my throat. I remember the way Harmony looked the day we left Anna there. It'd be nice if the memory grew fuzzy, burned a little around the edges, but it hasn't yet.

"How long?" Another question I don't want the answer to, but really fucking need.

A long pause. "Fairly recent, Warner." She doesn't sound soft and apologetic now. Her voice grows in strength, it's muscles flexing, steeling for a confrontation. "It didn't happen on purpose, okay? It just... happened."

I laugh bitterly. "So says every person who accidentally fell for someone else while they were married."

"Give me a little more credit than that. We weren't without our share of problems before I went to Harmony, and you know it." She sighs. "Jordan didn't break up a happy marriage."

Ouch.

I look out the window as I drive, my eyes on Hayden land but not really seeing it. Instead, I see pictures of our relationship, snippets of joyful moments, and then they are replaced by darker memories. My own resentment when I couldn't coax Anna from bed. Couldn't make her smile, no matter what I did. How broken I began to feel, how I started to see myself as a failure.

"I'm sorry, Warner. I really am. I know it sounds like so little, especially in the grand scheme of things. My therapist says it's important I own my part of everything, and I want you to know I'm aware that most of what happened is my fault."

"It's not your fault." I'm so quick to defend her, even to her. An old habit dying hard, I guess. "You had a mental illness." Had or have? I don't know. It's been so long since she's discussed the details of her mental state with me.

"Yes," she confirms. "And it hurt everybody around me."

She doesn't say the words, but they hang there anyway, bright red and silent between us. *It almost killed me.*

Anna's confession that she was having suicidal thoughts

had been my wake-up call. I'd been sticking my head in the sand and pretending everything was going to work itself out, but her admittance forced me to finally admit how sick she was. That night I found Harmony and got her booked for treatment. She left the very next day. I didn't know it was the start of a long, slow, excruciating breakup.

"We're divorced." I say it matter-of-factly, trying it on the same way I tried on Jordan's name. It doesn't taste any better.

"Yes." Anna's voice is small, something I could fit into one of the silver thimbles my grandmother kept beside her sewing machine. "I can hardly believe it either, if it makes you feel any better."

"What happened to us?" A lone tear snakes down my face, but nobody is here to see it, so I don't bother wiping it.

"*I* happened to us, Warner."

I make a face. It feels like a cop-out. I want more. I want specifics. Times, dates, concrete evidence. I want to know where we went wrong, what turn we took that we were incapable of coming back from. "I need more than that, Anna."

She doesn't say anything, and I picture her looking down at the ground and biting the inside of her lip. It's what she does when she's uncomfortable.

I pull into the school parking lot and gaze out to the soccer field. Charlie is easy to identify. I'd know his gait anywhere. He has a jaunty, jubilant run. Completely unlike the other Hayden males. Wes, Wyatt, and I all run in a compact way, head lowered and shoulders tucked.

"Waiting on you," I say to Anna.

"I don't know how to say it."

"Just spit it out. Whatever you have to say will only hurt until it stops hurting."

She laughs, a quiet chuckle, devoid of whatever it is that

makes a laugh sound happy. "This would've happened no matter what. This destination was always where we were headed."

"What are you talking about?" I'm baffled. Our divorce happened because Anna was diagnosed with clinical depression, because life threw a fast-pitch curveball into the heart of our family. Not because *this destination was always where we were headed.* How can she even say such a thing? All those nights with Charlie, colicky and screaming, when we took turns holding him and trudged through the house, willing our exhausted bodies to stay awake. And when Peyton took too many of her gummy vitamins, declaring them candy, and we rushed her to the ER. Soccer matches, dance recitals, toddler tantrums, and bandages on injuries that were barely a scratch. We were a team. Me and Anna. High school sweethearts. Living on love. Our couch was hand-me-down but our devotion was pristine. Until it, apparently, wasn't.

"How could you not agree, Warner? How could you not see what we became when we were married? We were parents first, people second, and somewhere too far down the list we were lovers. We lost what we had when we were young. It... happens." She sighs for what has to be the seventh time since I called her. "Are you trying to tell me you don't see what I'm saying? None of this is resonating with you?"

My jaw clenches against her questions. I don't want her to be right, but it doesn't change the fact that she is. Mostly, anyway. We did become parents instead of lovers, and it happened quickly. Nearly as soon as Peyton was born.

"Warner, I'm going to ask you a question, and you don't need to answer me. I'm not the one who needs the answer, because I know it already." I'm silent, and she continues.

"When was the last time you remember being in love with me? *In* love."

In the distance, Charlie crosses the ball to the center of the field and the striker attacks, scoring. The boys cheer. A pang twists in the center of my chest, a sense of nostalgia that hurts more than it should. I was like Charlie once. Looking out at life and wondering what awaited me. Not knowing it would hold all this.

"Charlie's practice is almost over. I better go." The boys stride toward bags thrown haphazardly on the sidelines.

"I'll see you tomorrow, Warner. Six o'clock?"

It's her weekend with the kids. "Six o'clock," I echo, hanging up and placing the phone in my cup holder.

Charlie is just about to my truck, so I reach over and grab the handle, opening the door. He climbs in, tosses his bag in the back seat, and fastens his seat belt.

"I'm starving," he announces.

Despite how sour I feel on the inside, I smile. The kid is always hungry these days. On the way home, I swing by a drive-thru and grab a burger for Charlie.

"Don't tell Grandma," I instruct, thinking of my mom. "She said she's making your favorite tonight and she'll be irritated if she knows I fed you."

"Don't worry about me," Charlie says around a mouthful of food. "I'll eat Grandma's tater tot casserole."

I feign a look of confusion. "Tater tot casserole? Sorry, Son. She's making sushi."

Charlie sticks out his tongue. "Very funny, Dad."

He finishes his food, balling up the wrapper and tossing it into the paper bag. He drinks from his water bottle and drags the back of his hand over his mouth.

"Mom's tomorrow?" he asks.

I glance at him. I don't know what it's like to have

parents who are no longer married. My parents have been together so long I think of them as the same person sometimes, like an object someone stuck in a tree and the tree grew around it. Dislodging would be impossible.

"Yeah, bud. Mom's tomorrow. Or, Grandpa Brock and Grandma Susan's, anyway."

"It would be nice if we could go back to that house mom had with the pool and the water slide," Charlie says, looking out the window. "What happened to that house?"

I shake my head slowly, as if I don't know. The truth is, it was a sort of halfway house. A place where Anna stayed after the treatment center, with a person who'd gone through treatment years ago and volunteered her home to people exiting. I saw the wisdom in Anna staying there, almost like stairs. Leaving Harmony and coming home would've been like jumping from the third stair onto ground level. She'd said she needed it to be gradual, and I agreed. I just didn't realize she'd never be coming home again. Now she lives in an apartment, processing mortgage loans from her dining room table, and drives up to Sierra Grande every two weeks to have her kids at her parents' house. She still doesn't trust herself enough to be on her own with them. From what I've seen of her, maybe it's time.

"She was just renting it, and the lease was up." I detest the lies, but the kids aren't ready to know about Anna. She'll have to be the one to tell them.

"Too bad. It was a cool house."

Charlie hasn't said a lot about his mom or me. I wish I could crawl into his head and watch the thoughts pass. Maybe he feels more than he's letting on. He was eight when Anna left. Old enough to remember. Old enough to absorb what it meant? I don't know. I did everything in my power to cushion the blow.

I pull up outside the homestead. Charlie makes it inside before me. My mom is in the kitchen, pulling the casserole from the oven. It smells like my childhood.

"Hey, Mom."

She looks over her shoulder as she slides the glass dish onto the range. "Hi, Warner. Smells good, doesn't it?"

"Yes ma'am."

"Why don't you go invite Tenley to have dinner? I heard what happened the last time she tried to eat by herself in town. I'm worried the poor girl doesn't have enough to keep her full out there in Wyatt's place. She'd probably enjoy a home-cooked dinner. And it wouldn't hurt her to put a little meat on those bones."

Tenley's body is about as perfect as it can be, but I keep that thought to myself. I pull my phone from my pocket. My mom reaches over, batting at the screen. "No," she says.

I make a face. "You just told me to invite Tenley."

"I said *go* invite Tenley, not send her a text. Knock on her door and invite her to dinner like the big boy you are." She winks at me and makes a clicking sound from the side of her mouth, then slips her hands from the oven mitts and walks from the room.

My mom is tough, and she's never been a meddler. I was too young when I proposed to Anna, and looking back on it I'm almost positive everyone around me knew it. Maybe my mom should've said something then, but would it have even mattered? Probably not. I couldn't see the forest, because all the trees were in my way. Perhaps that's why she's poking her nose in my business now. The mention of Tenley is absolutely my mom's way of guiding me toward her.

I move through the house, checking on Charlie and saying hello to Peyton, who gives me little in the way of a real greeting, and head out the door. Pulling my ball cap low on my head, I take my truck over to Wyatt's cabin.

Something acidic races across my stomach. Nerves? Is that what this is? I've seen Tenley every day, hell I even saw her already today and had a beer with her a couple hours ago. But inviting her to dinner at the homestead, with my kids, feels like *more*.

And these nerves feel like more, too. Like excitement.

This is why I called Anna, even though she's the last person on the planet I want to talk with.

Closure. Not all of it though. Not yet. But what I do have, is enough for right now.

I pull up and cut the engine. Tenley is sitting on the porch swing, but I don't see her until I'm on the second step. She shifts, my attention is caught, and I halt. Her eyes are on me, cornflower blue reaching out to my light brown, and her face is excruciatingly gorgeous. She's an actress, so of course she's beautiful, but it's not just that. It's the layers underneath her skin. She's funny, and she's always game to learn. I can't think of many people who'd shovel shit just to learn how to hold the shovel the right way.

"Did you forget something?" Tenley's head tips to the side, her long hair fanning out. She tucks one knee up into her chest, but keeps her other foot on the floor. She pushes off, and the swing moves slowly.

"My mom told me to invite you to dinner." That's not what I meant to say. Or maybe I just wish I'd said something smoother. But how can I be smooth when I'm inviting her to dinner at my parents' house with my two kids? Nowhere in that scenario is there room for anything even remotely romantic.

She smirks. "Your mom?"

"Yes, but in the interest of full disclosure, she's not the only person who'd like you to be there."

"Charlie, too, huh?" She grins, teasing.

I huff a laugh. "Yeah. Charlie."

The swing slows and Tenley stands. She sails past me and into the cabin, stepping out a moment later with a jacket. "It gets chilly here at night."

"Lack of humidity." I follow her to the passenger side of my truck and open the door for her. It gives me the opportunity to appreciate her backside, and it's not one I miss.

I nod my head at her when she's seated, and she narrows her eyes in response. She knows.

We're quiet on the short drive to the homestead. She climbs the stairs to the front door ahead of me.

"Tenley?" Her name has left my lips before I've had time to consider what it is my brain would like to say.

She pivots. The setting sun casts a dull glow on her, turning her blonde hair amber and her eyes a darker shade. She gazes at me, expectant, but I'm too afraid to do what I want right now.

Instead of pulling her into my arms and tracing her lips with my own, which is what I'd do if my parents and kids weren't on the other side of the front door, I do the lamest thing possible. I offer her a high-five to make up for the one I missed earlier.

She stares at my offered palm, then slowly presses her palm to mine. Her gaze lifts.

"Another time," she whispers, then turns back around and walks inside.

17

TENLEY

CASSEROLE.

Tater tot, to be exact.

I've never had it, but it smells good enough to have kicked my salivary glands into working order. Just one look at the glass dish in the center of the Hayden dinner table tells me I'll be hooked for eternity.

"Juliette, that smells incredible." I smile at Warner's mother as she leans over the table with a large wooden salad bowl in her hand.

"Well, eat up," she replies. "There's plenty." She sets the salad in front of Beau, as far from me as possible. Either she's sending a message to her husband, or she's sending a message to me. Somehow I think it's the latter. She's always trying to get me to eat more food at breakfast.

The dishes are passed around the table. I take a bite of my dinner. *Oh my God.* It's as good as it smells. I chew and swallow, then open my mouth to compliment Juliette a second time, but decide not to. Twice would be overkill. Juliette doesn't seem the type to appreciate a barrage of compliments. Instead, I focus my attention across the table.

"Peyton, how was school?" I look at Warner's daughter and arrange my face into polite interest.

The look she gives me back could cut ice, slay a demon, maybe even scare the robe off Voldemort. "Fine," she answers, the answer sounding more like 'fine-uh.'

Oh Lord. The '-uh' ending. I did it. My sister did it. A hallmark of teenage girls, both past and present. I nod enthusiastically, as if Peyton has just told me that today she was elected president of student council. "That's great."

Warner meets my eyes. His shoulders lift, his eyes squeeze tight. He releases them both, the frustration clear. His mouth opens, but the voice comes from the far end of the table.

"You can be rude to used car salesmen and boys trying to get you to do something you don't want to do." Beau's voice is low, and he doesn't look up from his plate. He doesn't need to. He might have used a megaphone for all the attention he commanded the moment he spoke. "But you will not be rude to a guest in my house."

Peyton ducks her head, and I feel bad for her. I want to defend her, to tell them I was a teenager once too, that I had the same attitude. What I didn't have was an intimidating grandfather to tell me to knock it off.

I decide to keep my mouth shut. Drawing the ire of Beau ranks pretty low on the list of things I'd like to do anytime soon. Peyton can weather this one on her own.

Now it's awkward. Quiet. Forks and knives scrape plates. And then, in a miracle that rivals manna raining from heaven, Dakota walks from the kitchen into the dining room. She's holding a dinner plate.

She stands beside Juliette and grins at the table. "Would you believe me if I said I smelled dinner all the way from my house?"

Juliette snorts. "No." She takes Dakota's plate and passes it to Warner. He adds casserole and salad to her plate, then lifts it above his head.

Dakota walks up behind Warner, mussing his hair before taking her plate. He shifts it back into place. Dakota takes the empty seat beside me and starts to eat.

"So good," she says around a mouthful. She looks down the table. "Nice work, Mama H."

Juliette lifts her two eyebrows in acceptance, and that's it. My mother would have purred her pleasure at having her cooking skills complimented, would have rushed to write down the recipe and passed it off as her own when it was most certainly someone else's. It's amazing how different people can be.

"Dakota, do you know if the wine bar is booked solid tomorrow night?" Warner asks.

She shrugs. "Not sure, but I can text Jo and ask. Why?"

Warner looks at me. "It's Tenley's birthday tomorrow."

I narrow my eyes at him. He chuckles.

"She thought she was going to keep it a secret, but her cover was blown, so—"

Dakota interrupts him by clapping her hands together. "Yes, I love it. Perfect idea."

"I haven't even told you what I'm thinking."

"You don't have to. I'll take it from here." Dakota beams at me and pulls her phone from her pocket. She types out a message and puts the phone down.

"I don't usually do anything big for my birthday," I tell her. "I'm really low-key about it."

Dakota's phone buzzes and she looks at it, then back up to Warner. "Bring Tenley to The Orchard tomorrow evening at seven."

Warner's eyes meet mine. "I can do that."

"Good," Dakota replies, taking a bite. "I'll take care of everything else."

* * *

It's only seven in the morning and I've already fielded phone calls from my parents, my sister, and Gretchen. I haven't left the bed yet. It's too warm in my spot, I can't get up. And there isn't anything pressing to get out of bed for anyway. Warner has to do something with Wes so there won't be any ranching lessons today. My phone, still warm from my most recent conversation, rings again. *Morgan.*

"Hello there," I say as I press speaker.

Morgan's off-key voice floats into the air, the 'happy birthday' tune bobbing up and down like it's avoiding punches in a fight.

I thank her when she's finished. "It was like the sweetest symphony."

"So good, right?" Morgan laughs. "How's the big three-oh?"

"Very much the same as two-nine and 364 days."

"Do you have plans? I wish I were there."

"You can be. Get on a plane to Phoenix, rent a car, and drive two hours. Boom."

"I can't..."

"Because...?"

"I met someone last weekend and tonight I'm meeting his mother. We might be in love. Me and Pax, not me and the mom."

I sit up. "Wait, what?"

Morgan does this embarrassed giggle thing. "I know. It's crazy."

Throwing the comforter aside, I get out of bed and make

it as far as the couch, Libby in tow. "Tell me all about him."

"No. I don't want to jinx it."

"Telling me about him will jinx it?"

"Possibly."

"You're weird."

"I know. Tell me about your plans for tonight."

I frown. I don't like letting her off so easy, but I know Morgan, and she won't budge once she's made up her mind. "Dinner at a local place."

"With whom? Calvin?"

I shake my head at the same time I tell her no. "Remember the family I told you about?" I don't wait for her to respond. "I'm going out with some of them."

"The instructor?"

I clear my throat and shift so I'm parallel with the cushions. "Among others."

Morgan groans.

"What?" A defensive edge creeps into my tone.

"You like him."

I sigh, as if her accusation is an egregious transgression. Actually, I'm buying time.

"Quit stalling."

Dammit.

"He's nice, Morg. Just a friend. I told you that already."

"Right. Three times. And that's all you've said. Which is how I know you like him. Economy of words isn't something you've been known to practice."

"Are you calling me a motormouth?"

"I would never. I'm just saying that you tend to clam up when you like someone. You're not a gusher."

"Ew." My lip curls. It's official. I do not like the word 'gusher.'

"I know. I don't like it either. Strike it from the record."

"So stricken."

"Anyway," she says with exaggeration. "Are you going to come clean, or what?"

I sigh. "He's... pretty great."

"Can you do any better than that?"

"Gorgeous. Charming. Funny. Tall. I like his nose." It's a good nose. Straight. "But he's also fresh out of a divorce and has two kids, one of whom is basically a teenager and she's figuring out how much she doesn't like me."

"If she's basically a teenager then she doesn't like *anybody*."

"Especially me."

"Understandable."

"I agree." I can see it from Peyton's point of view, and it's not pretty. "But it doesn't even matter. Warner and I have agreed to be just friends. It's not the right time."

"Leave it to you to create your own real-life romantic comedy when you're shooting your last one."

"I don't know if I'd call this a romantic comedy." I pick at a speck of lint on the cushion. "Maybe a Greek tragedy."

"Let's hope not. Those end very..."

"Tragically?"

Morgan laughs. "Yes." She pauses. "Go have fun tonight, okay? Don't think about all your stuff. Your parents are fine, I saw them two days ago. Your mom was bitching at your dad and he ignored her. Nothing has changed. Your handsome, funny, and charming cowboy won't have his daughter with him tonight, right?" She doesn't wait for me to answer. "So you don't have to worry about her, either."

"True."

"I want a full report tomorrow, got it? And it had better be good. If you tell me you were in bed by nine, I'm going to be pissed off."

Morgan's using her mother's stern voice. It makes me smile. "I promise when we talk tomorrow, I'll have something good to tell you."

There's a knock on the door. A zing shoots through me. I'm almost positive it's Warner with coffee. Last night when he dropped me off after dinner with his family, he mentioned birthday coffee. Libby jumps off the couch and races for the front door.

I open the door, phone tucked between my shoulder and my tipped head. I was only half right. A smile spreads across my face. Warner stands on the bottom porch stair, and Charlie stands on the threshold, a handful of flowers thrust out at me. "Happy birthday," he says. "I picked these for you." Libby jumps around his feet.

I take the flowers. Earth clings to the flower's roots, showering down on my foot as the arrangement changes hands. "Charlie, you shouldn't have." I wink at him, and he beams. My eyes find Warner. One side of his mouth lifts into a smile. Into the phone, I say, "Morgan, I need to go. I'll talk to you tomorrow." Using my free hand, I slip the phone from my head and tuck it into my pocket.

Warner walks the rest of the way to me in the open doorway. He's holding coffee. "Morgan, huh? She's a real person?" He must see my confusion, because he follows it up with, "That's the name you gave me the first day we met."

I press two fingers to my lips, suppressing a laugh, and step back to welcome Warner and Charlie inside. "Morgan is my best friend," I explain, watching Warner stride into the kitchen. He pulls two mugs down while I rinse the dirt from the flowers and drop them into a cup with water. Charlie hops onto a stool that faces the kitchen counter and watches.

"These are lovely flowers, Charlie." I tap the glass holding the bouquet. "Where did you get them?"

He pushes hair off his forehead, dirt beneath his fingernails. "There's a meadow behind our house. But they grow nearly everywhere this time of year. They pop up out of nowhere."

I nod. "Wildflowers?"

"Yep." He glances behind me at a cabinet. "Uncle Wyatt keeps hot chocolate here for me..."

Warner laughs. "Is that your way of asking?"

Charlie shrugs. "Maybe."

"I think that's something we can do." I turn around, and Warner is close, so close I almost run into his outstretched hand with the mug of hot coffee.

"Thank you." I look up at him, towering over me. He presses the coffee into my hands, my fingertips raking across his hand as I take it.

Though no sound comes from him, his face is anything but quiet. His lower lip separates from his upper. The tip of his tongue slips out, curling over his bottom lip. His pupils dilate, black overtaking caramel. Blood warms his skin half hidden beneath two days of stubble.

The increasing heat of the coffee mug forces me to disrupt the moment. I place the mug on the counter and step around Warner to fix Charlie's hot chocolate. Like he said, there's a jar of pre-made mix in the cabinet.

"Here you go." I place the mug in front of Charlie. He thanks me, then glances at his feet. "Can I take Libby outside to play?"

I look to Warner. "Fine by me."

He nods his yes to Charlie. Charlie walks out of the cabin, two small hands wrapped tightly around his cup. Libby trots beside him.

My attention swings from the closing front door to Warner. He's looking at me over the brim of his cup.

"Happy birthday," he says. His voice is deep and low, curling into me like the steam rising from his coffee.

"You said that already." It's a light, teasing admonishment.

Warner shakes his head. "Charlie did. I didn't."

"Right." I look away. If I could keep my gaze trained on Warner, I would. But he's doing this thing where he's looking at me too closely, too intrusively, and it's making me squirm. It's safer to avert my gaze.

"Ready for tonight?" Warner asks. "In case you hadn't noticed, Dakota is pretty excited."

"She really didn't need to—"

"Stop."

"Stop what?"

"Trying to insist you don't need a celebration."

"I don't."

Warner rolls his eyes toward the ceiling. "I swear, woman, you are so damn hardheaded."

Laughter bursts from me, almost spilling my coffee as I shake. "That's the most cowboy thing I've ever heard you say."

Warner's eyes narrow. "Cowboy thing?"

"Yeah, you know. Western, or whatever." My palm slices through the air as I gesture, but really, I'm only digging myself deeper into a hole.

A smirk plays at the corner of his mouth. "No, I don't know. Why don't you enlighten me?"

I make a sound of playful disgust. "Quit playing dumb, Warner. Cowboy stuff like 'yeehaw.'" For emphasis, I twirl my hand in the air like I'm wielding a lasso.

Warner's smirk turns into a full smile. "To be fair, I haven't heard you say anything too 'actressy'."

I snort a laugh. "And what would be considered 'actressy'?"

Warner shrugs. "I'm not sure."

We look at each other for a long moment, the humor of our conversation disappearing like the sun ducking behind the clouds. The air between us thickens. How is it that two people who are still recovering from the pains of the past could possibly be tasked with the handling of a new opportunity? It seems too much. An embarrassment of riches.

But wouldn't it be crazy to let it pass us by? This kind of chemistry is rare. I know this, as surely as I know anything.

I reach for Warner's hand, my fingers sliding into his. "Warner, I—"

Charlie bursts in, panting. "You should have seen how fast Libby chased a stick I found."

I release Warner's hand and take a step back. His eyes search mine, but only for a second. Charlie is still talking, as oblivious to the climate of the room as any ten-year-old boy would be.

"...you should get Libby a ball, Tenley." Charlie marches into the kitchen, directly between Warner and I, and sets his empty mug in the sink. He turns to face us, an imperfect line of hot chocolate half dried above his upper lip. "Ready, Dad? I don't want to be late for school."

"Yeah, bud." Warner's voice is thicker than usual. "Let's go see if Peyton is ready yet."

Charlie fist-bumps me on his way out. Warner leans in, his lips near my ear, and says in a low voice, "I'll pick you up this evening."

I nod, a shiver of excitement making its way down my spine.

18

WARNER

When I was young, I thought this was all going to be easy. My life was a road, paved in smooth sandstone, and I was just stepping onto it. If I turn around now and look back, I see what I couldn't then. Rocks jutting up from below, forced through the sandstone by seismic interruptions.

I'd consider Tenley a seismic interruption of gargantuan proportion. Nothing else explains these jittery nerves in my stomach. Or the bouquet of pink roses lying on the passenger seat.

I'm wearing a collared shirt. Cologne. I'm a thirty-five-year-old single father of two and I'm taking a woman on a date.

Sort of.

We haven't called it a date, but the preparation feels like one. We call ourselves friends, but it's a farce. We both know it. Friends can feel attracted to one another, but I'm not sure they can feel *this* attracted.

Tenley is waiting out front for me. She's leaning against the pillar beside the top step. She wears a reddish-orange dress the color of a summer sunset, and a jean jacket. Her hair is loose, curled, swinging around her shoulders. My heart sinks down low, taking a seat next to my navel.

I hop out of my truck and hurry around the front, opening the passenger door for her. She walks closer, smiling at me.

"Birthday girl," I say to her, sweeping my arm toward the open vehicle.

She laughs, a tinkling, happy sound. Instead of climbing into the truck, she steps closer to me. Rests her hand on my forearm. Leans in. Brushes a kiss on my cheek. She smells like a hundred different good things.

"Hello," she says, and when she pulls back, I catch the faintest scent of wine on her breath.

She exclaims over the roses, acting as if they're the best gift she's ever received. That must be a million miles from the truth.

We're pulling out onto the main road, the roses nestled in her lap, when she admits she drank half a glass of wine while getting ready. "I'm nervous," she says, shrugging lightly. Her fingers trace the outline of a rose, curling inward toward the center.

It's hard for me to imagine. Tenley seems more confident than any woman I've ever met.

"Why?"

"You all are being so nice, and I know it's genuine. It's off-putting." Her tiny chuckle sounds embarrassed. "I know that seems ridiculous, but aside from Morgan and Gretchen, I don't have any true friends at home. A night out for my birthday might include twenty people, but I'd feel mostly alone surrounded by all of them." She shrugs again. "Everybody wants something. From me. From everyone else. One gigantic means to an end."

Well, that's... shitty. I feel bad for her. I reach for her hand, lifting it from her lap and resting it in mine over the console. "When you have people around you tonight, you're not allowed to feel lonely."

"Honestly, Warner, since I've come here, the last thing I've felt is lonely."

I'm trying not to let her words affect me, but it's no use. They shift and squirm in my chest, settling into a space beside my heart. Tenley being comfortable in my hometown, on the ranch that I love, means everything to me.

When we walk into The Orchard, Jo is the first person to greet us. She has long blonde hair with pink ends, and today it's wound into a thick braid that hangs over her shoulder.

"Warner, hi!" She walks around the hostess stand, smiling, and offers a handshake. I've known her since we were young, but she's always been reserved.

"Tenley, this is Jo. Dakota's general manager and friend."

Jo shakes Tenley's hand, too. "I'm going to be really honest here," Jo says, her cheeks growing pink. "I'm a huge fan of your movies and I had to tell myself not to freak out when I met you. It was a legit pep talk."

Tenley laughs, but it sounds different than every other laugh I've heard from her. Not fake, necessarily. Practiced.

"Thank you," she answers, and the handshake finally ends. "I've been looking forward to meeting you too. Dakota talks about you a lot."

The pink on Jo's cheeks deepens. "Come on." She pivots with a wave. "I'll show you where we set you up tonight."

Tenley goes first, and I start after her. Two knuckles on my right hand slide the length of her back, parallel to her spine, and I hardly realize I'm doing it until I feel her deep intake of breath.

"Here we are," Jo announces when she reaches the little

room off the main building. The French doors are open, facing the courtyard where all the oversized party games are set up. Connect 4, Cornhole, Ladder Toss, Jenga, and a few others I don't know. Inside the room, the long wood table is covered in a white lace tablecloth, some kind of fancy plants in the center of the table, and candles.

Tenley squeals. Her hands go to her mouth. The sound draws Dakota from the room, and she steps through the French doors just as we reach them.

"Dakota, I'm..." Tenley shakes her head. "This is incredible."

"It was fun." Dakota smiles at Jo. "Jo and I put it together earlier."

"You're joining us, right?" Tenley looks hopefully in Jo's direction, but Jo's eyes are on something inside the private room.

Wyatt. She doesn't look happy.

"I have some things to finish up," she answers, eyes coming back to us. "But I'll join you later."

Dakota pulls Tenley inside and Jo leaves. Tenley is more excited than I've ever seen or heard her. She comments on everything. The greenery in the middle of the table (Eucalyptus), the white wine Dakota pours for her (Sancerre), the folksy country music playing (a local band).

Wes stands talking to Wyatt, bottles of beer in their hands.

"How did you get beer?" I ask, interrupting them. "I thought this was a wine bar."

Wes points at the floor. A six-pack sits trapped between his feet. "Helps to know the owner."

I bend and grab one. It's a bitter IPA, not something I'd usually drink but like hell I'm going to complain about it to

Wes. He'd revoke my man card without hesitation or mercy. With one hand, I catch the bottle opener Wes tosses at me.

Tenley and Dakota laugh loudly, holding their hands over their mouths after they realize we're all looking over at them. Tenley's cheeks are flushed. Not from the wine. From pleasure. Sheer happiness.

And I'm the fool smiling at it all.

"Anna who?" Wyatt says, drawing my attention from Tenley. He does a head shake smirk combination that's pretty fucking obnoxious.

"Go fuck yourself," I mutter, my mouth poised on the rim of the bottle as the murky brown liquid fills my mouth.

Wyatt laughs. "Too late, I've already done that once today."

Wes snickers. Wyatt grins, proud to have made his oldest brother, and usually the most unyielding, laugh.

Wyatt irritates me. He's milking the youngest son act and it's starting to grate on my nerves. Today is a perfect example. Wes and I spent the better part of the day in the Gator, riding the perimeter of our property. Wes is hell-bent on keeping his eyes on our land, and I was roped into joining him simply because I'm his right-hand man.

Where was Wyatt today while Wes and I were working? Who the hell knows. He's a horse whisperer, a veritable magician of the equine variety, and this skill appears to have granted him carte blanche. He comes and goes from the ranch as he pleases. I don't understand it, and the one time I broached the subject with my father, I was instructed to put my nose back where it belonged.

I am a grown ass man. When is my little brother going to grow up as well?

"You don't have to get your pretty panties in a bunch,"

Wyatt says, winking at me in a way that makes me want to deck him. "You're allowed to move on."

I snort. "You're handing out relationship advice? That's rich, coming from the guy whose number of serious relationships were equal to Wes's up until he met Dakota. That is to say, *none*."

Wyatt gives me a hard look. Jo walks in carrying a gigantic board bearing too many different foods to count. Meats, cheeses, tiny pickles, dried fruits and nuts, and other things I can't even name.

Derrick and Andrea, Wes's friends from high school, walk in behind Jo. Dakota makes introductions with Tenley, and I watch both of them try not to lose their shit over meeting her. Tenley pretends not to notice their stammering. Her lips curve into a trained smile, much like the one she gave Jo when we walked in.

Dakota orders us to sit. Tenley motions for me to sit beside her, and I try not to let it show how happy this makes me. Dish after dish arrives at the table. Dakota keeps ordering, and I quickly realize some of what's coming out isn't even on the menu. I switch from Wes's IPA to wine and ignore his dirty look. It's a wine bar, for Christ's sake.

Tenley sparkles, as if a thousand diamonds live inside her. She is witty, sharp with her comebacks when Wyatt displays the chip wedged in his shoulder blades, and dry with her responses to Wes when his gruff sarcasm comes out. My brothers love her. Far more than they ever cared for Anna, and they aren't trying to hide it at all. It has nothing to do with her being a famous actress, either, because neither of my brothers give a shit about fame. *Doesn't matter how pretty your outside is when you're rotten inside.* That's what our grandma used to say.

Tenley laughs, a big belly laugh, at something Dakota

said. I miss the joke entirely. I'm too busy sitting in the ambient glow of Tenley, soaking up her goodness.

Dessert wine appears on the table, but I decline. "Driving," I remind Tenley, pointing a finger back at myself. A grin slips out the side of her mouth. Her eyes are glossy, her motions fluid. The wine has loosened her movements.

Wyatt reaches under his seat and stands. His gaze zeroes in on Tenley as he thrusts a small white box in her direction. "I got you something."

I bristle. Isn't it enough Wyatt has Tenley sleeping in his bed? While I'm three hundred yards away thinking about her lying between my little brother's sheets.

Tenley takes the cube-shaped box. She glances at Wyatt as she lifts the lid, reluctant. She, like me, has no idea what could be inside. Because of this, she leans her body back, angling the box away so nobody can peek. Her eyes widen, and she quickly puts the lid back on the box.

She stares at Wyatt, who's sitting across the table looking way too pleased. "How?" She's astonished, and the rest of us are clueless.

Wyatt shrugs as if it's no big deal, but the asshole can't seem to wipe the satisfied smirk from his face. "It wasn't hard to track down, once you learn people's motivations."

Her lip curls up in disgust. "Were they being sold?"

His answering nod is tiny. Tenley groans.

"Fucking Christ," Wes complains, raking a hand down his face. "Tell us what the fuck is in that box."

Thank God someone besides me said it. I'd look like a jealous asshole if it'd come from my mouth. Wes just looks like a regular asshole.

Tenley glances around the table, lips twisting. To Andrea, Derrick, and Jo, she says, "I've been staying at the Hayden ranch because someone broke into the house the studio rented for me. They only stole one thing, and Wyatt somehow managed to get it back." She runs a finger over the box now sitting in front of her on the table.

Her underwear. Inside that box are her underwear. Touched by my brother, because they didn't grow legs and climb in by themselves. Wyatt and I have been in plenty of fights over the years, but I've never wanted to snap off his fingers more than in this moment.

"And that would be?" Wes motions with a cupped hand that bounces through the air like a rock skipping the water's surface.

"My underwear."

Jo, Dakota, and Andrea gasp. Wes's eyebrows scrunch together, and I know he's already trying to work out who the hell took them. Derrick's head shakes, and he shares a *can you believe that?* look with Andrea.

Wes adjusts the way he's sitting in his chair, threads an arm over Dakota's shoulders, and asks Wyatt, "Do I want to know how you retrieved those?" He sounds proud, which isn't surprising. Protecting people is a cornerstone of Wes's personality.

Wyatt leans back in his chair. I can't see it, but I'd imagine the front two chair legs are off the ground. "Probably not." Wyatt looks at Tenley. "Let's just say that from now on, you shouldn't have any reason to hide out on the ranch. Nobody in Sierra Grande is going to fuck with you."

"Thank you," Tenley says quietly to Wyatt. She melts back into her seat, the box placed in front of her like it could be the next course. She sips her wine. Leaning over, I capture Tenley's hand under the table. Her fingers flutter at my touch. She is warm, her skin buttery soft.

My fingertip traces the top of her hand. Topples off her

thumb as it passes by. Glides across the spot where it landed. Her thigh. Her muscles constrict. She turns to me.

"Do friends do this, Warner?" The question rides on the low side of a whisper, and if I weren't watching her lips move, I may not have heard it at all.

"Some do sometimes, others not at all."

Her lips press together as she holds in a laugh. "You're confusing."

My finger circles her knee. "I know."

Her head tips, and the light from the flickering candle dances in her eyes. "What do you want, Warner?" I like the way she says it. Quiet and strong, she's holding me to my words. Making me answer for the way I'm touching her.

My response comes from deep within, rumbling against my chest, my lips and tongue shaping around each letter. "You."

Tenley holds my gaze. Says nothing. Across the table, Jo laughs. Glasses are lifted and set down. Tines of forks scrape across plates.

Tenley breaks first. She looks away, rejoining the conversation as if she were never absent. They are talking about Andrea and Derrick's weekly front yard happy hour, how the concept has grown and made people feel closer to their neighbors. The words float around me like fog. I'm having a hard time concentrating, until Andrea speaks to Wyatt.

"Wyatt, I want to know something." Her voice is heavy from more than enough wine. She leans her forearms on the table and looks at him.

Wyatt lifts his eyebrows and his chin at the same time, waiting.

"A little bird told me your truck was seen leaving Sara Schultz's house early in the morning last week." Andrea makes a pointed face. "And that her husband was out of town."

Derrick sighs irritably and puts his hand on Andrea's shoulder, pulling her back to upright. He says something in her ear and she frowns.

The reactions around the table are varied. Wyatt's face has turned to stone, his cheekbones taut, waiting for someone to speak out against his behavior. Wes pinches the bridge of his nose. Jo looks away, to a wall bare of anything interesting, and Dakota keeps her eyes on Wyatt, her gaze soft and curious. Of all people, Dakota is the most open to understanding other people's choices.

Tenley looks up at me. *Awkward*, she mouths. I nod.

Taking Tenley's hand, I stand up and pull her up with me. "On that note, we're going to take off." I clap both my brothers on the back and stop at Dakota. "Thank you for tonight." Tenley leans down, wraps Dakota in a hug, and says something in her ear. I take a few hundred dollars from my wallet and drop them into the purse hanging from Dakota's chair. She'd never accept the money outright.

We walk away, and behind me I hear Andrea apologizing to Wyatt, who I'm certain doesn't want to hear it.

I open the truck door for Tenley and wait for her to climb in. She pauses in the seat, the seat belt stretched midair in her hands, and says, "And here I was thinking a small town couldn't possibly hold as much drama as LA."

"Believe me, Tenley," My fingers tighten around the door as I move to close it. "This place holds plenty."

19

WARNER

Tenley's entire frame is relaxed. I don't think she's asleep, but it's hard to tell in the dark cab of my truck.

The sky is navy blue, and the moonlight slices through the pines and into my windshield at haphazard angles. I pull up to Wyatt's, cut the engine, and take a few long seconds to look at her. Her hair frames her face, and her dress has ridden up her thighs. Her eyes are closed, so maybe she is asleep.

I shift in my seat, open my door, and the movement stirs her. She glances around the cab of the truck, mildly confused, then realizes where she is.

"Wine makes me sleepy," she explains, her tone apologetic.

"No worries." My hands flick the air, waving away her apology. "Your snoring made for nice ambience."

Her mouth drops open and her eyebrows draw together. "I do not snore."

"If you say so."

She jabs a finger into my side, but I saw it coming and braced myself a second before, so it doesn't hurt. "Kidding," I tell her, my hands up in surrender. "You don't snore."

Tenley pulls her purse from the floor and threads her arm through the straps. "I better go," she says slowly. "Big day tomorrow. Running lines with Calvin." Each word is spoken with an open end, like she's leaving space for me to object, to suggest a different ending to our evening.

I want to. I really, really want to.

But I don't. That hurdle feels bigger than all the others, and I'm still working up the speed needed to clear it.

She opens the door and gets out. "Good night," she says softly, and closes the door.

I wait until she gets inside before driving away and spend the short drive to my house berating myself for being the dumbest man on the planet.

* * *

I HEAR her before I see her.

The crunch of twigs, the displacement of pinecones and pine straw as she walks. My fingers are wrapped tight around the cold longneck bottle, and I know there's no way she can see me out here. Not with the porch light off, and the tall trees filtering out most of the moonlight. I came out here after I dropped her off, needing the crisp night air to clear my head. I've been out here for a while, trying to sort through my thoughts.

I don't want to frighten her, so when she's at my porch stairs I greet her. "What happened to your big day tomorrow?"

She startles anyway. Grips the post, a hand flying to her chest.

"Sorry. I didn't mean to scare you."

She recovers, coming closer. "Why are you sitting out here in the dark?"

"I do my best thinking in the dark."

She's in front of me now. She changed her clothes. I think I prefer her in sweats.

Instead of sitting down in the second empty seat, she leans a shoulder against the wall. "What were you thinking about?"

"You," I answer immediately. No point in lying. It's too dark to see her features clearly, but I can still see her movements. Her arms cross in front of her chest, and I wish I could see her expression.

"I meant what I said earlier. You're confusing."

I don't need to see her face to know she's bothered by my behavior. Her tone is enough.

I pull at the neck of the sweatshirt I changed into before coming out here. "I don't mean to be."

She sighs. "I know. I'm sure this is hard for you."

"It is," I confirm. As true as that may be, there is one thing I know for certain, and that's the fact that I have to move on. Stagnation is not the place for me.

I stand up, setting my drink on the small table, and step closer to her. Her arms uncross.

"Confusing you is not my goal." I want to touch her, but I make myself wait.

"What is your goal?"

"For the future?" I had so many, and most of them have changed.

She shakes her head. "For right now."

I wish I could see her. If I could just see her face, determine her emotions in her gaze, this would be easier. But no. I'm going in blind. Maybe that's a good thing. I should let my heart lead.

Brutal honesty. That's how I'll handle this. "I like you. I'm attracted to you. And that scares me. I've never been with anybody but Anna. This house is a godsend because she never lived in it with me. I want to take you into my bedroom and remove your clothes. I spend a stupid amount of time thinking about the first time I saw you, and how different things might have been if I hadn't been in denial about the end of my marriage. And as scared as I am to be attracted to you, I'm more terrified of refusing how I feel about you and making the kind of mistake I'll think about when I'm an old man. To make a long story short, my goal right now is to kiss you the way I did that day in the field, and I hope to God you're okay with that because it's happening in three." I pause, giving her the opportunity to approve. Or refuse, but Christ I hope that's not what she does. "Two..."

"One," she says, stepping into the space between us, pressing her chest against me, her hands finding the back of my neck.

Her lips are on mine. My arms wind around her body, and her muscles relax. She melts into me, covering me in her warmth and her desire. She is sweet like sugar, but she has heat too. Like her spicy peach candy. The thought makes me smile, and she feels it.

"What's funny?" she asks, her question spoken against my lips.

"Later," I groan, because talking is the last thing I want to use my mouth for right now. My tongue slides against the seam of her lips, parting them softly. She moans into me, and the kiss grows deeper.

I walk her backward until she is pressed against my house. My hand drags down the length of her side and back up, settling on her hip. The fistful of sweats in my hand isn't enough. I need more. I push against her, and she pushes back, meeting me.

Wrapping two hands around her, I hoist her up and onto my waist. She laughs against me, the sound a vibration in my mouth.

"Hold on," I tell her, pulling back only long enough to speak.

Through the front door we go, and all the way back to my bedroom. Tenley's thigh muscles clench around my middle, her hands running through my hair. I pepper kisses across her collarbone as we clear my bedroom door.

What happens next is easily the best thing that's ever happened to me. Tenley crawls to the center of my bed after I lay her down, and removes every piece of her clothing. My throat tightens at the sight of her, open and inviting, on my bed. She is luscious curves and sexy smiles, beautiful and bold, and I am the luckiest man.

I undress as quickly as possible without embarrassing myself. Tenley crawls to the edge of the bed, reaching for me. Her touch, her stroke, sends a hiss of breath between clenched teeth.

I pull myself from her grasp in an effort to make this last as long as I possibly can. This experience with her is a gift, and I'm going to squeeze every last drop of pleasure from it.

Gently I guide her onto her back, and cover her mouth with mine. Her nails scratch lightly over my back, and the heat from our kiss builds. I pull away to take a breath, but I'm unwilling to keep my mouth off her for long. I drag kisses over her collarbone, down her chest. She pulls my hair while I take my time with each of her breasts.

"Mmmm," I moan against her, and my lips travel down, over her stomach. Down, down, down my lips go, until I'm nipping at the top of the insides of her thighs, and Tenley writhes with anticipation. She makes an incoherent sound at my first pass over her. I grin against her, and settle in.

It's not too long before her legs stiffen, her back arching off the bed. I hold her still when her hips begin to buck, making sure I finish the job.

Her body quiets, and I sit up between her open legs. She has a hand pressed over her mouth, but there's a smile in her eyes.

She looks down, staring at the part of me that's dying to get inside her. "I'm on birth control," she whispers.

Oh fuck, thank you.

I lie back down on top of her, hold my weight on one forearm, and reach down. Once I'm lined up with her, I don't pause for even the shortest second. Swiftly, maybe even brazenly, I'm inside her.

She guides me with her hips, pushing up and silently asking for more, but I respond by cupping her cheek and consuming her mouth.

"Warner, please," she says against me.

Her plea obliterates any shred of my remaining self-control.

Together we are intense, needy for each other. She wraps her legs around my back, and I kiss every part of her I can reach. We fuck hard, Tenley matching me even though she is beneath me, and she never indicates she wants anything less than what I'm giving. I place a hand between the top of her head and the headboard, and it's a good thing I do because pretty soon her head presses to my palm and the headboard bangs into the wall.

Tenley grips my back, squeezing me tight, and tells me she's close.

"Look at me," I say, pressing my nose to hers. She does as I've asked, allowing me to watch her approach her climax, and then she comes apart beneath me, shuddering and clamping a hand over her mouth to muffle her cries.

She needn't be quiet. We're alone out here, more alone than most people, and when the tremors of my impending climax start, I thrust into her once more.

With my release comes a guttural groan of her name, and she tightens her thighs at the word.

My head drops onto her chest. "I… I…" There's no way I can finish that sentence, and I'm so out of it I'm not sure what I'm even trying to say.

Her chest dips with her small laugh. "Same."

We stay in this position, my cheek pressed to the swell of her breast. I feel weirdly hollow, but also like I'm a starving man who has been given a morsel of food.

Eventually it becomes clear we need to move, and we each take turns in the bathroom. I'm lying in my bed when she steps out. She looks at me, then at the scattered clothes. She moves to put on her bra, and I stop her with an outstretched arm that touches nothing but air.

"Will you stay?"

Tenley straightens. She nods and climbs in beside me. I reach for her, pulling her in close. Neither of us say anything, because what is there to say? Everything that needs to be said was spoken with our actions.

She falls asleep first, and I am not far behind her. My last thought is of how good her hair smells.

20

TENLEY

In the movies, there are three types of morning after scenarios. The first is the regrettable one, where they wake up and look at one another, equally astounded and revolted to see the other person. The second is where they wake up and peek at each other, have awkward but endearing conversation, and agree to see each other again. And the third is my favorite: the belated realization that prior events were a mistake, and keeping it friendly is best. I just hope I'm not experiencing it in real life at this exact moment.

Warner is still asleep, but it's very likely that when he wakes up, he will blame last night on a lapse in judgment. We've already established once that he is capable of taking one step forward and two steps back. For that matter—

"You look worried." Warner's voice, thickened by sleep, breaks into my negative thoughts. For the past half hour, I've been lying on my back, alternating between staring up at the ceiling and glancing over at him. His hand hovers over my face, two of his fingers gently pushing apart my cinched eyebrows.

I roll to my left, prop my head on my hand, and look at

him. His hair is rumpled, his eyes squinty. It's another of his looks, and just as handsome as the rest.

My finger traces an invisible design on the white flannel bedsheets between us. "It's not easy, in my industry. Sometimes there are...expectations."

Warner closes one eye and says, "I'm not sure what you mean."

"People have sex with a fantasy, but wake up to reality." The small but persistent worry has been there since I woke up, even though I can't see it being true of Warner.

He takes a moment to process what I've said, then shakes his head as much as he can while it's lying on his pillow. "Wait, I'm confused. Are you famous or something?"

I bite back a smile.

"Because I thought you were just a regular person I helped on the side of the road one day. But knowing you're famous? That changes..." Warner pauses, his grin teasing, "nothing."

I move with the intention of playfully shoving him, but he rolls over suddenly, taking me by surprise. He pins me beneath him.

His mouth is on my neck, my collarbone, drifting down to my breasts. His words are muffled against my skin, but I understand him anyway. "You taste so good."

I open up for him unabashedly, fully in the knowledge I've never been like this with anyone else. Warner makes me feel safe and cherished. There is no room in me for timidity, not when I'm so full of heat and hunger, eagerness and desire.

Warner lines himself up with me, and I swallow hard. He fills me swiftly and sets a pace similar to last night. I love that he is not careful with me. I am not fragile like hand-blown glass, and I don't want to be treated that way.

Warner's face is buried in my hair, his lips on my ear and his hand holding onto my hip. I reach up, pressing a palm against the headboard, bracing against it, stopping us from moving too far up the bed.

Warner groans against me. He reaches down, his hand between my legs, touching me. It's not long before I'm rising.

Higher. Higher. Higher.

I reach the pinnacle, the muscles in my legs tensing, my toes curling around the bedsheet.

"Yes," Warner growls. He continues for just a minute more, and when his back muscles flex, I tighten around him.

Warner presses his nose to the space behind my ear, holds on to my hip and jerks, then stills. He takes a few moments to catch his breath, and as he's rolling off me, he says quietly, "I think you've ruined me." I'm not sure I was supposed to hear it. I'm not sure he meant to say it.

He pushes hair away from my face and kisses me so tenderly, it's hard to believe only five minutes ago he was fucking me.

Warner pulls back, staring down at me, his brown eyes warm. "I fell asleep in the shallows, and I woke up submerged."

Oh. *Oh.* My hand settles on my chest to keep my heart from galloping away. Warner brings me my clothes, and I sit up.

"Are you hungry?" he asks, watching as I thread my arms through my bra straps.

"Starving."

He grins. "Let's make breakfast."

"Bathroom." I point through the open door as I say it.

"Right." He nods. "Meet me in the kitchen."

I've just finished up in the bathroom and am walking

back through Warner's room when I spot his bookshelf. I honestly don't know how I missed it. It's gigantic, nearly the length of one wall, and stuffed with books, not decorated with tchotchkes and books on art history like a show bookcase. This is the collection of someone who loves to read.

I walk the length of the case, running my fingers gently along spines. I recognize many of the names. Warner has a little of everything, from Atlas Shrugged (a mammoth book, something I've heard of but never attempted), to Where The Crawdads Sing. From what I can tell, there are classics and bestsellers, fiction and non-fiction. Warner, it appears, is well-read.

"Did you get lost?" Warner's voice trickles in from somewhere else in the house.

I leave the room to find him, wrapping my arms around myself against the slight chill in the air.

Warner is in the kitchen, a mixing bowl in one hand and a whisk in the other. Coffee percolates from a machine on the counter.

"Pancakes okay?" he asks, motioning to the bowl.

"Pancakes are perfect." I hop onto the kitchen counter and look around. Warner's cabin is similar to Wyatt's, but larger. Where Wyatt's cabin is sparse, Warner's looks more like a home. A magnet keeps a list of spelling words held up to the fridge, kitchen gadgets compete for space on the countertop, a pair of boots with dirt caked to the edges next to the back door. I look back into the living room and see more proof that this is a home. A gaming console next to the television, framed pictures of Charlie and Peyton, a tie-dye hoodie haphazardly lying on the back of the couch.

And then I remember the books. "I think I figured out why you're not a cinephile."

"What's your theory?" Warner asks, glancing over at me as he butters a pan.

"You're a bibliophile instead."

Warner finishes pouring batter into four rounds on the griddle. He sets the bowl on the counter, then comes to stand between my legs, resting his palms on my thighs. "It's my thing. Reading. It gave me something to do when things with Anna started going downhill."

Her name is a reminder that I know nothing about his marriage. His ex-wife. Or if what's between us is ever going to amount to anything.

Warner walks away to check the pancakes. I watch as he flips them, lets them cook for another minute, then places them on a plate and pours more batter. He hands me the plate with the pancakes and pushes the syrup my way.

"Eat while they're warm."

I'm so hungry I eat every crumb on my plate. By the time I'm finished, Warner's pancakes are ready. He eats leaning up against the counter. I get down and set my plate in the sink. Warner finishes too, stacking his plate on mine and grabbing two mugs. He fills them, then motions for me to follow him.

We walk into a room off the kitchen, about halfway to his bedroom.

"This is my office," he says, striding behind a wooden desk. A laptop sits open on top, and a few different colored notebooks are scattered across the remaining space. Warner sweeps a hand in the air an inch above the notebooks. "Can you keep a secret?"

My head tilts, unsure of where he's going with all this. "I like to think so."

"I just finished my master's degree. In English literature."

The surprise makes me flinch. How have I been spending so much time with him and not known this by now? "English literature." I nod slowly. "Warner, that's great. I mean, you obviously love to read. Are you going to do something with the degree?"

Warner runs a hand through his hair. "I always wanted to be a college professor." He glances at the bare wall to his left, like he's envisioning a framed degree he feels belongs there. "I managed to get my bachelor's before Wes left for the Army, and then my dad needed me here. And also, well, Anna..." Warner looks at me, his eyes probing, trying to read my thoughts. "Does it upset you to hear about her?"

I shake my head no, but it's a lie. Maybe a little more like a fib. It's natural not to love hearing about someone's ex.

"Things just didn't really go my way, I guess. Not that that's a bad thing. I have a lot to show for the things that did go my way, and some other blessings that came from the unknown." Warner rounds his desk and comes closer, but he stops short and sits back on the edge of his desk. "I heard about a spot opening up soon at the local community college."

"Will you keep working for your family?"

Warner looks down, crossing one bare foot over the other. "I can't be in two places at once, and ranching is a full-time commitment. There's never a shortage of tasks." He frowns as he speaks, and I wonder if he realizes it. "I'll have to choose. Either the ranch, or what I love."

"You don't love ranching?"

"To a point. Not like Wes does."

"But you're so good at it." Snippets of his lessons come back to me.

"Do you love what you're good at?"

He has me there. This is my last film for a reason.

I reach for him, wrapping my arms around his neck. "Wes doesn't know, does he?"

His hands run the length of my back and he buries his head into my neck as he shakes it back and forth.

"Your secret is safe with me," I whisper into his hair.

We stay that way until I remember I need to feed Libby. Warner offers to come with me, but I need to shower and I'm ready for a little space. I'm not sure what this has meant, and I'm even more unsure if I should ask.

"Are you busy later? Do you want to do something this afternoon?" Warner asks when I've picked up my purse off the ground where I dropped it inside his front door last night.

My mind travels to my fridge. My very *empty* fridge. "I have to run lines with Calvin. And I need groceries. Maybe you can come with me and be my security?" I say it jokingly, but after what happened with my underwear, I guess it's not much of a joke.

Warner chuckles. He palms the open door, and it makes his bicep ripple, and then it makes my whole body do a melty, ripply thing alongside it.

I pause in the open door. "I must be missing the joke."

Warner shakes his head. "Do you know how Wyatt got your underwear back?"

"No..." The word is drawn out as I realize I have no clue how he retrieved my unmentionables.

Warner's eyebrows raise. "Me neither. But my guess is that Wyatt is right and nobody around town is going to give you any more trouble."

I eye him. "Does that mean you're not interested in grocery shopping with me?"

"I didn't say that."

I give him a challenging look. "What did you say?"

Warner smirks. "I'd be happy to accompany you on your trip to town. I'll even hold your bags."

I press a hand to his chest. "You're quite the gentleman."

Warner's expression changes, his eyes knowing and hungry. "Not always."

* * *

In LA, I rarely did my own grocery shopping. I would have preferred to do it myself, but Tate insisted on ordering groceries or having his assistant go on a run. Unless, of course, he wanted to be seen. Then he had his assistant call the paps and tip them off. It wasn't a big deal to Tate if he missed a photo op, because he would just *create* them instead.

But grocery shopping at a small, adorable grocery store like the Sierra Supply? That's something I can see myself doing regularly. Between this place and the Merc, which I'm told sells Cow Tales candy (a must-try, Warner insists), I think I'd have all I need. Sierra Supply is loaded with fresh produce grown by local farms. It also has an aisle for basic hunting and fishing supplies, but that was added a couple years ago according to Warner. Its addition made steam shoot from the ears of Maia, the owner of the Merc, who also carries basic hunting and fishing supplies. But, Warner added, for those who do more than dabble in hunting and fishing, there's a real store for that a few miles away. I nodded at all the inside information, then moved on to the next aisle. What I didn't tell Warner was how much his stories are making me fall deeper in love with the small-town charm of Sierra Grande.

"So," Warner starts, peering into my cart. "Is this what you eat before a movie begins shooting?"

My gaze doesn't follow his. I know what's in there. Carrots, leafy greens, apples and berries. To be fair, we've only just begun shopping.

"Sort of," I answer. "This movie allows for a little wiggle room. It's not like I'm shooting a beach vacation film."

Warner scowls. "That top you wore in the photo shoot looked like half of a bikini."

Playfully I tap the tip of his nose. "Does that upset you?"

He tosses a frozen pizza into the cart. "Not after what happened this morning." He runs his hand over my lower back, as if remembering what it looks like without the fabric of my shirt to cover it.

My scar. The playful atmosphere evaporates.

Warner's hand stills. "What's wrong?"

"You saw my scar." I couldn't hide the embarrassment in my voice even if I wanted to.

His eyebrows knit together. "So?" He points a finger at his brow bone. "I have a scar too."

"That's nothing like mine." I picture the long strip of mottled flesh, the color three shades darker than my skin.

Warner's hand drifts again, then stills over my scar. Quietly, he says, "I fell asleep in the shallows, and I woke up submerged."

I swallow. It's the second time today he's said that. "Is that from something? Lines like that are usually delivered to me from a script."

He raises two fingers, holds them over the center of his chest, and taps twice.

It's in this moment that I realize I'm in danger. Warner is too good to be true. He must be an apparition, a mirage, a delusion. I'm torn between wanting to run from these feelings, and accepting everything Warner has to offer, soaking it all up like the parched desert I drove through to get to this town.

I opt for the latter.

Leaning in, I tuck my leg between his knees and grip his arm. He lowers his lips, I arch up to meet him, as if this is the most natural thing in the world to do. His mouth presses to mine, gentle and perfect, and my eyes flutter closed.

I don't see the person at the end of the aisle. Nor do I see it when they pull their phone from their pocket and take our picture.

21

TENLEY

"I knew it." Barb smacks her hands together, and Shirley startles.

"Knew what?"

Barb pushes her glasses higher up on her nose and shows the phone to her friend. A whole minute is wasted when Shirley tells her she can't read it. Barb enlarges the font and silently thanks her grandson for showing her how.

"I'll be damned," Shirley whispers.

* * *

"You ready for this?" Calvin stands two feet from me, stuffing a donut from the craft table into his face.

"All set." I nod, grabbing a pear and adjusting the front of my cream silk blouse. Wardrobe has me in a navy blue skirt and matching jacket for today's scene, but it's too warm to wear the jacket while I'm standing around waiting for filming to begin. I bite into my pear, taking care not to drip the juice onto the jacket folded over my forearm.

"Thanks for canceling on me at the last minute on

Saturday. I was almost to the coffee shop where you told me to meet you." Calvin tries to tuck his left hand into his pocket, but his jeans are so tight he barely manages to fit in anything more than up to his knuckles. "It would be good for us to be seen together. People love it when they think the leads are getting together in real life."

I have to resist curling my lip. There's nothing wrong with Calvin, like some really obvious fatal flaw. He's just not the handsome, charming, intelligent cowboy I want to spend time with. "I told you I had to go grocery shopping."

"Great excuse." He rolls his eyes and finishes his donut. "Have you been to The Orchard yet? It's the only place I can stand to eat in this small-ass town."

"Apparently it's either that or the craft table for you." I swipe a finger over the chocolate at the corner of his lip. "It's too bad we don't have a kissing scene today. I could've enjoyed your donut vicariously."

They call us to the set, and we stop being Tenley and Calvin, longtime friends. I become a big city lawyer addicted to her job and her email, and Calvin turns into a stoic, irritated cowboy. We maintain those roles for the next five hours, until the director, Ari, tells us he thinks he has what he needs.

I'm in my trailer, washing the makeup from my face, when my mom calls. I look at Lauren, the person who has been tasked with dog sitting Libby while I'm filming, and thank her for her time. She slips out with a quick wave as my phone rings. I hit the button for speaker and begin talking.

"First day went well, I know that's why you're calling." My robe falls open as I lean into the mirror, dragging a cotton pad dipped in makeup remover over my eyes. "We shot the scene where I first arrive at the ranch and I'm horrified. Calvin was great. Very convincing as a cowboy."

My mom's quiet for a second, then says, "Have you not seen Dirty Laundry today?"

"No, I have not, because I don't waste a moment of my precious life on that nonsense." As I say it, I remember how recently that *nonsense* turned out to be *truth*.

My phone dings as I rub moisturizer on my face. I lean over and see a message has come through.

"Take a look at what I just sent you," my mother says, her voice terse. I'd bet fifty dollars her lips are pursed right now.

I stifle a sigh and navigate to my messages, opening up the newest one at the top.

My fingers fly to my lips and I suck in a very audible breath.

"Uh-huh. Now do you see what I'm calling about?"

My mind races, thinking back to two days ago in the grocery store. Nobody bothered us. Nobody said anything, or stared, or acted differently at all. The cashier was polite and friendly, joking with me and asking Warner how his kids were doing.

"Mom, I—" I look into the mirror and picture her on the other end of the line. "I'm not sure what to say. The man in the photo is Warner Hayden, the guy who was teaching me about ranching. I'll be more careful from now on. I'll—"

"Don't change a thing."

"What? Why?" Libby's collar jingles from the ground beside me, and I stoop to scratch her between the ears.

"Are you serious? Tenley Roberts and a mystery man? Especially after what Tate did to you? Gold, Tenley. Brilliant."

I bristle. I don't like reducing Warner, or the feelings that are developing between us, to a publicity stunt.

"I have real feelings for him, Mom."

She laughs. "That's obvious from the picture."

"I'm serious."

"So am I."

I fall quiet, not sure what to say next. I focus on pulling on my jeans and T-shirt and wait for her to move onto the next subject. I know she will, because she's not good at reading between the lines, or hearing what's unspoken. And I'm not good at telling her when I'm upset.

"Can you keep seeing him?"

I give the phone a hard look. "Yes." I still haven't told her I'm staying on the Hayden property, and right now I'm not feeling much like sharing the news.

"Perfect. I couldn't be more excited." I hear her hands clap together.

"Wonderful," I say tightly. Normally I'd bury my irritation. I've been doing it for years, and I'm pretty good at it. But today, I don't want to. Today, it has to do with Warner.

"Is there anything wrong?"

"I don't like the idea of using Warner, Mom." I finish tying my shoes and grab my purse.

"You're not using him, it's just—"

"Making sure I'm seen out with him? Conveniently being in the place where I know someone with a camera will be? If you don't like the word *using*, let's choose a different word. How about manipulating? Or scheming? Are those more palatable?"

"Tenley." She's shocked. I can practically hear her mind scrambling, trying to understand my about-face. I have never talked to her this way. But something like this has never been asked of me. Not from her, anyway.

"Mom, I'm not going to orchestrate opportunities for

Warner and me to be seen together."

"Ok. I get it. I understand." I think she wants to say more, but she's holding back. "We need the publicity, Tenley. You know how much this movie means to me and your father. So can you just maybe not *hide* your relationship?"

I pinch the bridge of my nose with one hand while holding the phone in midair with the other. "After this picture, Warner might want to do exactly that."

"There's always Calvin."

My nose wrinkles. First Calvin mentions being seen together, now my mom? "Mom, I'm going to do everything in my power to make sure this movie is successful and you can pay… you know." If I say the name out loud three times, will they appear like Bloody Mary? Best not to find out. "Or you can just let me pay it off now and this can all be behind you."

"No way, Ten. We're your parents. This is our mess."

We talk for another minute, then my mom says she has to go. "I love you, Mom."

"I love you too, babe."

I hang up with her and leave the trailer. I wave goodbye to the crew, poke my head in Ari's trailer where I know he's watching dailies, and say goodbye.

It's almost thirty minutes out to the Hayden ranch, and I'm grateful for the drive. Pearl helps me clear my head. Top down, hair tangling in the wind, with Libby on my passenger seat.

***

I'm almost positive Warner isn't home. When we spoke this morning over coffee, he told me Charlie had soccer practice this afternoon. I didn't ask, but I took that to mean

Charlie and Peyton are back in his care. It's hard for me to understand why Anna has such limited access to her children, and by now I'm pretty curious, but I know it's not something I should be prying into.

I park Pearl in front of Warner's house and slip from my car. There's just a little something I want to drop off for him.

I don't know if Warner knows about the pictures of us kissing in the grocery store, and I'm not sure how he's going to react. Having my private affairs plastered all over the place is part and parcel with my career, but Warner... not so much. This jar of candy I'm leaving on his doorstep will either be a peace offering or a way to butter him up before telling him we were spotted.

I've just set the candy on the mat when the front door opens suddenly.

I jump back in surprise, my hand resting on my wildly beating heart. Peyton stands in the open doorway, looking every bit the sullen, angry thirteen-year-old.

"Sorry, I, uh..." I point down at the candy. "I was just leaving a surprise for your dad. And you, too, of course." I scoop it up and hand it over. "It's my favorite candy from LA."

Peyton eyes the jar but takes it. "Thank you," she says slowly.

"Sure, no problem." Silence. "Well, okay, that's it. I'll see you around." I pivot, making my way down the steps.

"Wait." Her voice is bumpy and unsure, as if she's about to do something and she hates that she has to.

Slowly, I turn around. "Yes?"

Peyton drops the act. Her lower lip trembles, and her eyes are fearful. "I need help."

My gaze sweeps over her quickly, looking for evidence of injury. None, from what I can see. "Are you hurt?"

She shakes her head. “I’m, um…” She glances around, as if we’re not in quiet seclusion. “I think I got my period.”

Whoa. “Okay. No big deal.” I come closer. “Do you have anything to use for it? Pads or…” I trail off. Something tells me Warner wouldn’t love the idea of his daughter using a tampon. Ultimately it will be her choice, but I remember when I got my period. My dad was horrified by the idea that something was entering my body, even if it was only a stick of cotton.

Warner probably hadn’t thought to buy something ahead of time. Peyton shakes her head. No.

“No worries, I have some stuff. Hang tight, I’ll be right back.” Libby barks from her place in my car. “How about…” I walk to the passenger side and open the door, “Libby keeps you company while I’m gone?” I motion for Libby to get down, and she jumps out. She runs over and Peyton scoops her up, smiling when Libby kisses her face.

“See you soon,” I tell Peyton. She closes the door to Warner’s house, and I go to mine. I grab a handful of panty liners, a couple pads, and a second jar of my precious candy. Peyton shouldn’t have to share with her dad and her brother when she’s on her period.

When I get back to Warner’s, I let myself in. Peyton sits at the kitchen table, Libby on her lap.

“I brought a couple things.” I place everything in front of her, explaining when she should use each one. Nudging the candy, I say, “This is because no woman on their period should have to share their candy.”

Peyton looks up at me. “Does this make me a woman now?”

Oh shit. I am so not qualified to be answering questions like this. I am, however, the only adult around, and I’m certainly not going to leave Peyton hanging.

"Well." I take the seat beside her. "That question has many answers. From what I can tell, there is no one time when you become a woman. I think a lot of little developments and experiences add together, and one day you realize you're a woman." My lips twist as I consider what I've just said and realize it applies to something else. "It's the same for becoming an adult, in my opinion."

Peyton nods, slowly reaching out for the stash on the table. She stands. "I knew I wasn't dying or anything. When I saw the blood, I mean. I knew what it probably was. It was just scary."

I have the urge to reach out, to touch her forearm and reassure her, but I don't dare. I'm just grateful for the progress we seem to have made so far. "I understand."

When Peyton leaves the room, I call Warner and tell him what's happened. He's completely silent.

"Warner?"

"Processing," he answers.

I tap my thumb on the table. "Process faster. She's going to be back soon, and I don't want her to walk in while I'm talking to you."

He sighs. Not like he's irritated, just that this is all a lot for him. I get it. He's a single father to a girl who is now considered a young woman. "What do I need to do?"

"Stop at the store. She needs supplies. I'll text you the list."

"Okay. Anything else?"

"Yes. You need to lose the horrified tone of voice by the time you get home. It's the last thing she needs to hear."

Warner chuckles. "You're pretty good at this."

"I have some experience in this department."

We hang up, I send Warner a text with what he needs to buy, and Peyton comes back into the kitchen. "Did you call my dad?" Her expression tells me she already knows the answer.

I nod. "I had to. I didn't have enough supplies for you."

Peyton turns away, her cheeks pink. I reach for her, and this time I actually do touch her. Just lightly on the forearm, so she'll turn to look at me. "Don't be embarrassed. This is a completely natural part of life."

She shrugs. "Yeah, I guess so."

I stand, lifting Libby into my arms. "We'll get out of your hair now."

Peyton's arm shoots out. "Stay! I mean, can you stay?"

I set Libby back down and try not to show my shock. "Sure, no problem."

We look at each other, the quiet of the home turning awkward. Peyton sucks her lower lip between her teeth.

A memory surfaces, and I snap my fingers. "I have an idea. Do you trust me?"

A ghost of a smile tugs the corner of Peyton's lip. "I guess so..."

I head for the couch, and Peyton follows. She sits down beside me. "When my sister and I were younger we'd watch this show together." Using my phone, I open the internet and find the show. The opening music starts, and Peyton looks at me in disbelief. I have just outed myself as the most uncool person to walk the planet.

Oh well. Might as well seal the deal. I open my mouth, and I sing every word of the theme song. Before the opening line of the show, Peyton's laughing hysterically.

When Warner walks in a half hour later, he stops just inside the living room, his arms loaded with bags. Charlie is right behind him, toeing off his cleats. Warner clears his throat. "What are you two up to?" His gaze swings from me to Peyton and back again.

I open my mouth, but Peyton answers. "Girl time." She casts a glance at me, then gets up from the couch. I smile at her.

Peyton has to cross in front of Warner to leave the room. Their collective embarrassment permeates the air. Charlie has moved on already, probably to change out of his sweaty uniform.

"Here," Warner holds out the bags with the drugstore logo. "I got you some, um, stuff. For, you know..." He looks to me, his eyes desperate for help. My fist is pressed to my lips to keep my laughter inside.

Peyton yanks the bags from his hand, mutters a barely audible *thanks*, and leaves the room. I get up from the couch and go to where Warner is frozen. He looks down at me, and that's when I see it. *Tears.*

"Are you okay?"

He nods. The tears are unshed, but there's just enough moisture to make his eyes shine. "If you tell Wes I cried about this, I will withhold sex for approximately one month."

I make a noise in the back of my throat. "Good to know you're not above using sex as a weapon."

Warner grabs my hand, curling his fingers through mine. "All's fair in love and war."

My heart thrums and my mind goes blank. He just said *love*, and the panicked look in his eyes tells me he is perfectly aware.

To cover up his panic, I tell him, "I promise not to tell Wes."

His thumb runs over the top of my hand. "It's hard, watching her grow up. I swear I can still feel her in my arms on the day she was born." He makes a cradle with his other arm.

My heart melts into a puddle. Would anybody believe me if I told them the tough, rugged, handsome Warner Hayden has the soul of a poet and the emotional depth most women only dream of?

"Did Peyton call you for help? When she... you know." Warner leads me by the hand into the kitchen where he starts pulling out ingredients for dinner.

"You can say it," I chastise. "There's nothing wrong with naming the event. Normalize it now, so she doesn't feel like she can't come to you later about other things having to do with her body." Warner adopts a look of horror, like he'd never considered there could be other things occurring, so I put the poor guy out of his misery and continue talking. "I happened to come by." The candy is there, on the table, so I go get it and bring it back, sliding it across the counter toward the potatoes waiting for Warner's peeler.

"I was dropping off some candy when she answered the door. She told me what happened."

Warner stops what he's doing and opens the jar. He fishes out a peach ring and eats it. "I'll never have something peach flavored and not think of you." He eats two more and closes the jar. "How many of those did you bring with you from LA?"

"An ungodly amount. I have a very real problem."

Warner resumes peeling, the conversation about Peyton presumably finished. I suppose a father can only take so much. I lean against the counter in the same spot I was in when he made pancakes. I think it's safe to assume he hasn't heard about the picture of us or seen it. He would have mentioned it by now. Here goes nothing.

"My mom called me after I finished up today, and—"

Warner whips around, his hand against his forehead.

"Shit, I'm sorry. I can't believe I forgot to ask you how your first day of filming went. What an asshole."

"Something else kind of big was happening," I remind him. "And it went well. Until my mom called afterward. She sent me a picture from a gossip site."

Warner pauses, giving me a wary look. "Do I even want to know?"

My eyes squint as I make a bare-teeth face. "Probably."

His eyes widen, urging me to just say it already.

"Someone in the grocery store took a picture of us kissing. And sent it to the tabs." Warner doesn't say anything, he just stares at me. It's probably a look very similar to when I called him and told him about Peyton. I pull up the picture from my messages and offer it to him. He looks at it.

It's... sexy.

If I had to use a unit of measurement, I'd say it's *sexy as fuck.*

There we are, a moment of time captured, our bodies pressed so close we could be sewn together. His hands are on my face, my hands grip the front of his shirt. The picture also tells the story of what we've done in the moments the camera didn't capture. The intensity, the passion of that kiss, makes a wager we are lovers a safe bet.

Warner lets out a long, slow breath. "That's fucking hot."

It's the last thing I was expecting him to say, and also the perfect response. "You're not mad?"

"What's there to be mad about? I can't change it. Nor would I want to." Warner drops what's in his hands and moves closer to me. He pins me against the counter, one hand on either side of me, his hips grinding into me. He leans down, his voice rumbling against my ear. "I was on the receiving end of that kiss. Pretty sure that makes me the luckiest man in the world."

My hands wrap around his middle. "It's actually good publicity for the movie, but don't worry. You won't have to experience any more invasions of privacy. My mom suggested Calvin and I act like we're a thing, and I can go that route."

Warner leans back, looking down at me with hooded eyes. "I hope to hell you're kidding."

His serious tone takes me by surprise. "I'm not. Should I be?"

"Yes." His tone is possessive. I love it. Warner leans back in, running his nose along my jaw. He is hard against my stomach, and I feel my grip on reality loosening. "You're real dating me, Tenley. Not fake dating that asshole."

"We're dating?"

He breathes next to my ear. "What do you want to call it?"

I know better than to say much more. Like an animal, Warner could spook and run away. Besides, with his lips dragging across my skin like this, I'm having trouble focusing on my words, so all I manage is, "Calvin's not an asshole."

"Right now, he is."

A grin pulls at my lips, but Warner swallows it with his mouth. His lips are on mine, and desire curls through me, my pulse racing, and—

"Dad!"

Warner rips himself away from me, and I turn just in time to see Charlie's dark brown hair exiting through the back door. Warner hustles after him without a backward glance, not that I expect one.

I stand there, still in shock, two fingers pressed to my mouth where Warner's lips were only seconds ago. I gather my purse, and my dog, and walk out of Warner's front door.

22

WARNER

GODDAMMIT.

I should've known better. What was I thinking? That we were invisible?

It's Tenley. That woman, she does things to me. She's a tidal wave, and I'm the innocent bystander, awestruck as I watch her envelop me.

Poor Charlie. It's not the way I would've told him.

But if I'm being honest, I don't have a clue how I would've told him I like Tenley. This territory is as uncharted as all the territory I've traversed in the past two years. How can a man know what to say, let alone how to guide a child, when he's still discovering? This entire time, I've had my own experiences to draw from. I could parent Charlie because, like him, I'd been a young boy once too. But this? A divorce and stepping into a relationship with someone new? Unfamiliar ground.

I told Tenley we're dating because it seems logical, but the truth is that I don't know what the fuck we are doing. I know I like her. I know that when I'm around her everything feels possible. I'm not Warner the son, Warner the brother, Warner the second Hayden boy, Warner the dad, Warner from the big cattle ranch.

I'm just Warner, a man who likes a woman. And there's Tenley, a woman who likes a man. When I'm with Tenley, I don't see her roles, the one she acts in or the roles she occupies in real life. She is a woman I can't seem to stay away from, a woman who simultaneously takes the breath from my lungs and gives me more oxygen. A paradox, a contradiction, a pain that feels like pleasure.

None of which I can say to a ten-year-old.

When I find Charlie, he is hiding beneath the shade of a tree. The late afternoon sun filters through the skinny branches, sparsely illuminating his body.

"Hey buddy," I say, settling beside him in the pine straw. Compared to my frame, he seems so small, but I know his emotions right now are big. Hell, my emotions are big right now, too.

Charlie gathers dried needles in his palm, transferring them from one hand to the other. "Hi, Dad."

My boy. I fight the urge to take him in my arms, the way I would've done when he was younger, back when my touch could heal his bumps and bruises. There was a time when his pain needed only a kiss from me or his mom, and he would declare it gone.

This ache will not be magically soothed, and it's something I know firsthand. The divorce has injured us all. Charlie is just a kid trying to understand it, and I'm the adult blindly leading him.

"Charlie, I'm sorry for what you saw back there."

He lets the pine straw fall to the ground. His palms are caked in dirt-covered sap. When he looks up at me, I see his childlike confusion. “I guess you like Tenley. You were kissing her.”

I take a deep breath and let it go. “I like Tenley. She is a very nice person.”

“I like her dog.”

His response makes me smile. “Did you know Tenley found Libby wandering around and rescued her?”

Charlie squints as the breeze moves the tree branches, sunlight slipping over his face. “That was nice of her.”

I nod. “Mm-hmm.” I’m not sure what to say or how to direct the conversation.

“Am I going to have two moms?”

I lean back, putting my back against the tree trunk. “Tenley and I are just getting to know each other. And you have a mom already. She’s your only mom.”

“Colton on my soccer team has parents who are divorced, and they remarried and now he has two moms and two dads. Will that happen to me?”

“I don’t know for certain what’s going to happen.” I wish I could give Charlie something concrete, but I can’t placate him just for the sake of trying to make this better. He trusts me to tell him the truth. And the truth is that I don’t know. But, there is one thing I’m certain about. “Charlie, your mom and I love you very much. We have ever since we first laid eyes on you. You are my son, and no matter what happens, I will always love you.”

I lean forward and put my arms around him. His dirty hands, small but growing every day, return my hug. “I love you too, Dad.”

We’re on our way back to the house, walking side by side, when Charlie bumps my arm with his. “I like her, too. Tenley. She’s nice. Plus, she’s famous, which is kind of cool.”

I chuckle at his assessment of Tenley. "Yeah, she's cool."

We go inside the house, and Charlie heads for his room. The potatoes I abandoned are still on the counter, and the oxygen has turned them from yellow to yellow-brown. Tenley isn't in the kitchen, and a quick check out front tells me she has left. Her Bronco is gone. I check my phone and find two texts, one from my little sister and another from Anna.

The first, from Jessie, says *Warner are you fucking kidding me???!!!!!!!!* and is followed by four wide-eyed emojis and one purple heart.

The second, from Anna, says *We need to talk.*

Neither woman identifies a subject, yet I already know they are referring to the same one.

A picture of me and Tenley, wrapped in the same kind of embrace that Charlie walked in on. I have a hard time believing it was someone from Sierra Grande who took that photo. The people of this town might not have a problem gossiping about its inhabitants, but they'd never sell out one of their own. Like the rules of family, I can talk badly about my siblings, but somebody else better not say a word against them. This is how I know whoever took that photo and sent it out had to be associated with the movie. Besides, whatever Wyatt did to get Tenley's underwear back probably put the fear of God into whoever it was, and the Sierra Grande gossip mill helped spread the fear around like butter on warm bread.

To irritate Jessie, who I know was the most excited of all when we learned a movie was being filmed in our town, I respond with one word: *What?*

Then I finish making dinner and sit down to eat with my kids. Charlie finishes first, and bolts to do his homework.

This is as good a time as any to tell Peyton about Tenley, before she finds out from someone else. Or, God forbid, if she sees the picture for herself and then—

"Savannah sent me a picture of you and Tenley." Peyton pushes her food around with her fork, her eyes on her plate.

Fuck. Every step in this conversation feels like a landmine. This is when parenting is the hardest. Some days I'm hanging on for dear life.

"I'm sorry you had to see that," I start, taking the first step into the minefield.

"It's not like it came as a shock, Dad." She gives me a look that conveys how utterly hopeless she thinks I am. "You and Tenley couldn't be more obvious."

I bite my lip, not sure where to go from here. Movement in any direction could get me blown to bits.

Peyton saves me by continuing to talk. "I was mad, at first, but then Tenley showed up here, and..." Her cheeks redden. "...you know."

As much as it embarrasses her, I place my hand on hers. "Parents don't always know what's right, and your mom and I are doing the best we can. I'll tell you what I told Charlie, and if you have any questions you can come to me." I look at my beautiful daughter. Her face is steadily losing it's roundness, her cheekbones emerging and making her look less like my little girl. "Your mother and I love you more than anything, and you are the most important thing to us, okay?"

Peyton nods, brushing away her hair when it falls into her face. She's ready for the conversation to be over, so I stand up and gently remind her it's her night to do the dishes.

She parks it at the sink after mild and expected complaints, and I feel relief that although everything in this house feels different now, it is also still the same. I step out front and make sure the door closes behind me, then call Anna.

* * *

"YOU SHOULD'VE TOLD me you were dating someone. I don't appreciate finding out from the internet."

"I didn't appreciate finding you wrapped in someone else's arms in the shadows at your parents' house." I regret it as soon as I say it. I didn't call Anna so we could verbally spar. What's done is done.

"This is different, Warner, and you know it. They're calling you 'the mystery cowboy.'"

Anna sounds jealous, but I know better than to point that out. She'd deny it, and it wouldn't get us anywhere.

"An actress, huh?" Anna's voice turns soft. "My parents told me there was a movie being filmed there, and the kids told me you'd been helping someone learn about ranching, but I didn't put it all together. I'm surprised Peyton didn't tell me who that someone was. I'm sure she knew."

Anna sounds reluctant and suspicious, so I put that to rest immediately. "Peyton probably didn't think to tell you. She wasn't keeping something from you on purpose. What you saw in that picture is a recent development." Mostly, anyway. Our first kiss, in that field after we saw the antelope, was a few weeks ago. But nobody else knows that happened, and it's not something that needs to be made public.

"I don't like it. Seeing you with another woman." Her voice is sheepish.

The admittance feels good inside. Whether or not our marriage is over, Anna rejected me, and what once stung unbearably now only smarts periodically.

"I know what you're going to say." Anna rushes forward, not giving me a chance to respond, which is fine by me because it's one hell of an awkward conversation. "You're going to tell me I made the bed and now I'm lying in it."

"Something along those lines."

"I'm not saying we should be doing anything different, Warner. Our marriage is over. I mean, obviously. We're divorced."

"Right. So why did you think we should talk? That's what you said in your text message."

She sighs. "We're co-parents now, so going forward, I think you should give me a heads-up when you're dating someone. Don't let me find out from my sister-in-law when she sends me a screenshot."

I roll my eyes. I've never liked Anna's brother's wife and was more than happy to help them pack their moving truck when they left Sierra Grande seven years ago.

"Agreed. Same goes for you."

"Agreed."

The connection falls silent, and I find it amazing we have nothing to say to one another. I was by her side both times she gave birth, fed her ice chips and encouraged her, and here we are now with very little to say to each other. The dissolution of marriage, the unraveling of lives, is the most uncomfortable thing I've ever experienced.

A light turns on in the distance. It's Tenley, stepping from her back door. Her blonde hair shines in stark contrast to the dark brown log walls, and above the tree line, the sky is streaked with hot pink and purple-blue.

I say goodbye to Anna and slip the phone back into my pocket, fighting the urge to stride across the small expanse of Hayden land that separates us. I want to pull Tenley into my arms and finish the kiss we started in my kitchen. But I don't. My kids are home, and they come first.

I wave to Tenley, hoping to somehow convey all my thoughts. She waves back, then goes back into her cabin. I wonder why she came out at all? Maybe it was just to check on me.

23

TENLEY

It's not that I've been avoiding Warner, exactly, it's just that it's been three days since Charlie walked in on us in the kitchen and I haven't gone out of my way to see him. We've exchanged text messages and talked every day, but I'm treading lightly. I've never dated a man who has children, and I need Warner to lead.

Tonight, there won't be any not-exactly-avoiding Warner because Juliette has invited me to dinner at the homestead. With '*the whole fam damily*' as she put it. I finished up on the set a little later today than previous days, because I'd had a later call time. I'm even more behind because afterward, Ari pulled me aside and asked if I could talk to the Haydens about letting a drone onto their property, for the sake of getting good aerial shots. What the empty Circle B ranch gives us in terms of setting, it's missing in an actual herd of cows. I told him I'd ask, but not to expect much. Beau doesn't strike me as someone who wants a tiny recording device flying over his land. Or Wes either, for that matter.

I have approximately thirty minutes before I'm due at the homestead and I've just stepped from the shower. I keep going over the conversation I had earlier with Morgan, on my drive back to the ranch from the set.

She called to tell me my plants were healthy, that Tate had brought by a box of my things, and that I was a dirty rotten scoundrel for making her learn about Warner through the gossip rags. I'd explained to her the timing of events, how quickly everything had happened, and she said she only partly forgave me. We ended the call with her promising to send me a picture of all my happy plants, and me vowing she wouldn't have to learn about her best friend's love life secondhand.

Warner's truck is out front when I pull up to his parents' house, so I park alongside him. I walk inside and see Juliette wasn't kidding when she said the whole family would be here. Wes, Dakota, Wyatt, Warner, Peyton, Charlie, and Gramps. They're all in the huge living room. A young woman I've never seen before sits in an armchair, and when I walk in, she leaps from her seat. She comes closer, and I know right away she's Jessie, the youngest Hayden. If the eyes hadn't given it away, the confident swagger would. The Haydens come at life with a sure foot.

"Ahh!" She throws her hands in the air. "I can't believe it's you. Wait until I tell Marlowe. She's going to lose her shit." She says the last word with so much emphasis it sounds more like *shii-iiit.*

Juliette's stern voice cuts into my smile. "Jessamyn Hayden, watch your mouth, young lady."

"Sure, Mom," Jessie says, with the ease of someone who's been placating her mother her entire life.

Just behind Jessie, I see Warner. He's shaking his head slightly, his eyes on his sister. He may be embarrassed by her reaction, but it doesn't bother me.

Jessie sticks her hand out for a handshake, but I do her

one better and pull her in for a hug. "It's nice to meet you, Jessie. Who's Marlowe?"

"My best friend. Her dad is the mayor."

"Mayor Cruz. Right." I nod my head. Mayor Cruz was more accommodating than any other public official I can remember. Not that I've had a lot of dealings with them, but people talk, and I've heard some horror stories.

Juliette steps in. "Jessie, give Tenley some breathing room, for Christ's sake. Come with me to check on dinner." She tugs on Jessie's arm, pulling her away from me. Jessie rolls her eyes at her mother, but allows herself to be led from the room.

Dakota ducks from under the arm Wes has over her shoulder. "Tenley, do you want to help me pour wine?"

"You can't have wine," Wes says quickly. Every head turns to him.

Dakota gives him an exasperated look, and he mouths the word *sorry*.

Warner is the first to react. He grabs his brother, pulling him in for a hug and a solid thump on his back. "Congratulations, man."

"What the hell am I missing?" Wyatt asks, a confused look on his face.

Warner smacks the back of his head. "Dakota's pregnant, you half-wit."

Wyatt lands a playful punch in Warner's side. "You're not supposed to assume shit like that about ladies."

All heads swing to Dakota. There's no way for her to avoid the spotlight now. "We're pregnant," she confirms, a wide, beaming grin taking over her face.

Juliette and Jessie reappear. "Did I hear that correctly?" Juliette asks, her hands cupping her mouth in excitement.

Dakota's grin is probably answer enough, but she adds, "Yep."

Juliette throws her hands in the air, and suddenly there is so much commotion it's hard to distinguish one voice from the other. So many hugs, tears from Dakota, who swears she doesn't know why she's crying, and all-around palpable joy.

I sneak off to the kitchen to pour wine. Jessie finds me just as I've finished and helps me carry out the glasses. Wes has already poured whiskey. Apparently it's the preference of every Hayden man, because they all hold a tumbler. Jessie and I distribute the wine, and Dakota looks longingly at my glass while she sips her water.

"Sushi and wine." Dakota pats her still-flat stomach. "I'm going to gorge myself on Yellowtail sashimi and a good Spanish red after I have this baby."

Juliette half-hugs Dakota and tells her she hopes the baby likes pasta because that's what she made for dinner.

The dining room table is larger than normal, with the leaf pulled out. Warner sits beside me, and his nearness makes me happy. Three days without physical proximity was harder than I'd like to admit. I don't know what that says about the future. Once dinner is underway and conversation fills the room, Warner leans closer to me. Quietly, he says, "I've missed you."

"Same," I whisper.

"Avoiding me?"

"Maybe a little," I admit. I peek down the table at Charlie. He's smiling while he eats lasagna.

"He's okay. We talked. He likes you."

"I'm not sure how all this is supposed to go."

"None of us do."

"I—"

"What are you two whispering about?" Gramps cuts into our side conversation.

I smile at the old man. "Warner is giving me some pointers for a scene I'm shooting tomorrow."

Gramps squints. He knows I'm lying, but he doesn't call me on it. Under the table, Warner presses his knee against mine. The meal continues, but Warner's leg doesn't move.

Juliette has made enough for twice as many people, and after dinner is over Jessie says she's going to take the third lasagna out to Cowboy House to see if any of the cowboys are hungry.

"Fuck that," Wyatt says under his breath, pushing back from the table. "You're not going out to where all the cowboys live by yourself. I'll go with you."

"You don't think I can walk my ass over there in the dark? Afraid I'll trip over a tree root?"

"It's the cowboys I don't trust," Wyatt says to her back as she stalks from the room, heading for the kitchen. He looks back at us. "Lies. It's her I don't trust. She'll go out there with a lasagna and end up playing strip poker." Wyatt shoves his chair in and looks directly at Wes and Warner. "Calamity is home for the summer, boys. Get ready."

I turn curious eyes on Warner. He sees my question and answers it. "When she was little, we all called her Calamity Jessie. Mostly because she had a mouth on her that would make a grown man blush, and no amount of soap would keep her from using it. But also because everywhere she went, chaos followed."

"I like her." It feels like something that needs to be said. Jessie's three much older brothers seem to still view her as a child, instead of an adult who has just finished up her freshman year of college.

"There's not much to dislike," Dakota adds.

Wes's upper lip curls to one side. "Is this some girl power thing?"

Dakota elbows him, not exactly gently. "You'd do well to remember that Jessie is an adult. She is no longer walking chaos, if she ever was at all, and"—Dakota turns her stern look on Wyatt— "if she wants to walk into Cowboy House and strip down, that's her choice."

All three Hayden brothers share a long look. Wyatt smacks his hand on the back of his chair and says, "Fuck that. I'm going with her."

Dakota sends me a *can you believe these guys* look, and I laugh.

Warner rakes a hand down his face. "It's a good thing my kids are helping with the dishes. I don't need Peyton getting ideas about the cowboys and strip poker."

Warner refills my wine and adds a finger more of whiskey to his and Wes's glasses. We go out to the front porch, where the sky has turned navy blue, and wind streaks through the trees, creating a melody of its own. Wes and Dakota settle into a love seat, and opposite it is a single chair. Warner offers me the chair, but I decline, opting to sit on the arm of the chair while he sits down.

Dakota asks me about the movie, and I tell her about how this week went. Warner's arm slips behind me, his hand coming to rest on my hip. Dakota interrupts me to ask questions, and I answer them. Mostly it's basic stuff about how movies are made, and how long scenes really take to shoot, and then she asks, "Did you have to kiss that handsome costar of yours this week? Rough life."

Warner's hand tightens on my hip. I look down at him, then back to Dakota. "We're shooting the big sex scene next week." Talking about the movie makes me remember what Ari asked me before I left the set this afternoon. "Wes, do you think it would be okay for the crew to fly a drone over some of the Hayden ranch? Just to get some aerial footage? The Circle B obviously isn't a working ranch, and if it doesn't come from you guys it may end up being stock footage, which nobody wants. The movie might be a romantic comedy, but it still needs authenticity."

I steel myself for his response, which I'm positive will be a *hell no*, but he shocks everyone by agreeing. Warner sips his whiskey, then motions toward Wes with the glass. "Either the whiskey has given you the warm and fuzzies, or you're high on the pregnancy news."

Wes doesn't laugh, but his eyes hold mirth. My response is decidedly different. Instead of Warner's joke making me laugh, it's forced a realization that's been in front of me this whole time and I've ignored.

Warner knows what it's like to be high on pregnancy news, two times over. Warner knows many things I don't know, all of which suddenly seem like creatures creeping from the shadows. Marriage, pregnancy, birth, infancy... How likely is he to want to do those things again? I don't want to marry the guy tomorrow, but I can't ignore the facts. Eventually I'm going to want all those things. But what about Warner?

I start to fake a yawn, but it quickly turns real. Warner looks up at me as I cover my mouth with my hand.

"Tired?" he asks. He uses the outside edge of his palm to lightly rub my thigh. The last sip of amber liquid in his tumbler swirls around, the scent curling up to my nose.

I nod, standing. "I'd better take off. I have an early call time." False. I'm not due in until noon.

Warner stands also. "Can I drive you back to your cabin?"

I can't help but smile. "Don't you mean Wyatt's cabin?"

Warner bites down on his lower lip. "I've come to think of it as yours."

I wink. "A girl could only be so lucky."

Dakota chuckles, but Warner sees through my casual tone. His eyes narrow, his gaze turning shrewd.

"Anyway," I continue. "I drove here. I can drive myself back."

"Right." He nods. "Are you up for some fun this weekend? I was under the distinct impression we're supposed to be letting people see us together."

I might be confused about what's happening with me and Warner, but I know my role, and it's more than the one I'm playing in the movie. Stirring up interest in the movie is tantamount to making a good film. My parents are depending on me.

I place my hand on Warner's upper arm and give it a light squeeze. "Of course. You just tell me where to be."

I say goodbye to Wes and Dakota, then duck into the house to thank Beau and Juliette for dinner. When I come back out, Warner is waiting for me on the top step. He leans against the post, arms folded, making his broad chest and shoulders look even bigger.

"Are you walking me the thirty feet to my car?"

He nods once. "Yes ma'am."

I stop when I reach him. "And they say chivalry is dead."

Warner's hand finds the small of my back. "It's alive out here."

He guides me down the stairs and around to the other side of his truck, where I'm parked. The lights from the homestead don't reach this far, and hazy clouds are moving in, making quick work of the moonlight.

He steps closer, one hand gripping my hip. I draw in a surprised breath when he cups my breast with his other hand, his thumb drawing back and forth over the thin material covering my nipple. "So much for chivalry," I whisper around the sensation. "I think I know why you wanted to walk me out."

Warner leans in, his lips hovering above mine, and says, "A man can be both chivalrous and want a woman the way I want you."

"Is that right?" I'm practically panting. How embarrassing.

Warner's lips brush mine. "Do you doubt me?"

His question throws me off guard, makes me remember my thoughts from earlier. "No, but..."

Warner pulls back slightly. "What?"

I don't want to tell him. Not right now. Not when he's pressed against me, when everything feels like it's where it's supposed to be. I just want to live in this moment, in this time devoid of previous marriages, of publicity stunts and the fallout from gambling addictions.

I don't answer. Instead, I wrap my hand around his neck and pull him down to me. He allows it, allows me to slip into him, to kiss him in a way that turns us both inside out.

Finally, I drag my face away, turning my head so I can suck in a deep breath of much-needed air. Warner takes a step away, opening up Pearl's driver side door. I climb in. "Let me know about this weekend," I tell him.

He presses a thumb to the center of his lower lip, regarding me with that perceptive gaze of his. Maybe with most men I could get away with hiding my feelings, but Warner is not most men. His sensitivity doesn't allow for smoke screens.

"You'll talk when you're ready?"

I nod. His willingness not to push is another reminder

he is practiced in the art of relationships. Anna has taught him not to force a woman to talk when she doesn't want to.

I turn the car on, Pearl's engine coming to life with a roar. Warner closes my door, smacking it once with an open palm and striding back to the homestead as I drive away from it. On my way past Cowboy House, I spot Jessie and Wyatt coming out. They pause in the front porch light. She looks irritated. He looks exhausted. Maybe he was up late last night. Maybe he was with the married woman again. Far be it from me to judge.

I grab my phone as I lay down in bed and open up my text app. Just as I hoped, there's a message from Warner.

Good night, beautiful.

I answer him with ***Good night, handsome.***

24

TENLEY

"You said you had an early morning."

The voice comes from across the room. I open my eyes, blink against the sunlight, and hold back the groan rising up.

Warner has one eyebrow raised. He holds his coffee carafe and a white paper bag.

Sitting up, I pull the comforter up around my middle and push my hair from my face. "What time is it?"

"Nine. I took the kids to school and stopped for a treat" —he raises the white bag— "it's blueberry muffin day at The Bakery. Thought I'd just be dropping it off for you to have when you returned, but when I drove up and saw Pearl, I went to my house and made coffee, then came over."

"How did you get in?"

"You didn't answer my knock, so I used my key."

My mouth opens. "You've had a key this whole time?"

He shrugs. "Technically, you have a key to my house also. It's near the front of the junk drawer in the kitchen."

I frown. "Doesn't count if I didn't know it was there."

"Are you mad I let myself in?"

I cross my arms and pretend to be upset. "Maybe."

"Are you going to let me make it up to you?" His tone changes from apologetic to flirtatious.

"Depends on what you have planned."

Warner grins. It's not his normal, happy, nice guy grin. This is wolfish, causing frenzied excitement to flutter in my core. He sets the coffee on the dresser, but keeps the bag in his grasp. "First, I have for you a blueberry muffin that will put all others to shame." He stops at the foot of the bed and hands me the bag. The mattress dips when he presses a knee onto the bed and leans forward on both hands. "And I'm wondering if you, perhaps, have a muffin for me to eat."

My lips press together at the boldness of his words. Who would have guessed that the respectful man who pulled over to help a stranded stranger could talk like that?

Warner grips my ankle tucked safely under the sheets. "Did I embarrass you?"

"A little."

Warner grins again, and I think he *likes* that he made me blush. He grips the comforter in one hand and yanks, throwing the entire thing on the ground behind him. I laugh, and he does the same thing to the sheet, leaving me sitting there in my oversized T-shirt clutching the crinkly paper bag.

Warner's gaze runs the length of my legs, his eyes hooded and hungry. A predator. I've never seen him like this. I… well, I love it. He lifts my leg, and I fall back on my elbows. Pressing a kiss to the inside of my ankle, he says, "I've missed you."

"You saw me last night."

His lips draw back and forth over my skin, his scruff scraping gently. "I don't want to go three days without seeing you again."

I swallow against the sensation. "I was waiting for you to take the next step."

Warner drags his lips over my calf, pausing to nuzzle into the crook of my bent knee. His gaze meets mine, and everything inside me tightens and relaxes at the same time. It's delicious and heady and confusing and I think that maybe I'm drowning.

"I'm here now, Tenley. I'm taking the next step."

We stop talking after that.

* * *

"DOES it weird you out that this is your brother's bed?" I press back into the warmth of Warner's bare chest.

He waits a beat to answer, then says, "It does now."

I laugh and roll over onto my stomach, my cheek pressed to the pillow. "Fresh sheets," I mumble.

"Thank fuck," Warner answers.

The postcoital glow is dulling, and my worries from last night come creeping in. I'd rather not have these thoughts right now, while I'm lying in bed with him, but they feel too big to ignore.

"Warner?" My fingers graze the few inches of space between our bodies.

"Hmmm?" His voice is thick. Tired. Sated.

I close my eyes. "Would you ever remarry? Or have more kids?"

Silence.

I open my eyes. He's staring at me.

"I'm not trying to race down the aisle and then catch an Uber to labor and delivery, but I need to know what you see in your future. I'm only here in Sierra Grande for a set amount of time, and it'd be nice if I had some idea of what's happening between us." He's still quiet, and now it's a cringe-worthy level of awkwardness. "Should I save my frequent flyer miles for an exotic vacation, or plan to start using the Merc for all my shopping needs?"

Warner's still frozen, and I'm wondering if maybe I can snap my fingers and go back in time forty-five seconds. Instead, I ramble, because I can't seem to make my mouth be quiet. "I'm thirty, and this is my last film for the foreseeable future, and I need to start thinking about what's next for me."

Warner thaws. Blinks. Takes a deep breath. "What I feel for you is..." The skin around his eyes pinches and he looks pained. I fight the urge to jump in and save him from the agony of having to put his feelings into words. I'm not going to save him though, because I deserve to know.

He draws a breath and continues. "What I feel for you is unlike anything I've felt before. But as of right now, I can't imagine getting remarried and having kids. I checked those boxes a long time ago. And while I love my kids and wouldn't change anything that gave me them, the whole marriage thing didn't work out so great for me."

I knew it. I could've written his reply, word for word, like a script. And even though I saw it coming, it hurts. Far more than I'd like to admit, even to myself. Absent of my permission, Warner burrowed deep under my skin. I never stood a chance.

I lie there, quiet now, and so does Warner. After a few minutes, his fingertips begin to dust my back with the lightest touch. After a long, quiet minute, he says my name tentatively. "Hmm?" The sound reverberates in my throat.

"Tell me about your scar." His hand stills, touching the blemished skin.

Morgan is the only person I've told about my scar. Not

even Tate. When he asked, I'd made up a lie, and maybe since he's a spinner of elaborate yarns, he readily accepted mine.

I hate how I got the scar. I hate my origin story.

I open my mouth, astonished because I know that the truth will follow. I guess I just needed to find the one thing that makes me sicker than telling the truth. And that one thing is holding myself back from Warner.

Whether we last until tomorrow or until we're old and gray, I want him to know me. The good, the bad... and the ugly.

Warner's hand resumes its caress, and he probably thinks I'm going to ignore his question. His hand startles when I speak, bumping against me.

"It happened when I was eight." My voice is small, almost as small as my body had been back then. My eyes flutter closed, and I see it all so clearly, the wood paneled hotel room, the sheets tinged an odd yellow from time and use and who knows what else. She's there, too. The woman who birthed me. She gave me life, and questionable care.

It hurts to talk about, but I forge ahead. "My parents, the ones I talk about, adopted me when I was eight. Before that I lived in a shitty hotel with my mother. I didn't know it at the time, but as I got older, I started to understand what she was. A prostitute. Addicted to various things." Warner's fingers continue their dance, his touch featherlight but reassuring.

"Sometimes I'm not sure if what I remember from that time are separate events, or if what I can see is the same thing happening over and over, like a loop. Maybe I only have a few really bad memories, not a hundred. The worst one, though, is the day I got my scar." Tears prick my eyes. "She'd come back the afternoon before and laid down on the bed. I don't know if she took something, or was already on it, but she fell asleep. Or so I thought. She didn't wake up, which wasn't all that uncommon. We had a little food, so I fed myself and watched TV." My breath catches as I remember her lying there, her stringy hair across her face. I'd brushed it back on my way to the bathroom.

"I decided to take a shower. I remember wanting her to wake up and see how capable I was, how I was clean and fed. It was a glass shower door, and a piece of shit one at that. I must've closed it too hard when I was climbing out, because the glass fell from the door and broke all around me. I called for her, but she didn't answer. I took a step, but there was water on the floor, and I slipped. The glass cut me in a few different places, very shallow. Except my back. It wasn't horribly deep, but long and jagged, like it had been dragged across me. I'd watched a medical drama on TV a few weeks before, so I knew it needed pressure. I made my way to the wall, where I pressed my back against a towel, and pushed myself against the wall as hard as I could. I called for her, over and over. Eventually I fell asleep, and when I woke up, the bleeding had stopped. I put on my clothes and went back out to the room. My mother hadn't moved, and I checked for her pulse the way I'd seen on the TV show. I didn't really know what I was looking for, but I understood that I didn't feel *anything*. No heart beating, no breath coming in and out of her mouth. I ran to the front desk, and they made two phone calls. First to the police, and one I couldn't hear, because they'd walked away after they dialed. Child Protective Services came and took me, and I spent twenty-nine days in foster care. A couple who didn't think they could get pregnant wanted to adopt, and they didn't care that I wasn't a cute, sweet cooing baby. The day I met the people who I consider my mom and dad was the best day of my life. The day they brought my sister home from the hospital was the second best day." Finally, I roll over so I can look him in the face. "Very few people in my life know that story."

The sadness in Warner's eyes is profound. "I'm sorry your life started out that way."

The small smile that curves my lips contains grief and pain. "Me too. But I'm incredibly grateful it didn't keep going that way."

The pad of Warner's thumb grazes my jaw. "I understand the trust you're putting in me by telling me all that. I will not break it." He kisses me. Sweetly. Gently. He says, "I like you more than I should." His tone is melancholy. So is mine when I say, "Same."

His brown eyes pour into me, searching. "What are we supposed to do?"

The timing is wrong. The circumstances are heavy. A Greek tragedy, star-crossed lovers doomed from the beginning. I've never considered myself a martyr, but maybe that's because I've never been in a position like this.

The thought of not having Warner, not touching him or seeing him, is too painful to bear. Whatever agony is in my future, I'll gladly take it if it means I can have Warner while I'm in Sierra Grande.

I kiss him, just as sweetly as he kissed me, and whisper my answer. "We ride the ride."

25

WARNER

"I'M SURPRISED YOU SHOWED." I PULL OVER A CHAIR FROM AN empty table near us. Wyatt rolls his eyes as he takes his seat. I knew when I invited him out on our double date with Wes and Dakota tonight there wasn't a huge chance he'd join us.

"Surprise," he grumbles, giving me a half-ass version of jazz hands. "Where are the girls?"

"Bathroom," I answer, shrugging because I know his next question is why they had to go together. I asked the same thing when Dakota stood up and grabbed Tenley's hand. She'd told me it was girl code. Whatever that means.

A hand slides across the top of my back. Tenley drops down, kissing my cheek as she sits back down in her seat.

"Did you make it okay?" My tone is sarcastic and playful.

Tenley nods, grasping her beer bottle. "Power in numbers, you know?"

I press a kiss to her temple and push away the impulse to end our double date early and drive her straight back to my place. Every moment with her now feels quantifiable. She'd said we're on a ride, and I know it will eventually be over. I can't count the number of times I've had to stop myself from feeling too much for her. There's no way I can care this deeply about someone so soon. It's irrational and crazy as hell.

Tenley leans into me. Wes pushes Dakota's sparkling water with lime closer to her. I stop short of telling him to chill with the overprotectiveness. Dakota's not going to get dehydrated and harm the baby.

"Did Jessie try to come with you?" Wes asks Wyatt.

Wyatt nods. "I told her she had some turning twenty-one to do before she was allowed in a bar with her brothers, and she told me where I could stick my lecture." The corners of Wyatt's mouth turn up as he talks. Sometimes I forget that Wyatt had the most time around Jessie while she was growing up, so he knows her the best.

"She's feisty," Dakota says with affection, wrapping her lips around her straw. She makes a face at the straw and plucks it from her drink. "I wish they'd use paper straws."

Wyatt takes the straw from her and ties a knot in it. "Where do you think you are, The Orchard? This is the Chute. No earth-friendly paper, and not a damn thing is local except the beef."

Over the loudspeaker they announce it's time for the bull riding. Tenley squeezes my arm. She's been excited about it since I asked if this is what she wanted to do for our date this weekend. "Seriously?" she'd asked, eyes wide. "That's some real cowboy shit."

Now she's the first one out of her chair. She bounces on her toes. Her excitement amuses Wes, who does this half grunt, half laugh.

We go outside and find seats on the metal bleachers. It's not packed, but there are plenty of spectators. The emcee is a middle-aged man in a tan suede blazer, and he stands off to the side of the arena, one forearm propped against the metal fence. He brings the microphone to his lips.

"Hello there all you fine folks! The Chute is happy to welcome you to tonight's bull riding competition. Remember to cheer on the participants in a friendly manner only, and for those of you who've already had your fill of alcohol, no hopping in the ring. The term 'mad as a bull' didn't appear out of thin air." He pauses to let the crowd laugh at his joke. Tenley chuckles, and even though I've heard his spiel twenty times by now, I can't help but smile at Tenley. She's into it, and I like that. I like that my beloved little town can bring her a piece of magic.

"And with that, let's get this party started!" He backs off the post with a flourish.

The first guy comes out. Tenley grabs my hand, squeezing it. Her eyes are fastened to the rider. My eyes never leave her.

"Six seconds," she breathes when the rider is bucked and the clock stops. She looks at me. The excitement on her face dulls. Her breath turns shallow, she swallows. Leans in. Our lips touch. It's short, it's sweet. It's perfect.

Tenley watches as they pull the next gate. My gaze wanders around the crowd. Right into the eyes of my ex-mother-in-law.

Susan's mouth forms a sad smile. She nods at me slowly. I return the gesture. We look away.

Tenley never notices the exchange, and I don't tell her. Rider after rider goes, and I can tell Tenley is worried about them. "It looks so painful," she whispers.

"It is."

"Have you done it?"

"Once, when I was younger. I didn't last long, and it hurt like hell."

"Why do they do it?"

"Why does anybody do anything? It appeals to them, in the same way any sport appeals to the athlete who plays it. Also"—I point to the small group of women near the arena floor—"the buckle bunnies might have something to do with it."

Tenley follows my gaze. "Buckle bunnies..." She draws out the word as she understands what I mean by it. Nodding, she says, "Gotcha."

Dakota begins yawning, which makes Tenley yawn, and Wes announces he's taking Dakota home.

Tenley says she's ready to leave too, so we all get up and file out of our row. We're in the parking lot when someone calls Tenley's name. It's a dude with a big camera, and he's pointing it at Tenley, taking pictures as he asks, "Can I get your photo?"

Tenley slips into her gracious actress version of herself. "Sure." She steps away and poses, angling herself toward the light coming from an old wooden post with a lantern hanging off the top.

"More," the guy says when she stops.

She laughs, but I'm positive she's not finding him funny. "I think you got your shot."

"Is this the man you were seen kissing recently?" Now he's peering at me, camera pointing. *Snap, snap*.

Anger bursts through me. "She said you got your shot already." I'm talking through clenched teeth, trying to keep my anger in check, for Tenley's sake.

He ignores me. "Tenley, why are your parents rushing to sell their house in Aspen?"

Tenley's easygoing façade disappears. "I, uh..."

"Is it true they're having financial trouble?" He steps

closer. "How do you feel about Tate moving on so soon? Are you mad he proposed to her but not you?"

The next thing I know, there is a camera in my hand.

"Hey," the photographer screeches, reaching for the camera. I block him with an outstretched palm. "Now do you understand the lady said she's done having her picture taken?" He reaches again, and I push him. He stumbles back a few feet but manages to stay upright. Wes and Wyatt step between us. I remove the SD card from the camera and toss it to Wyatt. He takes a lighter from his pocket and waves the small rectangle through the lick of flame. No matter how much shit we give one another, there will never come a time when the Hayden boys don't stick together.

I fling the camera back to the asshole, who fumbles what is likely his most valuable possession. He doesn't give either of us a glance as he hurries back across the parking lot.

"Warner," Tenley says my name like she's not totally happy with me.

Wes and Dakota mutter a quick good night and move on to his truck, and without another word Wyatt walks back into the bar. Tenley steps away from the pocket of light she'd stood in.

A muscle along my jaw tics. "I couldn't let him keep bothering you. He should've listened."

Tenley sighs. "I've been dealing with that crap my entire life. My parents were famous, remember? I know how to handle those situations."

"You seemed caught off guard. You looked upset."

"Maybe I was," she concedes. "I didn't know anything about my parents selling their place. Or about Tate." She steps into me, pressing her cheek to my chest.

“Are you upset about Tate?” I’m hoping she gives me the answer I want to hear.

“Not sad. More annoyed than anything else. With myself.”

“Because…?”

“Because I should’ve listened to my heart. I dated him because it was easy. He was nice. He was my professional equal. Never mind all the feelings I was having on the inside. I should really listen to myself—” Her words cut off as she looks up at me.

“What?”

She shakes her head. “Nothing.”

I’m too stubborn to let that one go. “It must’ve been something.”

The palm she places on my chest is firm. She takes a step back and looks me square in the eye. “Just a memory of Tate.”

I know she’s lying. If it weren’t for the twinge in my stomach, the gut instinct telling me what I know to be true, all I’d have to do is look into her eyes. I see fear in them. Agony.

I swallow her words. I need the lie just as much as she does.

When we get back to my house, and I’m inside her, the lie in her eyes melts away. What she tells me with her body is the truth.

* * *

“WAY TO GO, WARNER.”

Sunday morning breakfast at the homestead always has some teasing, some laughter, and some foul language. It’s just not usually directed at me.

Jessie drops something in front of me, and it lands on the table with a dull thud.

"Christ," I say when I see the picture on her phone. Inches from my real, in the flesh face, is me in electronic format. I look angry, with my eyebrows drawn and my hand outstretched as I take away the photographer's camera.

Thank God I showed up this morning to find my mom had already fed Peyton and Charlie breakfast and sent them to help the cowboys throw hay to the horses. They don't need to see any of this.

I sift through my memory of last night, trying but failing to see a second photographer. Clearly there was one somewhere, hiding in the shadows of the shitty parking lot lighting at the Chute.

Jessie sits down across from me. Her smirk irritates me further.

Pushing the phone across the table, I say, "He was ignoring Tenley when she said to stop taking her picture, and I stood up for her. I don't know why my reaction amuses you."

"I'm not amused or surprised about your reaction. Protecting what's yours is so ingrained in this family, I don't know if it's nurture or nature at this point."

Protecting what's yours...

Is Tenley mine? Mine to have, mine to protect... mine to love?

I've been going over questions similar to those since I opened my eyes this morning. No matter what I tell myself about it all being too much, too soon, I can't seem to push it away completely. My brain understands that I'm a divorced single father trying like hell to figure out where to go from here, but my heart doesn't give two fucks. It's a needy, selfish bastard.

"What I'm saying, *Warner*," Jessie speaks my name with extra attitude, pulling my attention back to her, "is that it's painfully obvious you have strong feelings for her."

"What's that?" My mom walks up behind Jessie and looks down at her phone. The rest of my family files in behind my mom, all taking their places around the table.

Mom takes in the photo of me. Her gaze rises, stays on me for a long beat, then she goes to sit beside my dad. Everyone is quiet, waiting to hear what's on Jessie's phone. When nothing comes, my dad loses his patience. "Either say it or let's move on," he grumbles. He has zero tolerance for drama of any kind. He's a shoot straight and don't ask questions kind of guy.

Wyatt grabs the phone from Jessie. A cursory glance tells him all he needs to know. Besides, he was there. "Warner is experiencing a Wes and Dakota situation. He's in love with Tenley but he won't cowboy up and tell her."

"Fuck off, Wyatt."

Wyatt opens his mouth to respond, but from the end of the table comes the old, measured voice of my grandpa. "Warner, my eyesight might be closer to bat than man, but even I can see you've got it bad."

At first, it's just Jessie with a small, stifled giggle. Then it's Wyatt, and he doesn't hold back. Next, it's everyone, a cacophony of laughter. Even my dad wears a reluctant, bemused half grin.

"I hate all of you," I say, swiping bacon from the platter in front of me. I grab more than my share and stare at Wyatt. "And you, asshole, I'm eating your portion of bacon."

Wyatt laughs again and flips me off. There's bacon in my mouth when I return the gesture.

26

TENLEY

My mother's calling and I know what it's about, and I do not want to answer. But if I don't answer, she will call over and over. Then she will call Gretchen, and Gretchen doesn't need to be a part of that. Besides, I've already talked to Gretchen this morning.

"Hi, Mom." I tuck the phone between my shoulder and my ear and open the fridge. I'd like to make a smoothie, but Wyatt doesn't have a blender. It's the first time since coming to Sierra Grande that I've really missed something about my home. But then I remember that my blender was actually Tate's blender and he took it when we broke up.

"Hi, honey," my mom answers. "What are you up to?"

Her breezy tone is too *on purpose.* I see right through it like it's gossamer. "I'm headed into town in search of a smoothie." Last week on the set I overheard two crew members talking about a place they found in the middle of town. It can't be hard to locate.

"How nice. Anything new?"

I roll my eyes as I pull Pearl out onto the road that leads

around the homestead and through to the main road. "Mom, do you have something to ask me?"

"Your new... friend is making a splash this morning."

"Technically, he made a splash last night."

"What do you think about it?"

I sigh quietly. Warner looked pissed off in the photo, but he also looked strong. Protective. Capable and in control. And I still can't figure out how the picture was taken in the first place. Wyatt said nobody in this town would take a picture like that, not after what he'd done to get my underwear back. He still hasn't said what he did, but I believe him. The only logical explanation is that there was a second pap we didn't know about. In LA, they're everywhere. But here in a small town, I felt relatively insulated. That'll be changing soon, if what Gretchen said is true.

When she called this morning, she informed me that she'd heard there were paps headed here, hoping to catch Warner acting ill-tempered again. "America's sweetheart meets bad boy cowboy, or something like that," Gretchen had said.

"The photo isn't what it seems, Mom."

"It never is. Tell me more about it."

I open my mouth to answer, then remember what the pap said. "Why did you put Aspen on the market? I thought you had time."

She's quiet. It's taking her too long to answer.

"Mom," I nudge her on.

"The people your father owes grew impatient."

"How impatient?"

She's quiet again, and it frightens me more than anything else could. "They didn't hurt us, if that's what you're wondering. But you can't tell people like that to wait. The word 'no' does not exist with them."

"Please let me pay off the debt for you, Mom. Please. I can make this all go away in seconds."

"It's not your place to clean up your parents' mistakes. I won't put you in that position."

"So instead, you're putting yourself and Dad in danger?"

"We're not in danger. Honestly," she adds, which doesn't make me feel any better. "Are you?"

I make a face. "What are you talking about?"

"Your cowboy. He lost his temper."

My arms go rigid and my knuckles whiten as I grip the steering wheel. "He's not experienced with paps, Mom. Comments don't roll off his back like water off a duck."

"I didn't mean to upset you."

"I'm not upset." False.

She switches subjects. "I hear filming is going well. The sex scene is this week."

I take a deep breath and blow it out my nose, letting my defensiveness of Warner seep out of me. "Yep."

"Are you nervous?"

"Nervous about having to passionately kiss and pretend to have sex with my childhood friend? All in a day's work."

Mom barks a laugh. "You're only sarcastic when you're nervous."

"I'm not nervous, exactly, but I'll admit that it's weird."

"That's what I figured." She sounds pleased with herself.

"Mom, I'm pulling into a parking spot. Can we talk later?" We say I love you and hang up.

Ten minutes later, on my way out of the store holding a raspberry banana smoothie, I see a woman a few cars from mine, struggling to load something heavy into the back of her vehicle.

"Can I help you with that?" I call as I approach. When she looks up, I recognize her from my birthday dinner. "Jo, right?" I put down my drink and place my hands on the opposite side of a large, heavy box. Together we slide it into her trunk.

"Thank you so much." She grins at me. "I won't even pretend to only halfway remember your name. Hi, Tenley."

We finish loading the next two boxes, and she tells me they're full of wine. "The delivery truck broke down on the way up the I-17, so I had to run into town and buy out the local selection."

"Maybe I'll come in for a glass sometime soon." Sitting at a table at The Orchard with a glass of wine sounds like a good way to spend an evening.

"Please come in. Your first glass is on me." Jo closes the trunk and starts toward the front of the car.

I wave goodbye and head back to Pearl. Warner texts just before I back out of the parking spot. He'd been at his parents' house all morning, first for breakfast and then because Wes needed help fixing a tractor.

Warner: ***I've already seen the photo, and I don't give a shit. There's a beautiful woman who lives a stone's throw from me, but I stopped by her house and she wasn't home. Do you know where she's gone?***

I grin at his words, my thumb running over the screen.

I don't know where she went, but would you like me to pass her a message?

Warner: ***Tell her to get her gorgeous ass back here because I need to kiss her.***

Anticipation curls through my stomach, delicious and exhilarating. I press down a little harder on the accelerator.

***

Warner is waiting for me on my front porch when I arrive. With one foot out of the car door, he grabs me and spins me around. He sets me down, pressing me up against Pearl, and he's hard against my stomach. He kisses me like he's been without food for days, and I'm dinner.

He tastes divine, but he smells like sweat and grease. And while that may be some women's fantasy, it isn't mine.

"Ew," I complain playfully against his lips. "You stink."

"I was waiting for you. Thought we could shower together." I feel his smile. "Save water."

"Didn't get enough last night?" I murmur, remembering the cool feel of his kitchen counter against my body.

His face is buried in my hair, and he says, "I'll never get enough."

I stiffen, but he doesn't notice. I have to remind myself that deep down, Warner is a poet. He might mean what he says, but it won't make him change his mind.

I throw myself into the moment. I'd rather give in to the experience than hold back and regret it forever. Last night when Warner asked me about Tate, I'd told him I should've listened to my heart. Well, here I am listening to my heart, and I'm still going to end up hurt. At least this way, I'm in control. I'm choosing my ending.

It's me who leads Warner into the cabin. Me who takes him to the bathroom and starts the shower. Me who stands with him under the running water, soaps him down, then drops to my knees.

It's not safe for me to use words to tell him I love him.

So I do the next best thing. I use my body.

27

TENLEY

AFTER THE PICTURE OF WARNER GRABBING THE CAMERA CAME out, I tried to tell him he didn't have to go into town with me. I repeated what Gretchen told me about the paps coming, hoping for something juicy.

Warner refused. He said he didn't give a shit who said what about him, and he wasn't going to hide out in his own town. He's also been in a good mood because the sex scene was moved out a week. I explained to him it will have to happen eventually, but he silenced me with a kiss and that was the end of that.

Every day we're getting closer and closer to finishing the movie. It's been one of the easier films I've worked on. The years Calvin and I have spent together as coworkers and friends has come in handy. So far, we haven't needed to make any changes to the script, so we haven't had to add days to the shoot.

Each day we get closer to finishing brings me a day closer to leaving Sierra Grande. The end is in sight, and it's making my time with Warner just a little sweeter, and a little more desperate. Each kiss is deeper, each touch lingers.

We're in the Merc right now buying dog treats for Libby, and Warner's running a fingertip up and down my bare arm. Touching me constantly is another recent development. It's as if he thinks I'll disappear if he doesn't have a hold on me. I wonder if he knows how contradictory his actions and his words have become?

I'd be lying if I said it doesn't give me hope. But there's a difference between feeling hopeful, and letting it determine my future. Warner and I want different things, and no amount of hope will change that.

I grab the treats, plus two bags of peach rings. Warner raises his eyebrows. "I'm out," I say with a pout. "I met this dude, and it turns out he's addicted to spicy peach candy too, and he ate my stash."

"What a dick." Warner grabs two more bags.

After a stop at the feed store for a few items Juliette requested, we're on our way back to my place. I want to check on Libby and I need to call Christian, my publicist. He's called twice while we've been running errands.

"Hey girl," I say to Libby when we open the front door. She dances in a circle, and her head goes straight into the bag Warner's holding, sniffing out what she knows is for her. Warner opens the box and feeds one to her.

My phone dings with a text, then starts ringing. "Hey Gretch—"

"I just sent you a link to an article. Before you read it, I just want to say I'm sorry. Christian did his best to stop it."

"Stop what?"

Warner's watching me, responding to the dread in my tone.

"Read the article."

She hangs up. Stomach rolling, I open Gretchen's message. I've only read the headline and already my fingers are at my mouth, flattening my lips against the groan climbing up my throat. My stomach sours.

I begin to read.

Cowboy or Coward?

Curious about the mystery man Tenley Roberts has been seen with? Us too.

His name is Warner Hayden, and he's a member of a cattle ranching royal family. Next time you're shopping at Whole Foods, take a glance at where your pasture-raised beef came from. Chances are, it's the Hayden Cattle Company.

Warner Hayden is handsome, rugged, and... married.

Or was, until recently. Hayden's ex-wife deserted him and their two children, or so everyone thought.

Where did she go?

A treatment facility outside Phoenix. HIPAA regulations prohibited a source inside the facility from revealing why she was there, but said, "The husband never came to see her. The children never visited. It was all very suspect, if you ask me. Like taking out the trash. She was dumped."

Looks like Roberts' handsome new beau may be more coward than cowboy.

This is her second strike in relationships this year. Here's hoping she doesn't have a third.

"Tenley, what is it?"

Blood pounds in my ears as I look at Warner. The first time I met him, I knew I'd met someone good. A person with a warm, kind light glowing from the depths.

He doesn't deserve this.

He takes the phone I'm holding out for him and quickly reads the article. His eyes tighten and he swallows hard.

"Fucking shit." The words are low, dangerous, forced out

through his teeth. He tosses the bag of dog treats onto the floor next to Libby and strides out the door.

I go after him. "Where are you going?"

"To my kids. To Anna. This is going to kill her." He shakes his head as he stomps to his truck, one hand raking over the back of his neck. He stops in his open door and looks back at me. "The article got it wrong. They got everything wrong."

Tears sting my eyes. "I know."

Warner gets in his truck and turns it around. He's gone in seconds.

When I'm in the cabin and the door is shut, I slink to the ground and cry. Libby licks my tears.

28

WARNER

ANNA'S CONFUSED. I WOULD BE TOO IF I OPENED MY FRONT door and found her standing there.

I don't know what she's going to do when she finds out. It's her secret, *our* secret. Me and Anna. Brock and Susan. Created and kept at Anna's request. She didn't want people in town knowing.

She was mortified at what she'd done, at how swiftly and easily the mental illness had taken hold. At the time I said all the right things, but they fell on deaf ears. I used big words, but they gained no purchase.

Normalize.

Destigmatize.

Make mental health a part of the conversation. Remove the hushed tones. Whole-body health. I researched until my eyes dried and I could read no more. I said it all, but Anna couldn't hear me. She wasn't only in the throes of her clinical depression, she was fucking drowning in it.

She's better now. She's come so far, but I don't know how fragile it all is. Will the road she's traveled turn to dust under her feet when I tell her about the article? She sees herself as a weakling. To me, she's a warrior.

"Warner, what's wrong?" Anna glances back into the house, then steps outside. She's close to me, and reflexively I take a step away to give her space. There was a time when space was the last thing I'd give her. When I'd hover over her, watchful, worried sick about what she might do.

My teeth grind together as I try to put everything into words. I was so certain I had to be the one to tell her she's been outed, that the news should come from me, but now that I'm here, I'm at a loss for words. How do you tell someone you care about that the secret they've worked so hard to keep is now public knowledge, and it's your fault?

Anna speaks. "Did something happen with Tenley?" Her tone holds care, but also reluctance. She's mistakenly assuming I'm coming to her with relationship woes.

"Sort of," I start. "There was a situation with a photographer. Tenley told him to stop taking pictures and he didn't listen."

A small dimple forms in Anna's left cheek as she laughs. "Let me guess... you puffed up your chest and took care of business?"

Despite the heaviness in my heart, I chuckle. "Something like that."

Anna's head tips to the side. "Then what happened?"

I rub the pad of a thumb across my eye, stalling for time. "I think it piqued a whole lot of curiosity. One of the gossip sites must've started digging."

All traces of humor disappear from Anna's face. She crosses her arm in front of herself, like she can defend against whatever it is I've come to tell her. Instinctively, she knows this is about her.

"They were looking at me, I'm sure, trying to find something bad or interesting." A disgusted grunt tickles the back of my throat. "I'm sure they figured out I'm a single dad, which begs the question about the mom."

"Spit it out, Warner."

"They published an article saying you went to a treatment facility and I abandoned you."

A short, terse breath. A vacant gaze across the front yard. Anna's initial reaction is smaller in scale than I thought it would be.

I reach for her shoulder, wanting to comfort her, but I can't tell if she needs it. She's not retreating into herself, like I watched her do repeatedly. If anything, she is drawing strength from somewhere deep inside, filling in the chasms where sadness and uncertainty used to flow.

"We need to talk to the kids. Especially Peyton." Anna looks back to the house when she says our daughter's name. "All her friends have phones. They'll tell her the second they see her on Monday morning at school."

"And the town?" It was Sierra Grande that Anna had worried about. All the people who'd watched her grow up. Everyone who'd attended our wedding, celebrated the birth of our children. She'd thought she was letting them all down. She was supposed to be the perfect mother and wife. Anna could barely tell herself she wasn't perfect; she couldn't stomach other people knowing it too.

Anna places a hand on my forearm. Her touch used to feel warm on my skin. Right now, it feels like nothing. Like a touch from Dakota, or Jessie, or my mother.

Unlike Tenley, whose touch creates an odd buoyancy in my limbs, and a searing desire through the rest of me.

"Warner, do you remember when we were getting ready

to drive to Harmony? Do you remember what you said to me?"

I shake my head. I said a lot of things. I exhausted all my words trying to make sure Anna knew I loved her, that I was there for her.

"You told me this would not define me." Anna smiles gently. "And you were right. It won't. But only if I don't let it. So now, we're going to call Peyton and Charlie into the living room, and we're going to tell them why I had to go away. And then, my mom will tell the town gossips. One person will tell another, until they all know. I won't hide, and I won't duck my head." She smiles again, and I see the old Anna, the one who was happy a long time ago. "Normalize. Destigmatize. Those are also your words."

I'm fucking blown away by her bravery. "Anna, I'm sorry. I brought this on you. You're forced to do this because of me."

She pauses in the door she's just opened. "The day was coming. You just... expedited it."

I follow her into the house, and she calls for the kids. In the living room, as a family of four, with Brock and Susan looking on, Anna explains her departure to Peyton and Charlie. Tears prick the backs of my eyes as I watch my kids learn about what was happening under their noses, but I don't allow them to fall. They need me to be strong for them. The same way Anna is being strong for them now.

We may no longer be married, or in love, but we are partners in parenting. And our kids come first.

* * *

"I DIDN'T KNOW it was like that." Barb presses a palm to her chest, Scarlett O'Hara style.

"To think"—Shirley shakes her head—"we all believed the worst."

"We should pray for Anna."

"And for us. Gossip is the devil's work."

Barb eyes Shirley. "Hold your horses. The Lord knows our hearts were in the right place."

29

TENLEY

IT'S FOR THE BEST.

I shouldn't be here any longer. Wyatt's cabin. Hayden property.

What am I even doing? The last thing I want to do is make life more complicated for Warner and his kids.

In a few weeks' time I'll be back in LA. Figuring out what's next for me. Maybe I'll take a long vacation, bounce around for a little while. Maybe I'll hole up in my place with Morgan and eat an ungodly amount of ice cream.

The sound of the dryer's notification that it's done makes me jump. I place the last of my toiletries in a bag and go grab the sheets. Every step is wooden, every heartbeat hollow.

I'm almost done here. Fresh sheets on the bed. Bag packed. One more pass through the small cabin to make certain everything is in its place, and I'll be ready to go.

Not true.

I won't be *ready* to go.

I'll just go. One foot in front of the other, until there's enough distance to be considered gone.

30

WARNER

AFTER OUR FAMILY TALK, PEYTON AND CHARLIE ELECTED TO finish out their weekend visit with their mom. Despite the strength Anna showed just now, I saw the way the kids wanted to protect her. They are Haydens, after all.

I pass the homestead and Cowboy House, then continue on the dirt road until I veer off for Wyatt's cabin. In the distance, through the pine trees, I see Pearl.

Automatically, a smile curves my lips. It remains in place when I let myself in the front door, and stride all the way into the kitchen, where I can see a wash of golden hair.

Tenley turns to face me, and my smile slides away.

"What's wrong?" I step toward her, but halt when she shakes her head back and forth quickly.

"I'm leaving." Her voice quivers.

My head flinches back, her words hitting me with a painful force. I need a better explanation. "You're leaving Sierra Grande? But the movie..." Her meaning takes hold, and my next words disappear like my smile. "It's me. You're leaving me."

She shakes her head again, this time slower. "You can't expect me to stay, Warner. We want two different things, and the longer this goes on, the harder it will be. I thought I could handle the pain, but—" Her shoulders curl forward with her small shrug. "I can't."

I have to go to her. I need to touch her.

She doesn't stop me. My hand glides through her hair, cupping the back of her head. The momentum takes us back a few feet, and I cradle her lower back with my arm, buffering her from the edge of the counter.

"Don't go." My voice is hoarse, like I've been screaming for hours. Or maybe, I've been screaming silently for years. "Please, Tenley."

We're mere inches apart, and she looks into my eyes. "This isn't fair to me."

Shame fills me. She's not wrong.

"I want things you're not willing to give, Warner. And I chose to continue with you, knowing how you felt. None of this is your fault. But it's time."

"I'm sorry." In this moment, my apology means more than anything I've ever said.

Tenley leans closer. Her soft lips brush mine. I close my eyes. She kisses me harder. I kiss her back, crushing her to me, holding on for dear life.

My hands run over her waist, skimming her shoulders, trailing down her arms. Her skin is blazing hot, rising under my touch, and she moans into my mouth.

"Is this a good idea?" I ask against her.

"No," she chokes out, but doesn't stop.

I know it will be the last time, and it heightens every sensation. Into the bedroom we go, her legs wrapped around my waist, as we melt into one another. We fall down onto the bed, holding tighter, fastening like we can capture the liquid we're made of. We both know that when this is over, we'll have slipped through the cracks in our fingers. But for now, we get lost.

I lean down, pressing my lips to her neck, inhaling as I taste her, drinking her in. I do not need to commit her to memory. She is already there.

Tenley has never been timid with me, but there's something new about her now. Raw. Palpable. No second-guessing. No questioning. Her heart leads.

Legs apart, she invites me in. Looking into her eyes, I see it. The beckoning. The beginning of a farewell.

What am I to do except take it? I'll have her, in any way I can.

I lean forward, line myself up with her, and keep my eyes trained on hers. I've never been gentle with her, but I am now. Each moment is measured, ecstasy delivered in cadence.

A goodbye I can control.

And so, I make the most of it. So does Tenley. She grips me, holding on to my hips as I slip into her, and when she comes, she rakes her fingernails across my back. She's never done this before, and immediately I understand it. She's marking me, a basic, primal need to brand me as hers. Nail scratches or not, I am Tenley's. One day they will heal, disappear, and yet, they will be there. A permanent, invisible record of who owns my heart.

We lay breathless for a few minutes. Tenley goes to the bathroom, and when she returns, she gathers her clothes and dresses. I pull on my jeans and sit back down on the bed, watching her. She bends to pick up a bag I hadn't noticed until now. She straightens and tears roll down her face. My heart twists at the sight, but I don't dare go to her. It would only prolong the inevitable.

"I am going to tell you this because if I don't, I'll regret it for the rest of my life. After I say it, don't follow me. Let me go." She takes a deep breath and looks me squarely in the eyes, her chin lifted. "I'm in love with you."

She walks out of the room. The front door closes. Not a slam, but a gentle closing. Much like our time together. In like a lion, out like a lamb.

I sit motionless on the bed, for how long I don't know. My body feels like it's been drained of blood, my heart trampled on by the bulls we pulled from pasture. Finally I stand and start moving, my motions on autopilot. I strip the sheets. Place them in the washing machine.

I have all the time in the world, so I wait for them to go through the cycle. I walk around Wyatt's cabin, searching for traces of Tenley. On the kitchen counter I find a piece of paper, the pen she used beside it.

If you're ever in LA...

Her address follows. It's such an anticlimactic ending for an experience that stretched me beyond repair.

I go home. Open a beer. Stand on my front porch and drink it while I stare at the backside of Wyatt's cabin.

She's in love with me. This feels too big to wrap my arms around, too enormous to capture. Tenley's words have formed a fist, and it's stuck up under my ribs.

I know what this feeling is. *Heartbreak.*

But it's new. Not like it was with Anna. That was slow agony. This is sharper. More acute. Like someone has obliterated the rest of my life.

Before you can have a broken heart, you need to have love.

The thought nearly knocks me out. I don't know why. The signs were all there.

I grab a second beer. Drink it. Sit in my realization. Berate myself.

Knowing is worse. The lights are on and now I can see what a fucking fool I am. I fell in love knowing I was an emotional dead end. Tenley should have everything she wants; all I've done is given her a matching broken heart.

31

TENLEY

A DROP IN THE BUCKET. THAT'S WHAT TATE WAS COMPARED to Warner.

I feel like a worn-out dishrag.

In time I will feel better, I know that as certainly as I know that Warner will never be in my past. He is woven into the fabric of my soul, and I will carry him as I go.

Calvin has come to stay at the house with me. I'm not worried about my safety, not after whatever magic Wyatt performed to get my underwear back. I just don't want to be alone. It's been over a week since I left the Hayden ranch, and I've been a terrible roommate.

Calvin steps out on the back porch, a glass of wine in each hand. "You look like shit," he says, handing me one. "Makeup is clearly doing their job because those dark circles aren't noticeable when we're filming."

"Thank God for that," I say mockingly.

Calvin grabs a handful of carrots from the vegetable tray between us. I'm eating chips. Fuck the broccoli. "Did today's sex scene make you want to have actual sex with me?"

I snort. "Yes, your nude-colored ass floss was really doing it for me."

Calvin snorts back. "About as sexy as your pasties."

"Some guys probably like them."

He shrugs. "Not this guy." He shoves two of my chips into his mouth. When he finishes chewing, he asks, "Do you want to go to a real restaurant and have a glass of wine?"

I prop my feet on the chair opposite me. "Let me guess, The Orchard?"

"Well, yes. Duh. Everything else in this town is barely edible. We should ask the owner if she'll open up a location in LA."

I say nothing about his uppity attitude. It's just the way Calvin is. And I'm grateful to have him here with me, especially considering I've been shit company.

Calvin finishes his glass of wine, I store mine in the fridge, and we leave for The Orchard.

* * *

Jo is behind the bar, and when she sees me, she smiles and comes out to give me a hug. I'm taken aback by the show of friendship, and I lean into her embrace. Despite the sex scene I shot with Calvin earlier today, I feel like it's been so long since I've felt human touch. Libby's kisses are sweet, but they don't count.

Jo nods at Calvin and walks back behind the bar. "What can I get for you?"

Calvin orders a cabernet. I ask for sauvignon blanc.

"This one is my favorite," she says as she pours my white wine. "It's from a vineyard about an hour east of here."

I thank her and take a drink. Crisp. Cold. Perfect.

Two people settle in at the end of the bar, and Jo goes to help them.

"She's pretty," Calvin comments. His face is upturned as he takes a drink, but his eyes are on her.

"Beautiful," I correct. "Those cheekbones. No contouring happening on that face."

My wine is half empty when Jo makes it back over to us. She balances two empty water glasses in one hand and uses the other hand to fill the glasses with ice from an unseen station below the bar top.

"How's it going out at the HCC?" She fills the glasses with water and slides one to each of us.

I grab it and take a sip, buying myself a few more seconds. I wish I had something better to tell her.

"I've moved back into the place the studio rented for me." I nod my head at Calvin. "He's staying with me."

Jo nods her head once, slowly, scrutinizing me. I can tell she sees past my casual tone of voice.

She doesn't press for details about Warner, which I appreciate. Leaning her forearms on the bar, she says, "The Haydens are a tough bunch to pin down. They're modern cowboys with an Old West attitude. Makes for some interesting experiences." She doesn't elaborate, and I get the feeling she has some stories to tell.

Starting with Anna. I'm dying to hear about her, even if it no longer matters. Warner wouldn't talk about her, I didn't feel right pressing him, but my curious nature is berating me for never finding anything out.

I sip my wine, affecting a relaxed posture, and ask, "Jo, did you see the piece on Warner's ex-wife?"

Her hazel eyes narrow. It's like she has an uncanny ability to detect bullshit. "Anna?"

I nod.

"I saw it. I thought it was uncouth of that... reporter? Journalist? Can you even call him that?"

I shrug. I've never given much thought to the title. I just know they can make you glow, or they can stain your image, all with a few words.

Jo's irritation with the articles subsides, and her demeanor softens. "He went after one of our own," she explains. Her eyes flicker to Calvin. He's being abnormally quiet, to the point I almost forget he's here.

"Go on." He flicks his hand toward us and pulls out his phone. "Don't mind me. I'll just be over here playing poker."

I look back to Jo. "Warner never told me much about her, and that article took me by surprise."

She crosses her arms in front of her and leans a hip against something unseen under the bar. "Are you asking if he abandoned Anna at a treatment facility?"

I shake my head adamantly. It's not even a question. "Warner would never do something like that. It's more... general confusion on my part. I don't understand what happened with Anna."

"I'm almost as clueless as you. All I know is that Warner and Anna were the golden couple, high school sweethearts, blah blah blah, and then Anna slowly started fading away. Fewer and fewer town activities, I didn't see her at school events—" Jo pauses to refill my water. "I have a much younger little brother who's about Peyton's age, so I'd seen the family around for a long time by then. The family of four seemed like they went to a family of three, and then I heard Anna left town."

I stare into my empty wine glass. "I feel awful for Warner."

Jo smiles halfway and tips her head side to side. "You can if you want to, but Warner probably doesn't want your pity. He did what Haydens do. He pulled himself up by his bootstraps and moved on. Since then, he's been everything for everybody. He doesn't miss a soccer match, a school play, or a bake sale. He's Wes's second-in-command, and that's not an easy job. It's demanding, plus Wes can be an asshole." She jokingly looks around the place. "Just don't tell Dakota I said that."

"He's been nice to me every time I've been around him."

"Reformed asshole." Jo makes air quotes. "That's what Dakota calls him."

I laugh, but the sound is hollow. Much like everything else inside me. "Warner and I want different things. That's why I left. My heart couldn't take being with him and knowing I can never really have him the way I want him."

Jo touches my hand. "Those Hayden boys can make a girl go crazy."

"Personal experience?"

Something flashes in her eyes, and then she says, "I watched Dakota with Wes."

I get the feeling that's not all she's referring to, but I drop it. "Are you dating anybody?"

"Actually, I am. He works at the bank. It's only been a handful of dates, nothing major." She waves her hands, downplaying the relationship.

I smile encouragingly. "I hope it works out in whatever way you want it to."

She laughs softly. "I don't sound excited, do I?"

My lips purse and my head shakes. Jo looks down the bar. Her attention snaps back to me and she eyes my empty wine glass. "Do you want another?"

I decline and glance at Calvin. Normally he prefers to command conversation, but he's busy on his phone. "We have an early meeting with the director." I elbow Calvin to make him look up.

He gives me a blank stare and I roll my eyes. He'd been fully immersed in the game. "Anyway," I give Jo a look and she laughs. "We'd better get going."

"No check. I owed you a drink."

I thread my arm through my purse strap and stand up. "Thank you for the drink and the conversation."

The ticket machine at the end of the bar starts printing an order. Jo smiles and waves at us and goes to read the ticket. I leave a generous tip, then walk out in front of Calvin. His nose stays stuck in his phone the entire drive back to the house, the light illuminating his features. He looks focused.

I tap the side of his phone when we pull up. "You'd think there are naked girls on the screen, not playing cards."

"Poker is a skill, Tenley, and I like to win."

"Okay, Calvin," I say sarcastically and go inside. I've never known him to be much of a gambler, but then again, I didn't realize it about my father either.

I'm in the kitchen pouring a glass of water when he walks in, sans phone.

"Oh look, I got my roommate back."

He shoots me a dirty look. "Very cute."

I touch his shoulder on my way out of the room. "Thanks for staying with me."

Guilt flickers in his eyes. "Sorry I turned into a dud tonight."

I shrug on my way out of the room. "I had Jo." Just before I turn the corner, I glance back. Calvin has his knuckles pressed to his mouth and he's looking down at the floor.

32

WARNER

I CAN'T THINK, I CAN'T SIT STILL, I CAN'T CONCENTRATE ON A damn thing.

It's why I've come to the homestead for dinner. The kids are with Anna again, an unexpected midweek visit, and without them to distract me, I start feeling pretty damn sorry for myself.

Wyatt stomps onto the front porch. "The fuck's wrong with you?" he demands. He's wearing a half-tucked flannel print shirt and tight-ass jeans piled on top of boots that nobody in their right mind would call cowboy.

I lean back in my seat and stare openly at his choice of footwear. "Where's your motorcycle?"

Wyatt ignores the jab, pulling a single cigarette from his back pocket and lighting it. I frown. "Since when do you smoke?"

He shrugs. "Since when I decided that I fucking felt like it."

I join him at the porch railing. "You're in a foul mood." I hold my hand out for the cancer stick. "Let me have some."

He side-eyes me like he doesn't believe I want to smoke,

then hands it over. I bring it to my mouth but drop it right before it touches me, and stomp on it with my real-ass cowboy boot.

Wyatt's jaw twitches. "Prick."

I stare back at him. "Dumbass."

Wes steps out of the front door Wyatt left half open and stops, looking at us. "My money's on Wyatt."

I take a step back from my little brother. "Thanks a lot, Wes."

He shrugs. "Your heart's broken. No way you'd put up a real fight."

My lips turn down. "Maybe I'm angry and I need to take it out on someone."

Wes snorts. "Yeah, angry at yourself. Are you going to punch your own face?"

I'm somewhat seriously considering bull-rushing Wes, but a buzzing sound grabs my attention. Looking in the late afternoon sky, I spot a small object flying around.

"It's the drone Tenley asked me about." Wes searches my face after he says her name. "They were here earlier too, getting shots at different times of the day."

He doesn't say it, but the only way he'd know that is if he'd talked to Tenley recently. More recently than me. It's been two weeks since she left the ranch, but it feels like two years. I'm waiting for the sharp pain in my chest to fade to a dull throb, something I can learn to live with for the rest of my life.

I open my mouth to speak but the front door opens so forcefully that it looks like it's coming off its hinges. My dad treads heavily on the wood-planked porch, also wearing real-ass cowboy boots. I'm about to point this out to Wyatt because I can't resist giving him shit for wearing something so trendy, but my attention is pulled away by the swing of a gun. Dad steps from the porch, strides to the center of the yard, and takes aim. The drone explodes, fragments falling to earth like a clumsy firecracker.

Wes sighs. Loudly. Deeply.

Dad turns and stares at him. The look on his face is close to a sneer, but sneering requires a certain amount of emotion, which my dad isn't exactly known for displaying. "I told them no pictures of the HCC. Not by land, not by air, and if they create a sea in a landlocked state and send in a picture-taking jet-ski, I will torpedo them."

Gramps's laughter floats through the front porch window, and I tuck away the smile it puts on my face.

Wes shakes his head slightly. "Dad, I gave them permission."

"Like hell you did."

Wes looks to me for help. I was there for the conversation between Wes and Tenley, but there's no fucking way I'm stepping into this cow pie.

Dad grumbles on his way past Wes and into the house. Wes locks onto me with his death stare. "Thanks a lot."

"You would've done the same thing."

"I was coming out here to ask you to go get a beer with me, but maybe not. Maybe you should stew in that pulverized heart of yours all by yourself."

I ignore what he said and consider his invite. "I could go for a beer." I look at Wyatt. "You want to come?"

He nods. Without asking, I know we're going to the Chute.

I start for my truck. "Let me go get changed and—"

"I want to go!" Jessie leaps from the house, eyes bright and hopeful.

We all turn to look at her. "No." The word comes from each of us.

She presses fisted hands to her hips. "Why? Because I'm not a 'boy'?"

I'm not sure why she put the word *boy* in air quotes. "No, Calamity, because you're not"—air quotes—"twenty-one."

"You don't have to go to the Chute," she argues. "You can go somewhere I can get into."

Wyatt laughs snidely. "Yeah, let's go to the underage bar. I can't wait to have a Shirley Temple."

"Fuck you," she snaps.

"Watch your mouth," Wes growls.

"Oohh, Wes is practicing being a dad," Jessie taunts.

"Jessie," I say calmly, like I do when Peyton starts handing out the sass. "Cussing and being rude isn't going to help you get your way."

"Oh, right." She nods solemnly. "I should be quiet and amenable, like a good girl. Stand down and forget I have opinions."

If her goal was to make all three of us feel like shit, then it worked.

Wes is the first to break. "Fine, you can come. We'll pick up a six-pack and go to the overlook."

The overlook is the informal term for an area just outside town on the far east side, known for its higher elevation and views of gently sloping hills leading down into a valley. I haven't been there in years.

Right now, the thought of sitting there with my siblings and having a beer sounds like something I desperately need.

* * *

We said we're meeting back at the homestead, so I don't know why someone is knocking on my front door. I'm almost to the door when it opens and Wes steps in.

"Come on in," I say sarcastically.

"I need to borrow a shirt," he says, holding out his sleeve. A long swath of oily black covers him. "I stopped to look at that tractor we've been working on and must've brushed up against some grease." He starts for my bedroom.

"I don't think I have any clean shirts," I say to his back, trying to keep the panic from my voice. My bed is covered in papers. Books. My laptop is open. I'd been peering over my resumé when he knocked, quadruple checking for errors. The job opening at the Verde Valley Community College posted yesterday, and I'd like my application to be one of the first they see.

Wes stops in the middle of my bedroom. He looks around. "I know you've always liked to read, but I didn't know you were full-on obsessed."

Of everything in his line of sight, he starts with my crammed bookshelves?

"I found myself with more time on my hands after everything started happening with Anna. The kids went to bed and I didn't want to spend the rest of the night watching endless sports and drinking beer."

Wes nods, walking the length of the bookshelves. He glances at the bed, strewn with paper and the laptop with the bright screen that might as well have a blinking neon light on it. It's so obviously a resumé. The heading, the bullets, the format. Little else looks similar. He still doesn't mention it.

I could tell him to get the hell out of my room. He may be my boss and my big brother, but it's my house.

"I read Grisham. And some Stephen King, but it's scared me a few times." He sends me a warning look. "Don't tell anyone I told you that."

Through the disbelief I'm feeling that this conversation is taking place, I manage a smile. "It's in the vault."

Wes pulls open my closet and rifles through my shirts. "You going to tell me why you have an updated resumé open on your computer?"

I cross my arms and lean on the doorjamb. "That depends. Are you asking as my brother, or my boss?"

Wes pulls a shirt off the hanger. "Brother." He takes off his stained shirt and changes. "Though I can't help it if the information bleeds over. Nobody is *that* good at separating personal and professional."

I take a deep breath. "Reading isn't the only thing I've picked up in the past few years. I got my master's in English from an online program out of ASU."

Wes is quiet. I wish he'd look at me, but he's meticulously rolling up his sleeves, taking his sweet time. He steps back from my closet. "What are you planning to do with it?"

Here it is. The moment of truth. In true Wes fashion, he's looking the problem dead in the eye.

"Verde Valley CC has an opening for an English professor." If Wes looked at my resumé, he'd see how I tailored it to fit the role.

"You'd no longer work for the HCC?"

He knows the answer already. I cannot be a single father, second-in-command of the largest cattle ranch in Arizona, and a college professor at the same time. Anger boils. Why do people expect me to handle it all? Good old Warner, the wide net at the bottom. The catchall.

"You know the fucking answer, Wes."

"No, Warner, I don't." Wes's voice holds none of the anger of my own. "That's why I'm asking. I want you to say in plain words exactly what you want for yourself."

My teeth grind together. "I love this ranch, but I don't

want to bleed for it the way you do. There's something else out there for me. Whether or not it's being an English professor, I don't know, but I want the chance to try."

Wes lifts his chin to the ceiling. "Thank Christ," he mutters, lowering his gaze. "How long have you been waiting to say what's on your mind?"

My anger, my indignation, deflates. "A long time."

"Too long."

"Don't lecture me."

"I'm your big brother. It's my right, even if we are adults. Which leads me to my next question. What the hell happened with Tenley?"

My hands go to my pockets and I raise my shoulders, slowly letting them go. "She and I want different things. Simple as that."

Wes's chuckle is hollow. "It's never simple. In fact, there was a time when you told me to stop making everything so damn hard. So," he widens his stance and crosses his arms, like he's settling in for an argument. "I'm going to say the same to you. Quit making it difficult. If you love her, you love her. End of story. Everything else is just details."

"Now you're an expert?"

"I'm someone who has walked on the road you're currently on. I know what it's like to deny myself because I think what I want is wrong."

I've been married. I've had kids. Can those boxes only be checked once? Maybe for some people, but for me? What's my right answer?

I honestly don't know.

Wes can tell I'm done talking. We've given one another enough to think about. "You ready to go?" he asks.

We walk out, and just as I'm closing Wes's truck door he looks at me and says, "Do you know what this makes you?"

I sigh. "An asshole?"

"No." Wes clicks his seatbelt into place. "You're changing course. Taking a chance. You're a maverick."

The word turns over in my head. I like it.

We leave the house and stop at the homestead to pick up Wyatt and Jessie. Wes pulls off for a six-pack, and we arrive at the lookout just as the heavy, bright orange sun sinks halfway down the horizon. Wyatt hands out the beer and presses a lemonade into Jessie's outstretched hand. She scowls.

We sit under the sparse canopy of a large pine, away from the openness of the overlook, four Hayden siblings shooting the shit. We quiet down when we hear footsteps. Twenty yards out, two young boys walk past us. They can't be more than thirteen and probably know Peyton. Each has a pellet gun over their shoulder, and neither has seen us.

"Quail hunting," I whisper.

They walk on, and Jessie stands up. She creeps after them, parallel to the line they walk. Wyatt whisper-hisses her name, and she brushes him off with a wave. Jessie makes it to the next tree and palms the trunk, leaning around to keep the young boys in her eyeline.

I watch one of the two boys take a rock from his pocket. He throws it at a bush, and the quail inside scatter. Both boys take aim. They shoot.

Jessie howls like she's been hit. The boys look at each other for a split second, then break into a sprint. They tear off away from the lookout like someone lit their asses on fire, back the way they came. They don't slow down, and they don't see us.

Jessie's doubled over, slapping her thigh. Wyatt laughs so hard no sound comes out. I'm shaking my head and trying like hell to keep from laughing. It doesn't work. That was too fucking funny. With the three of us cracking up, Wes doesn't stand a chance. He lets go of his stoic leader of the pack routine and joins in.

"You're fucking crazy, Calamity," Wyatt says to Jessie. "Those boys think they hit a person."

"Can't grow up with you three and be sane," she shoots back. He sneaks her some beer when Wes isn't looking.

Later on, when I'm getting out of Wes's truck in front of my place, Wyatt rolls down the window and yells, "I found the home address of the guy who wrote that article about you and Anna. In case you want to drive out there and throw a bag of flaming dog shit in his face."

There are plenty of things I'd like to do to that guy, but what's the point? It'd be a lot of time and energy for not much benefit. I shake my head at his offer and go inside. The second I'm home, my mind drifts back to the place where it's been for two weeks, like a record stuck on repeat.

I open my phone and sift through pictures of her, serving myself a heaping plate of misery. Why the fuck not? There's one in particular I get stuck on. Her lips are poised to kiss my cheek, her eyes shut tight. My grin is as goofy as they come, but so damn happy.

When I go to bed, I leave my phone on the kitchen counter on purpose. If I leave it out there, I won't be tempted to keep torturing myself with pictures.

I lay down and do nothing but think of Tenley. She's beautiful and sweet and so damn funny, she's everything I want and everything I'm afraid to have.

I throw off my covers and go get my phone. Who was I kidding?

33

TENLEY

"THAT'S A WRAP." I WINK AT CALVIN AND OFFER MY HAND.

He takes it, pulling me in for a hug. We're in the kitchen at the rental house. Filming ended yesterday, and it's time for me to go back to LA. Calvin will leave later today, but I packed last night. There's nothing left for me in Sierra Grande, but I try not to think too much about that. If I can avert my gaze from my broken heart for just long enough, I'll make it out of this town. If I examine my feelings too closely, I'll wind up back at the HCC, in the arms of a man I'm positive loves me but refuses to acknowledge it.

I step back from Calvin and look at him pleadingly. "Would you mind grabbing my heaviest suitcase from my room?"

Calvin flexes his biceps and lopes off. I take two apples from the fridge and turn back just in time to see my phone flash with a text. I grab it off the table and realize too late it's not mine. The message has my name though, so I read it. I don't understand what it means. ***I need more on Tenley,*** from a number that hasn't been given a name in Calvin's contacts.

"Did you pack bricks?" Calvin jokes, bumping into the

wall as he hauls in my suitcase. He stops short when he sees me with his phone.

"Why does someone need more on me? More of what?"

Calvin palms the air like he's innocent. Ironically, this is what everyone who's guilty of something does.

"Calvin." I speak his name like a threat.

"It's just publicity, I swear."

I squint, trying to understand, but I don't. "Keep going."

"I have skin in the game, too. It's not just your parents who need this movie to be successful." He has a pleading look on his face. I don't like it.

"Nobody wants a flop, Calvin, but I still don't understand."

"Your dad came to me six months ago and asked me for a loan. He told me about the gambling and said he had an inside tip on a horse and he was going to win big. I gave him what he needed, but I was interested too. He introduced me to the guys, and I—"

"No." I shake my head, not willing to believe that Calvin is in the same hot water as my dad.

"Your dad was wrong. And he was smart enough to be done after that." His voice takes on a pleading edge. "But not me. And you know we get paid more if this movie does well, Tenley."

"What did you do?" I think I already know, the events arranging themselves in my mind, but I want him to say it.

"I sent pictures of you and Warner to the gossip rags. I told them Warner's name. I'd heard some talk when I was coming out of a store, two old ladies sitting on a bench talking loudly like they'd forgotten their hearing aids. I told my contact at Celebrity Dirt. It went from there."

He doesn't look at me. It's the smartest decision of his life. If he attempted eye contact with me now, I'd put a big bruise on that pretty, deceptive face. I can't think of what to do, or say, so I choose nothing.

I grab my suitcase and lug it out the door. I nearly break my back lifting it in Pearl, but once it's in, I hop in too. Libby wags her tail from her place in the passenger seat. Calvin wisely stays in the house, and as I pull away, I don't look back.

My first thought is to blame Calvin for costing me my relationship with Warner, but even I know that's a stretch. There is nobody to blame but ourselves. Me, for wanting something. And Warner, for not wanting it. Nobody could look at us and say we aren't being true to ourselves.

I'm on the outskirts of Sierra Grande when I stop for gas. While the pump runs, I pop into the convenience store for a bottle of water, then remember the twelve-pack of water my dad put in my car on the way out here. I grab four more bottles, plus a bag of pistachios for the road.

I'm standing by the pump waiting for it to finish when an SUV pulls into the spot beside me. A blonde woman climbs out, glancing at me as she goes through the motions of inserting the pump into her SUV. Recognition lights up her eyes.

I turn back to Pearl. I'm in a sour mood, and I really hope she doesn't talk to me.

"Excuse me?"

I sigh silently and plaster a smile on my face. "Hello," I greet her pleasantly.

She's a little older than me, lines around her eyes and across her forehead, but she's very pretty. She waves, and a diamond engagement ring sparkles in the sunlight. "This is going to sound awkward, but I'm Anna. Warner's ex-wife."

"Oh," I say before I can stop myself, "hello. I'm Tenley. Obviously. I mean, you already knew that."

She smiles kindly. “Yes. But it’s nice to meet the real you. Not the public you.”

Everything printed about her comes rushing down on me, like Gatorade poured on a winning coach’s head. “I am so very sorry for that article and what they said about you. It’s my fault. If it weren’t for Warner and me…” Could I make this any worse? First, I get this woman’s private information blasted on the internet, and now I’m reminding her that her ex moved on with me. Way to go.

She laughs in this small, uncomfortable way. “It’s weird, I know.”

I gesture between us. “This is all new to me.”

“It’s new to me too.”

The gas pump clicks, signaling my car is full.

Anna takes a step forward, and I stay where I am. “I want you to know I don’t blame you or Warner for that article. I don’t like it, and I don’t appreciate it, of course, but it’s not the end of the world. Warner probably acted like it, because he remembers how sick I was and how badly I wanted to hide what I was going through.”

“I understood why he acted the way he did. He’s a good man.”

“The best. So,” her gaze flickers over jam-packed Pearl. “Why are you leaving town?”

“The film is over.”

“And you and Warner?”

A lump forms in my throat. “Also over.”

Anna looks at me with a mixture of pity and understanding. “I don’t think you are.”

Pain slices across my heart. “Trust me, we are. We want different things.”

“I just dropped Peyton and Charlie back off at Warner’s place and believe me when I say that man is a wreck.”

"He is?" All I can remember is me standing in front of him, telling him I was in love with him, and him staring back at me like he'd swallowed his tongue.

"I think we've already reached the seventh circle of awkwardness, so I'm just going to come right out and say this. He is desperately in love with you."

Her words should make me soar. Instead, I plummet lower than I already was. Because it doesn't matter if Warner is in love with me. In fact, that makes it worse. Circumstances killed us, not lack of feeling.

"I've never been married and I want kids," I blurt out. "He wants neither. Us being in love with each other doesn't change that."

Anna nods slowly. "That's tough."

"More than tough. An impasse."

"Can I just say one more thing and then you can be on your way?" She doesn't wait for me to say yes. Maybe she's afraid I'll deny her. "Warner's picking himself up from the hardest experience of his life, and it's my fault. He's not a man to stay down long, and he also doesn't give up what he wants. You know that family crest in the living room at his parents' house? Legacy, Loyalty, Honor?"

I nod.

"That's embedded in Warner's soul. If he's in love with you, he'll never stop being loyal to you. You met at the same time his life was imploding. He just needs a little time to get back on his feet and recalibrate."

I'm mostly listening to Anna, but a small part of me is trying to understand why she's being so nice about all this. So I ask, because why the hell not? It's likely I'll never see her again.

"My kids deserve a father who's happy. I want Warner to have a nice life, even if we don't share it. And even though I barely know you, I know what you did for my daughter. Peyton told me how you helped her when she got her period, and I'm very thankful she had someone that day."

I brush off the compliment. "It was nothing."

Anna shakes her head. "It was something." Her gas pump makes the same sound mine did a few minutes ago. She steps back toward the pump. "And I hope you and Warner eventually figure things out. Drive safe back to LA."

I climb into my car and lean out the open window. "It was nice to meet you, Anna."

"Same to you, Tenley."

With a wave, I'm off. Down the blacktop road, I go. A long desert highway stretches out before me. On my way out to Sierra Grande, I'd been thinking about getting away from Tate and looking forward to this being my last film for the foreseeable future.

Now here I am, leaving this small town. This town that holds the man who stole my heart, the thief who snuck in under the cover of goodness.

A great, choking sob attacks my chest. It would be so easy to turn around, to drive back to the HCC, to point my headlights into Warner's front window. I'd get what I need, and almost everything I want.

But not quite.

34

WARNER

I've gone a month without Tenley, and here's what I've learned: everything is useless. I've worked so hard to exist without her, and it's all for nothing. I go through the motions. I make meals. I sit on the sidelines at soccer games. I doubt anybody could be more present and also completely absent.

How can I be a thirty-something man and still wind up someone else's cautionary tale?

The one bright spot in all this? Next week is my second interview at the Verde Valley Community College.

I thought Wes's eyes were going to come out of his head when I told him I needed time off for the interview. To be fair, the guy is doing the best he can, but he needs me. The ranch is too big for one person to run, even with the team he has.

My mom has called me into the homestead for a sandwich. I'm well aware of how spoiled I am to find a turkey and cheese with a pickle waiting for me when I get to the kitchen table. She stares at me from the end of the table.

She's not sitting, and there isn't food for her, so it's uncomfortable. I get the feeling I've been lured into a trap.

"What's up?" I ask, picking up the sandwich.

She calls for Jessie but keeps her eyes on me. "Warner," I say, pointing back at myself, as if she needs to be reminded who I am.

Her lip twitches in a smile. Jessie flies into the room, her hair around her face and her eyes wild. Unlike my mom, she sits right beside me. She leans forward on her forearms, her fingers drumming the table.

"What?" My tone is sharp. These two women need to start talking.

Jessie pushes her phone toward me. It was already open to what she wants me to see, meaning this was planned. I've been ambushed.

"Go on," she urges, lowering her chin to indicate the phone.

I sigh in irritation around my bite. This feels juvenile. If Wes was the one telling me something, I'd have known it three minutes ago. None of this song and dance.

Despite the bold font, the title of the article isn't what I read first. It's Tenley's expression in the accompanying photo. Her eyebrows are pulled together, her shoulders hunched. She looks protective and irritated. Then I read the headline. My chewing pauses, the turkey and cheese turns to mush.

Tenley Roberts Expecting. That's what the headline screams. And below that, in smaller font still larger than the rest of the piece, it says, Seen Leaving The OB-GYN And Buying A Crib.

I spit my bite into my napkin. Everything drops away. The homestead, my seat, my family. I feel like I'm floating.

Tenley… pregnant?

"Warner?"

My gaze refocuses. I'm not sure if my mom or my sister said my name. "Yes?" I say into the space between them.

"Is it true?"

I look back at the image still glowing on Jessie's phone. Tenley normally smiles for the camera. Here she looks... defensive.

My head shakes slowly. "It's not impossible." I don't know what to say.

"What are you going to do?" My mom's voice is hard, like tough love. She's trying to coach me through the shock.

There isn't a goddamned doubt in my mind what my next step is. "Mom, can you pick up the kids from school?"

She nods. "What are you doing?"

I push away my lunch and stand. "Going to LA."

***

I HATE THIS PLACE. The smog. The traffic. The sheer number of people. I've never been claustrophobic but being here is making me rethink that.

My phone spouts directions at me, and I do my best to follow them. As I get further from the city itself, the more I like the surroundings. Maybe it's not so bad.

I think I'm here now. Tenley's house. I gaze up at the tall fence, the metal gate. I lean out of my open window and press a speaker button on a keypad.

"Hello?" The female voice is excited. And it's not Tenley.

"Yes, hi. I'm looking for Tenley Roberts."

Sarcastic laughter. "You and everyone else. Is this Warner Hayden?"

"Yeah?" It comes out sounding like I'm unsure of my own name.

"The truck gave you away. Come in."

I look down at the side of the truck and remember the logo emblazoned there. The gate rattles as it opens. I drive in, and it closes behind me. Tenley's house is... not too huge. It's nice, but not ostentatious.

I get out of my truck. Take one big stride up the three concrete steps that lead to her front door. The door opens before I can knock.

A man looks back at me.

I stand up straighter. My chest puffs out. What the fuck is happening here? Has Tenley moved on? Is this guy the father?

"Hey dude." The guy sticks out his hand. He has a man bun. I hate him instantly.

Ignoring his offered hand, I ask, "Where's Tenley?"

He makes a show of dropping his hand, but I swear to God his eyes are laughing.

"She's taking a nap."

A nap... because she's pregnant. Pregnancy is exhausting. I remember. My stomach contracts.

I stand there, unsure of what to say, and whoever the fuck this is doesn't have shit to say either.

"Warner?"

Tenley comes from behind the guy. Her hair is gathered into a ponytail that drapes over her shoulder. She's wearing my T-shirt.

Every protective cell in my body springs forth. I go to her. I don't know who this asshat is, and I don't care. Tenley is mine. Everything I've felt since she walked out six weeks ago spews forth, a dam finally burst.

"Tenley, I—"

She shakes her head. Pulls me away. I don't look at the guy. He stopped existing the moment I saw Tenley.

I can't pay attention to her home, even as she's leading me through it. All I see is her in front of me.

She takes me out a set of doors and into her backyard. She sits on a lounge chair, and I sit on it too. There's no way I'm taking a seat separate from her.

"Why are you here?"

My hand rakes over my face. I had hours to prepare my speech, but the words have disappeared. I open my mouth and wing it. The words come from the center of my chest. "Every second since you walked out of Wyatt's cabin has been worthless. I thought I'd been through hell and back and didn't know something else could hurt more, and then you left, and I found out it was possible. I resigned myself to living a life where I was always going to be in love with you, but not have you. I thought I was being gallant, giving you up so you could go on to have the things you want out of life."

Tenley cuts in. "Warner, are you here because you heard I'm pregnant? I hate to break it to you, but—"

"Only partially. I'm here because I can't be gallant. I can't do the right thing and let you go. I love you and you're mine and I want the baby even if I'm not the father. I want the baby because it's yours and I love anything and everything that has to do with you." I'm well aware whoever the man is that opened the door is probably watching this exchange right now. "Am I going to be a dad again? Or is it the guy who opened the door?"

Tenley covers her eyes with her hands, fingers pressing into her brow bones. "Oh my God, Warner. Oh my gosh, oh my gosh. You just said you love me." Her hands peel away. Her eyes are glistening.

I grab her hand. Hold it in both of mine. Fuck that guy inside, whoever he is.

"That guy is the father. But it's not my baby." Her head shakes back and forth in double time. "I'm not pregnant."

My chest grows tight and a heaviness settles in. What in the actual fuck are these feelings? I'm... sad. Disappointed. And the rest of me is running around trying to figure out my reaction.

Tenley's free hand cups my cheek. "Warner? You look unhappy."

I turn into her touch. Kiss the inside of her palm, relish in the scent of her skin I thought I'd only smell in memories. "Not unhappy. Confused. I feel disappointed."

Tenley's head cocks sideways, her loose ponytail leaning precariously to one side. "You wanted me to be pregnant? Help me understand, Warner. Because this is the opposite of everything you said in Sierra Grande."

"I know. This change of heart is happening in real time. You're seeing it as I'm living it." I can't believe this. I'm floored. Fucking dumbfounded. What is happening to me? "I'm sorry, Tenley. I know this sounds crazy. It seems impossible and unbelievable. Life smacked me around and I assumed I wasn't supposed to have a second chance at anything. But I was wrong. My life didn't end at thirty-five." I stare into those eyes that have stolen my heart. "It feels like it's just getting started. And I refuse to miss out on you."

Tenley stares at me. Her lips part just slightly. Her face softens. And then, blessedly because I'm dying over here, a grin tugs up one corner of her mouth.

"Are you going to kiss me, or what?"

I don't have time to be slow or sweet. I have six weeks to make up for, and I intend to make good on every one of those missed opportunities.

I kiss her like she's made of air and I'm out of oxygen. I can't get enough of her.

Tenley melts against me, and I send up a quick thanks to the man above. Not only a second chance with Tenley, but a second chance for a happy, full life.

"Well, well, well," a voice says. A female voice. Probably the one who answered the intercom.

Tenley pulls away and brushes her knuckles across her lips. She looks at me from under her lashes and winks at me. "Morgan, this is Warner Hayden."

The woman standing off to the side of the lounge chair looks down at me with a narrowed-eye gaze that isn't *totally* full of distrust. I think I see some amusement in there somewhere. She's holding Libby, who wriggles in her grasp. She sets the dog down and her hands go to her hips. "I sure as hell hope so, or I'd be very confused."

Libby races to me and jumps on the chair. Tenley moves back to let her in, and she paws my chest and licks my chin.

Tenley laughs and points at Morgan. "If you haven't already noticed, Morgan is the one who's pregnant."

I hadn't, but Morgan turns to the side, smoothes her shirt over her stomach, and there it is. A little baby bump.

"Congratulations," I say.

"Thank you." She rubs her belly, but her eyes stay on me. "What are your intentions with my best friend?"

I hadn't thought much beyond getting to Tenley and telling her how I feel. I open my mouth to say that but Tenley answers for me. "I want a cozy house on a little bit of land. Maybe next to the Verde River, so Libby can play and swim."

I wind my fingers through hers. "You want to live in Sierra Grande?"

"Of course. Peyton and Charlie should be with their

family. And I kind of fell in love with small-town life." She grins. "And the rest of the Hayden family."

"What about your career?" I know she was planning to take a break, but can Tenley really be happy not making movies?

She shrugs. "If I want to go back later, maybe I will. I'll leave the door ajar."

Morgan taps her thigh and whistles, and Libby scurries over. "It was nice to meet you, Warner. We'll chat later." She takes Libby inside with her.

I lean in and nuzzle Tenley's cheek. "I met a Morgan once. On the side of the road."

"Weird."

"Mm-hmm."

My lips find hers. Against them, I say, "I love you." I want her to hear it and feel it.

"I love you too, Warner."

They are the five most beautiful words I've ever heard her say.

EPILOGUE

"Can we get out of here?" Tenley pounds her feet on the passenger side floorboard. Pearl's metal construction makes it sound like a drum.

I don't know that I've ever seen Tenley so excited. It thrills me to know moving to Sierra Grande makes her this happy.

Morgan and her fiancé, Pax, are standing in front of Tenley's house. Pax waves, and Morgan looks like it's all she can do to remain upright. She's nearing the end of her pregnancy and all she wants is to be off her feet.

I turn the key and Pearl's engine roars to life. Tenley turns around and sits on her knees, waving. "Call me the second you have a contraction," she yells at Morgan.

Morgan yells back, but Tenley can't hear her.

"What?" Tenley yells.

Morgan rolls her eyes and gives Tenley an exaggerated thumbs up.

Tenley laughs and drops down into the seat, buckling herself in. "She'll call me."

I pause when the gate closes behind us, using my phone to read Wyatt's last text and enter the address he sent.

"What's there?" Tenley asks as my phone starts reciting directions.

"You'll see." I'm afraid if I tell her where I'm going, she'll put a stop to it. Plus, it probably won't work. The timing has to be just right, and I'm not going to spend any more time on this than I have to.

I slow when I get to the residential neighborhood. It's mostly single-family homes, and at the end are the apartments I'm looking for.

"I wish I knew what you were doing," Tenley says, tapping a fingernail on the glove compartment.

"If I told you, you'd stop me." I give her a quick kiss and hop out. Time appears to be on my side.

The kid is around fourteen. He's walking a large Labrador retriever and holding a small plastic bag that looks to be in use. This couldn't be any better.

"Seriously?" the kid asks when I tell him what I want. I hand over the fifty and he shakes his head. "I can't wait to tell my friends about this."

The apartment is on the ground floor. It makes this a hell of a lot easier.

I have no idea if the guy is home. For all I know, I might just stand there and wait and end up watching to make sure the flaming bag doesn't catch anything else on fire.

Turns out, I don't have to. He's home.

I'm standing at the end of the sidewalk that leads to his front door. He looks down at the bag, eyes widening. Back up at me.

"Returning the favor," I call out.

"Who are you?" he yells as I walk away.

It makes me even happier I took Wyatt up on his idea.

That guy wrote a story that blew up my life, and he doesn't even remember my face. He might now, though.

I get back to the vehicle and find Tenley slouched in her seat, her face hidden behind my ball cap. "You're crazy," she says, her voice muffled.

"Crazy for you." I drive out of the neighborhood and get us back on the interstate.

Tenley tosses my hat on the floor in the back seat. She runs her fingers through my hair and settles her hand on my neck. "Let's go home."

* * *

Six months later

"Quite the wedding, huh? Did you see the bride's train? You'd have thought she was royalty."

"She kind of is, if you think about it."

"Guess all royal families have a black sheep..."

"Now, what's that supposed to mean?"

"You haven't heard?"

"Obviously not."

"The youngest Hayden boy got himself into trouble the day after the wedding. I heard he was at the police station, and it wasn't because he was delivering a care package."

"Ladies, how are you this fine morning?" Both women startle. I feel bad. At their advanced age, it's probably not good for their hearts.

The quieter of the two has the decency to look flustered over being caught gossiping. Her chattier counterpart lifts her chin in defiance.

"Congratulations on your nuptials," she says.

"Thank you." I nod at her. Tenley walks out of Marigold's carrying two to-go cups of coffee. She smiles at the old ladies and says hello. Neither has much to say about us now that we are here.

Not that they're wrong. It was quite the wedding, Tenley's train was a mile long, and Wyatt found himself an audience with the sheriff. And not in a good way.

It won't be me dealing with Wyatt's mess. Tenley and I are headed out of town. We stopped for coffee, and now we're driving down to Phoenix. We'll pick up Peyton and Charlie from Anna, who kept them after the wedding so we could have a few nights to ourselves. From there, we'll get on a plane to Hawaii. It's a family honeymoon, at Tenley's suggestion. We'll go on another trip later, just the two of us.

Tenley has read every book available on how to be a stepmom. She'd do fine even without all the instruction, but she says you only get one chance to do it right.

We timed the wedding and family honeymoon to coincide with the holiday break from school. Both for the kids and for myself. My students will be back the second week of January.

Tenley's movie won't release for another six months, and until she starts traveling we're focusing our free time on remodeling the old Stephens house, the one the movie studio put her in when she first came to town. Tenley confided in me how much the movie means to her parents' financial situation. She's worried and nervous the movie will be a flop.

I've researched Tenley's career, and if there's one thing I've learned, it's that a Tenley Roberts film has never flopped. Still, I don't want her walking around anxious for the next six months, so I called upon Wyatt. He used his mysterious contact, the person who helped him get back Tenley's underwear, to find the name of the guy Tenley's dad is indebted to. If Tenley's movie doesn't make money, she can pay off her parents debt like she has wanted to all along.

Wes has yet to find someone he trusts as much as me. He still gives me shit for leaving, and I help out when I can. Tenley pitches in too, putting to use those ranching lessons that started all this.

We say goodbye to the two old busybodies sitting on the bench outside Marigold's. "Were they talking about us?" Tenley whispers as we walk to our car, parked a few spots away.

I nod.

She slips an arm around my waist. "I see them there often."

"Just assume you're a topic of their conversation."

She laughs. "Wouldn't be the first time."

I lean over to kiss my wife before she gets in the car. "Won't be the last."

Tenley grabs me, keeping me in place. "Let's at least give them something good to talk about."

I grin against her lips and push my hips into her. "Woman, I love you."

Tenley kisses me hard. I bet those ladies have their hawk-like eyes on us, and they're saying it won't be long until the Haydens are adding another grandchild to the crew.

And in just two months' time, their prediction turns out to be true.

* * *

Wyatt Hayden takes his community service sentence in stride, until he hears who he'll be spending his time with. Jo Shelton has made it clear she despises him, but the more time she spends with the morally gray cowboy, the more she sees the truth that everyone else is blind to. And Wyatt? He'll do just about anything to steal her heart. Read about Wyatt's shenanigans in The Outlaw!

WANT MORE of the Hayden family? Visit jennifermillikinwrites.com to read a Hayden family prequel novella.

SNEAK PEEK AT THE OUTLAW

"He's coming home. Tonight. Right now."

It's loud in the Chute, the voice of the lead singer in the live band bouncing off the walls and ricocheting around me, but I can still hear the fear in Sara's voice as it travels over the phone line.

"I'm on my way." I end the call and push away from the bar, tucking the stool back under the bar with my booted foot.

Denny and Ham stare at me, quiet judgment plain on their faces.

"Stop," I bark, peeling off a couple twenties and stuffing them in the rocks glass that holds my tab.

"You can't save her for the rest of time." Denny's brave enough to say what he knows I don't want to hear. Around the longneck bottle poised at his lips, he adds, "Or him."

The muscles in my face flex. I know the truth as well as they do, but I'm not ready to face it. Sometimes a person needs to see something through, needs to bleed the situation dry before they can admit defeat.

I owe Mickey. Without him, I don't know where I'd be.

He saved me once upon a time. Now I'm saving him. From himself, of all things.

I nod my head at my friends. "See you back at the ranch." Denny and Ham are cowboys at the Hayden Cattle Company, but they've been my friends for as long as I can remember. They're also Mickey's friends, but they've washed their hands of him. Or maybe they're showing him tough love. I don't know which it is, I just know I'm not doing either.

The Chute is busy tonight, hosting both a live band right now and bull riding later. I weave through bodies, stopping for a moment to say hi to Jackson and his younger brother, Colin. Colin sips from a bottle of root beer and smiles wide at me, his arms opening for a hug. Colin has Down syndrome, and he likes me for reasons that have nothing to do with my last name. I hug him, the same way I have for years. He steps back, his frame bulky in this tight space full of bodies, and bumps into someone's back. The guy turns around, pissed. The front of his shirt is wet with what I assume is the other half of the beer he's holding.

"What the fuck," he growls.

His eyes never get the chance to land on Colin because I'm there, stepping in front of him. It's possible the guy would've seen Colin's disability and chilled the fuck out, but now we'll never know.

"I'm waiting for your apology," the prick says. He's wearing black jeans, leather lace-up tennis shoes I know are expensive as fuck because I own boots by that brand, and a shirt with a hole near the neck. The hole looks too on purpose, like the shirt was sold that way instead of earning a tear with hard work. I dislike the guy immediately.

"You should hold your breath and wait to see if that happens," I tell him, pulling myself to full height, expanding my chest and lengthening my shoulders. Along with giving me a good life and emotional wounds, my dad showed me how to be physically intimidating. The first two are woven into the fabric of my life; the latter I call upon every now and again.

I don't have time for this shit with whoever this newcomer is, but I also don't have it in me to back down. Behind me, I hear Jackson tell Colin it's time to take a seat, and that makes me feel better. I push past the guy, giving him a good shoulder shove, and continue on through the crowd and out the door.

The truth is, I have no business driving right now. Laws are arbitrary to me, but there are a few I abide by, and drinking and driving is one of them. Despite this, I keep hearing Sara's voice. The fear. The dread.

I get in my truck. Turn it on. Sit back. Grab the bottle of water from the center console and down it. Sara's house isn't far from here. It's later on a Friday night. There won't be very many people out right now.

Just as I go to shift into drive, a tap on my window stops me. The lighting in the parking lot is dim, so I can't tell who it is very easily. I roll down my window.

"Fuck," I mutter.

"What are you doing, Wyatt?" Shelby Trask crosses her arms in front of herself. Her stiff uniform doesn't ripple, which is an accurate metaphor for her personality. She has definitive beliefs about right versus wrong. Let's just say Shelby and I have never really seen eye to eye.

"I'm just sitting in my truck, Officer Trask." I smile at her. It gets me nowhere.

"Wyatt, are you aware that it's against the law to sit behind the wheel of your vehicle when you are intoxicated?"

"Who says I'm intoxicated?"

She sighs. She knows I've got her there.

"It's not a huge leap to assume that when Wyatt Hayden emerges from the Chute, he's put back a few." She eyes me knowingly.

She's not wrong. But, of course, there's no way for her to confirm she's right. I'd pass any field sobriety test administered. I don't have the time to continue this with Shelby though. I need to get to Sara's before Mickey arrives. Give him something else to hit besides his wife.

"Officer Trask, it was great catching up, but I should be going."

"Not so fast, Wyatt. You see, I happen to have this handy little tool back at the station called a breathalyzer, and—"

Shit. This can't happen. If I'm waylaid, I don't know what will happen to Sara. Or Mickey. "Shelby, how long have we been friends? Since seventh grade?"

She frowns. "Save your words, Wyatt. Nothing you say will work. I am bound by law to bring you into the station."

Time for some serious cajoling. "We're the only two people in this parking lot, Shelby. Nobody will know if you let me go."

Her head is shaking before I finish my sentence. She points to something attached to her uniform. "See that? It's a body cam. It's recording, which means even though it's only you and I here right now, it's not only you and I who know you're intoxicated and behind the wheel of a vehicle."

Fuck. There's nothing more I can do, short of taking off and leading her straight to Sara's house. Which will create a whole host of problems, far greater than the one I was trying to prevent. Sara vehemently refuses to involve law enforcement.

I unbuckle. Hop out. Walk beside Shelby to her cruiser. She spares me the hassle of cuffing me. Small town and all.

We pass the turnoff for Mickey and Sara's house on the way to the station, and I wonder if Mickey has already made it home.

The metal chair shimmers dully in the blunt overhead light. I don't know why they've stuck me in here. I'm not being interrogated.

I was fine in the large cell with James Croft, the idiot who set off a bottle rocket earlier this evening when everybody and their senile grandparents know it's illegal. And the other guy, the one wearing obscenely tight jeans, was brought in for trespassing on Hayden Cattle Company land. He's probably still crowing about how his wandering was inadvertent. I didn't believe a word out of his mouth, nor did I tell him my last name is Hayden.

Like a watched pot never boils, a watched door never seems to open. I've glanced at my watch so many times I've lost count, the minutes ticking by at a sure and steady pace. Every minute in this place feels like an hour, and my mind is filled with the bruises that are most likely just beginning to take form on Sara's body.

Finally, the door opens. Sheriff Monroe steps in. He's getting on in age, thicker around the middle than he'd like to be, and has a zigzag scar on the back of his head from riding a horse into a barbed wire fence when he was a teenager.

The sheriff opts not to sit down, but stands behind the chair opposite mine, his hands gripping the back. His knuckles are hairy and he wears a silver ring with a piece of turquoise in the center.

"Where were you headed tonight, Wyatt? Before Officer Trask brought you in."

I don't want to say, but I know my compliance will make it more likely he'll be lenient with my punishment. "To help a friend."

His bushy, salt-and-pepper eyebrows draw together. "By any chance would that 'friend' be Sara Schultz?"

I'm not surprised he knows, but doesn't he have better things to do? Like, I don't know, protect the town of Sierra Grande? Then again, his wife is a terrible gossip.

Anger, and a healthy dose of injustice, bubbles up inside me. This town notices my truck parked outside the Schultz's home when it otherwise shouldn't be, but they don't see what's right under their noses. How did nobody else see it when Sara began wearing long sleeves in July? How was I the only one?

I tamp down the anger, hold tight to the sting of injustice, and answer. "Yes, Sheriff."

Emotion flickers in his eyes. He's not disgusted. Judgmental, yes. Probably confused about my morals, or apparent lack thereof. "Doesn't matter to you that she's married with kids?"

He waits for my reply, but I don't have much of one. It *does* matter to me that she's married with kids. It matters a whole hell of a lot. Just not for the reason the sheriff knows about. I nod at him. At least it's the truth.

He chews on his cheek and watches me. I know he's thinking about what to do with me.

"Who should I call, Wyatt? To come and get you?"

"I can walk."

He tells me no with a shake of his head. "You're still intoxicated. If I let you go in this state and you cause more trouble, it's my head on the chopping block."

My hands fist under the table and I let go of my final shred of hope that I can make it to the Schultz's tonight. Sara called, asked me for help, and I failed.

"Wes." My voice is rough, a rock scraped over sandpaper. "Call Wes."

* * *

An hour passes. Maybe more. I'm torturing myself, running through scenarios of what could've gone down tonight at Mickey and Sara's. I pulled up memories of them as a happy family, like they used to be before Mickey lost his job and left to find work outside of town. When I'm sick of torturing myself, I run through a list of shit I need to do when I get out of here. The metal chair I'm sitting in started to feel like concrete about thirty minutes ago. My ass is asleep.

The sudden opening of the door startles me, and I sit up straight. The sheriff steps in, followed by my father.

My heart, my stomach, my whole body drops out of me, scattering on the cold floor.

Not my dad.

I'd specifically asked for my big brother, Wes. Not my other big brother, Warner, because he has kids and his wife is pregnant. Wes has a baby at home too, but my nephew is sleeping through the night now, and a call to Wes isn't as disruptive.

Wes is tougher than Warner when it comes to me, but he was the next best alternative to my dad. So how the hell did I get stuck with the man who regularly fails to hide his disappointment when he looks at me?

Sheriff Monroe stops on the other side of the table. He holds on to the back of the chair like he did earlier and levels his gaze on mine. My dad, who could just as easily have at least stood on my side of the table, steps up beside the sheriff. Guess I've never really needed to draw a line to know what side my dad's on. It's whatever is opposite mine.

The sheriff says in a tired voice, "We're not arresting you, Wyatt."

I nod, close to telling him I know that already, but keep my mouth shut instead. I might have a quick wit and a smart mouth that's gotten me into trouble more times than I can count, but I know how to harness it. "Thanks, Sheriff."

I dare a glance at my dad. Nothing moves. Not his face. Not his stance. Not even a muscle tic along his jaw. Beau Hayden is a beast of a man, a local legend, and a goddamn living statue.

My chair scrapes its protest as I stand. In this cold, quiet space, the sound bounces off the walls. "Ready to go home?"

My dad's steely-eyed gaze doesn't leave me. "Can we have a minute, Sheriff?"

The sheriff doesn't respond, but his booted retreat speaks his reply. The door closes.

Now the muscles in his face twitch. When we were younger, he'd flick our ears with what felt like the strongest, meanest fingers in the state of Arizona. Misbehavior was avoided because nobody wanted to draw his anger. A lot has changed in twenty years. Somewhere along the way, I stopped giving a fuck.

"Where's Wes?"

He crosses his arms in front of himself, partially covering the HCC insignia on his vest. "Wes doesn't need to come to your rescue. He has a son to raise." He eyes me meaningfully. "And so do I."

I bristle. "I'm an adult."

"A person would be hard-pressed to know it."

I mimic his stance. The last thing I want is to hear from

my father how I've managed to disappoint him yet again. "Can we go?"

His lips are drawn in a grim line. "You think drinking and driving is no big deal?"

"I wasn't actually driving. I was sitting."

A terse stream of air huffs from his nose. As sounds go, it's as ubiquitous as his flicking fingers. It means he cannot believe the sheer stupidity of the words you've just spoken.

"Quit playing cute, Son. If Shelby hadn't been there you'd have been driving."

"Does it even matter anymore? It's over."

"What was so important that you were going to do something you know damn well is illegal? Not to mention dangerous."

My lips tighten, an invisible needle and thread sewing a seam.

"Christ," my dad mutters, shaking his head at me. "I already know where you were headed, Wyatt. Just thought maybe you'd do me the courtesy of telling me the truth."

If I told him the truth, Sara would lose her husband, her sole source of income for her and her two kids, and Mickey would go to jail. Should Sara keep absorbing Mickey's liquor-fueled fists? Hell no. That's what I'm for until I can think of a better solution. Until I figure out a way to help Mickey long-term.

He turns toward the door. "Come on," my dad growls, dissatisfied with me once again. What the fuck else is new?

My entire existence is a letdown for him.

He loves me because he has to, because it's hardwired. One thing I've learned though, is that while a person can feel love for someone, they can also feel a hundred other emotions, and absolutely none of them have to be good.

ACKNOWLEDGMENTS

Readers. Thank you! Where would I be without you? I truly appreciate all the love and attention you give my stories. There are so many ways you could spend your time, and knowing you've used your precious time on my work means everything to me.

My beta readers. Thank you for accepting the misshapen story I hand you, and helping me mold it into what is eventually its best version.

My dad. Thank you for advising me on what a carburetor is, and what it does in a truck! And for allowing me to use some of your real life experiences in my work. They make my books come to life.

My kids and my husband. You believe in what I do, in the stories I create in my head, in the world of make-believe I sometimes drift off to. I love you guys.

To my tribe. You know who you are. Your love and support keeps me afloat.

ABOUT THE AUTHOR

Jennifer Millikin is a bestselling author of contemporary romance and women's fiction. She is the two-time recipient of the Readers Favorite Gold Star Award, and readers have called her work "emotionally riveting" and "unputdownable". Following a viral TikTok video with over fourteen million views, Jennifer's third novel *Our Finest Hour* has been optioned for TV/Film. She lives in the Arizona desert with her husband, children, and Liberty, her Labrador retriever. With thirteen novels published so far, she plans to continue her passion for storytelling.

Visit jennifermillikinwrites.com to sign up for her newsletter and receive a free novella.

facebook.com/JenniferMillikinwrites
instagram.com/jenmillwrites
bookbub.com/profile/jennifer-millikin

Made in United States
Troutdale, OR
02/28/2025

29360540R00177